RAVEN

The Raven Witch Saga

SG TURNER

Raven

The Raven Witch Saga Part I

The summer months were coming to an end when my parents disappeared. Although the day had begun like any other, it became one that I would never forget.

That morning, as usual, I sat at the kitchen table listening to the noises drifting up from outside – traffic, police sirens, people laughing and shouting – while I struggled to swallow the piece of dry bread that was shoved in front of me. "Eat," commanded my mother.

A small glass of milk just about helped it go down before she snatched the plastic tumbler from my hands, pulled me to my feet and shoved me out of the front door of our London flat without another word. Turning around to search her eyes, I attempted a smile in the hope that she might return it. But the door was shut in my face. A deep ache filled my stomach. I needed something that I had never experienced. I needed to know that she loved me.

Leaning against the door, I heard the familiar sound of her footsteps walking into the other room. She closed the door and locked it behind her. My mother and father had locked themselves in the spare room once again, just like they had done every day for as long as I could remember. I had always assumed they worked from home. I've no idea what they did, they never told me. I never asked. I wasn't allowed to ask questions.

Running down the four long flights of stairs, I pushed open the large, heavy door that led outside. The noises multiplied and hit me, as did the dull smog and the intense London humidity that seemed to accompany every hot summer. As my feet touched the edge of the pavement, I stopped for a moment to allow a few cars to pass by before rushing across the road to school. I had to be quick. She was watching, she was always watching. My mother would peer down, staring blankly at me from the fourth-floor window of the room she and my father spent their days. It was as if she was making sure I was actually going to school. Like I would dare do anything else. She never smiled. She never waved. She just stared. Sometimes it was almost as if she was looking right through me.

Returning home at lunchtime, as I was forced to do every day, she was there at that window staring at me again, as if her stare would physically guarantee that I came home. She had done it every day since I'd started school, so it was normal for me.

I unlocked the front door with my key and gingerly tiptoed into the kitchen, where I found her waiting for me.

"Eat and get back to school," she said with a glare as I perched myself onto the old metal stool and began spooning the cold soup into my mouth. It was the same cold soup I'd eaten every day. It would have been nice to have something else, a different flavour, perhaps, but I would never have asked. Oh no. I'd experienced my mother's anger one too many times before. It's not that she had ever hit me, but I knew. I just knew that she wanted to, so I avoided making her mad at all costs.

I believed that my mother's actions were the same as all other mothers. I imagined that she did what most mothers did. I didn't know any different. At least not until I met the newest girl at school, December Moon. When she had first arrived at the school, the other kids had sniggered and laughed when she had been introduced. Even I had thought it was a silly name to start with, but as soon as she spoke to me, I knew it was perfect.

After her introduction to the class, the only spare seat available was next to mine. As my fellow students were in the habit of ignoring me, I was a little startled to have this pale but pretty flame-haired girl smile at me as she approached and sat down. I shyly returned the smile as she quietly took out her books and a pencil case from the orange rucksack she had carried on her back. Her clothes were multi-coloured and flowing – a long, heavy purple flowery skirt was paired with an orange and pink striped top, and brown boots. A brown headband held back her straight shoulder-length hair, and when she turned, I noticed it had a pink flower sewn onto it. Ordinarily, the colours wouldn't work together, but on December, they just seemed to fit... perfectly.

When the attention was no longer on her, December turned to me and whispered "hello". She smiled again, and her whole face changed. It lit up.

It didn't take long for December and me to become best friends. We were both shy and quiet and were mostly ignored by everybody else. It made sense that we should spend school time together. More than anything, though, I wanted to be friends out of school hours. My mother, however, had always made it quite clear that friends of any kind were strictly forbidden. Fortunately, she couldn't see past the school gates, so December always waited for me inside, out of my mother's view. She was my secret.

December and I had spent many a break time chatting about each other's lives. She was an avid reader of all kinds of books, even magazines. In fact, reading was pretty much all she did when she was at home. I was in awe of her, and I knew then that she must know a lot more about other people's lives than I did. That was how I learned that my parent's actions were not entirely normal. Her own parents, however, could not be described as 'normal' either.

"My father died when I was three," she had told me soon after we'd met. "He was a very old man, and I was very young, so I don't remember him."

The edges of my mouth turned downwards as the heavy feeling of sadness took effect. "And what about your mother, December? Where is she?"

"She dumped me with my father's family shortly after he died and moved back to America on her own. She was from Seattle, Washington, apparently." Her response was so matter-of-fact that I didn't quite know what to say, other than "Oh."

"Basically, my Aunt Penelope – that's my father's younger sister who I live with – tells me that my mother married my father for his money but when he died, leaving her with nothing, she dumped me with her and took off."

"Aunt Penelope basically makes sure I am fed, schooled and clothed. Other than that, we don't have much time for each other." She shrugged her shoulders. "But that's fine with me. She doesn't like to be seen with me, especially when her super rich friends are around. Being my mother's daughter lowers the tone of her family... I even heard her say that to Monty once. Oh, Monty's our butler, chauffeur and sometimes gardener," she shrugged again, and that's when I saw a glimmer of something in her eyes. She wasn't quite so emotionless about it all after all.

Having never known anyone rich before... and with a butler too, I thought it was quite weird for her to be a student in the same school as me. "December?"

"Hmm?"

"Why doesn't your Aunt Penelope send you to a posh school?"

"Like I said, she'd rather I didn't exist so she'd rather keep me as far from her friends as possible."

"That makes sense, I guess. In which case, I'm glad! I would never have met you otherwise! So do you not know anything about your mother?" I asked, intrigued.

December shook her head, "Nope. Nothing."

The sound of the school bell put an end to our conversation and December didn't mention her mother or her father to me again for a very long time.

Discreetly waving goodbye to her on that fateful day, I knew there was something wrong the moment I stepped foot out of the school grounds. Looking up to the window expecting to see mother, a vision in white as usual, there was no sign of her. My heart began to thud faster in my chest as I ran as fast as I could up the stairs two at a time. I grappled with the key and pushed open the front door. She was nowhere to be seen. Neither was my father.

The spare room was locked as it always was, and no matter how hard I banged my fists on that door, there was no reply. I stopped and put my ear carefully against the solid wood to check for any sounds, but there was nothing. Just silence. Trying to kick the door down, I didn't even leave a single mark. I was just a slight girl with little strength, after all.

It was then that our neighbours, Dorothy and June, came rushing in.

"Oh, my dear, my dear! Whatever is the matter? What is all this banging about?" yelled one of the sisters as they tried to calm me down.

"It's mother," I said, "she's... she's disappeared. She's always here. I don't know what's happening. There's no answer at the door. Something's wrong," I sobbed.

Just at that moment, the sisters' black cat wandered in behind them. It immediately began purring at my feet and rubbed itself against my legs. It had never set foot in our apartment before, and it was strange that it did so then.

It jumped up so that it balanced on its hind legs and leaned against me. I momentarily forgot all about the commotion that I had caused and leaned forward to pick it up, cuddling it while it continued to purr. "That's strange," said June, "she's usually terrified of people." The cat was clearly not terrified of me. It was the first time I had ever stroked an animal, and I felt a strange affinity with it. It was a wonderful feeling as it rubbed its head against my neck. Looking into her deep, warm eyes, for a moment, I felt a strange sensation within me. It felt as though I was being loved. I didn't want to lose the feeling, so I sat down on the floor and stroked her soft fur, smiling.

"I'm going to call the police," one of the sisters said as the other tried to coax me off the floor. I didn't feel myself, for some reason. A strange trance-like state came over me.

"Come now, dear. Come and sit on the sofa. You'll catch your death on those cold floor tiles."

I did as I was told and followed her to our uncomfortable hard red leather sofa, where we waited until the police arrived. The cat sat on my lap, and the two sisters sat on either side of me.

"We know that your mother leads a strict routine, my dear, so to hear you banging on the door like that had us worried," said June.

"We've never known anything ever happen to you like this, so we thought we'd better come over straight away and find out what's going on," added Dorothy as she gently patted my hand with her own wrinkled, yet perfectly manicured, fingers.

My calm moments with the cat were cut short by the arrival of two young uniformed male police officers, followed by a third woman. The cat jumped out of my arms like a shot. She was clearly spooked by the presence of strangers and had vanished from our flat, presumably to return to the safety of her home. My calm feeling faded the moment she was gone.

The female police officer was very kind and polite and asked me a few questions about myself and my parents. When had I last seen them? Where did they work? Was it common for them to leave without telling me? Did they have mobile phones? I didn't even know the answer to the last question, although if they did, I never saw or heard them. Technology wasn't a word I heard used in our home. Not that there were ever many words used at all.

More questions were asked of me, and so I answered them as best as I could before the other two police officers managed to literally knock the door down. I wasn't prepared for what I saw, and I don't think they were either. There was almost nothing. Just a simple room, painted black – the floors, ceiling and walls all painted black. There were no chairs, no desks, nothing. The only things to be seen in the room were a small black shelf which contained two glass vials. One was filled with a thick deep red liquid, and the other contained what appeared to be something from the insides of an animal – I couldn't identify it, but it looked disgusting. A pang of fear shot through me. Fear for my parents' safety.

"Do you have any idea what substance this is, Miss?" asked one of the police officers.

I shook my head. "I've never been in here before."

The two men gave each other a sideways glance that was way too obvious for me not to have seen.

"Right then, Miss, would you like to wait outside while we gather some of this evidence together?" said the first officer as the other led me out of the black room.

Snippets of conversation could be heard as I waited for them to finish.

"This is definitely blood. What on earth do you think has been going on in here then, Pete?"

"Beats me, Dave. I tell you one thing though, it's weird, whatever it is. It's almost like something out of a horror film. Here... look at this."

The female officer appeared by my side and cleared her throat. The conversation in the black room suddenly became quieter.

"Don't worry, Lilly. We'll get to the bottom of this," she said, smiling. "We'll find your mum and dad."

After about half an hour, the officers appeared from the room, carrying the vials in two clear plastic bags.

"Okay, Constable Madley, we've all the evidence now. We'll take them to the lab for tests," said the taller of the two.

He tipped his hat to me and smiled before carrying everything out of the flat.

Following behind, the other one stopped in front of me and crouched down, looking right into my eyes. His dark brown eyes and the soft laughter lines around his mouth gave him a look of kindness. I hadn't noticed when they'd first arrived. "Lilly, we'll be in touch as soon as we have any information as to the whereabouts of your parents. Don't worry. We'll find them." He stood up then and patted Constable Madley on the back. They were clearly friends as well as colleagues. He smiled at her, "Thank you, Constable Madley. We'll see you back at the station."

❧ 3 ❧

My parents' disappearance continued to be a complete mystery. The police had told me that even though they had followed several lines of enquiry and spoken to countless people; they had come up without a single clue to go on. Not one person had seen them. I was the only one that had seen them that day. Well, I had seen her. I hadn't actually seen my father. I had just assumed he was there. I rarely saw him anyway, I rarely even heard him. Every now and then I would hear her speak to him, but I never heard him reply.

It had been a hot and humid summer and, unusual for England at that time of year, it had lasted for quite a few weeks. Naturally, there had been a hosepipe ban as happened every time the sun shone for more than a week there. I had only been aware of it because my teachers were keen to teach us all about current environmental issues.

Not that I noticed the ban. We didn't have a garden, we didn't even have any plants. Our home was a bare flat in London where I had lived all my life – all thirteen years of it. I can't say I was happy, nor can I say I was particularly unhappy because I wouldn't have known the true meaning of either word.

I was very much a loner with no friends until December came along. Luckily, the majority of kids at school were pleasant enough to us, but we didn't feel like we belonged with any of them, so we simply avoided contact. Of course, there were a few that taunted us every now and again, but we took little notice. They seemed to tease a lot of people at school, having silly nicknames for everyone - apart from December. The kids were amused enough by her name not to bother making up another. Mine was Mellow Yellow – probably because I was so quiet and wore a lot of yellow. Not by choice, though. The few clothes that I owned were bought by my mother, and for some reason, they were all yellow, not even a nice shade of yellow. All were second-hand clothes, and none fitted me correctly, but I certainly couldn't complain even if I hated them all. Like I said, my parents and I didn't really talk.

December and I preferred being in our own little world, alone with our thoughts or curled up with a sneaky book under the large chestnut tree in the playground.

At school, we blended into the background. We were courteous to most people, and most of them were polite to us. Yet if you asked anyone about me, even my name, I doubted very much that any of the kids would know. At least that was the case until my parents mysteriously vanished from the face of the earth. Then everyone seemed to know my name. Everyone knew I was Lilly Taylor.

Word had spread rapidly as I walked through the school gates a few days later.

Out of habit, December had waited hidden behind the walls for my arrival. She needn't have, of course. She hugged me tightly but didn't say a word. Somehow she just knew how I felt.

Shame the other kids didn't have a clue. Fingers pointed, people whispered and stared at me. Not a single other person approached me. Had it not been for December, I would have felt even more alone than I had ever felt before. I could easily have cried on her shoulder, but the tears did not come. As much as I wished they would, they wouldn't come, perhaps because I had never really had much of a relationship with either parent. I never felt loved. I never even felt liked. But they were my family.

The closest people to me at that time of my life, other than December, were the kind neighbours who had offered to take care of me until my parents were found. Or, in the event that they did not return; until plans were made for me to travel across the world to stay with my grandfather in Canada. A grand-father I knew nothing about. December would be crushed. I was her only friend, and she needed me as much as I needed her. I would hate to have to leave her, but deep down, I knew that it was likely.

Rather than put me into temporary foster care, Social Services had agreed that my staying with the sisters was the best thing for me. Familiarity, they said, would be better than handing me over to complete strangers. Dorothy and June were spinsters. They had never married but had been happy enough living together their entire lives. They were kind and honest, and they were trustworthy. I couldn't really have stayed with December even if I had wanted to. She didn't have the best relationship with her aunt. What her wealthy aunt gave to December in financial security, she lacked in love. She was as lonely as I was, and her aunt would never have allowed her to take me home with her.

Later that afternoon, I had rushed out of the school gates and looked up at the window to see if my mother had come back. She wasn't there, of course. No vision in white.

As I stood there, it occurred to me that for the very first time in my life I could do anything I wanted. Anything in the world. But I had no idea what to do. I looked around and watched many of the other kids laughing and joking. Some kicked around a football, others sat on the wall sneakily smoking cigarettes, while some of the younger ones were collected by their loving parents. December sadly waved goodbye from her chauffeur-driven car.

Instead of heading 'home', I gingerly walked in the opposite direction, looking back over my shoulder afraid that someone might swoop down and pull me back. Yet for the first time ever, I felt no pull to return to that place. If it weren't for Dorothy and June, I would probably have just carried on walking, but deep down I knew I couldn't hurt them like that. Especially when they had shown nothing but kindness to me.

So I turned around and headed back up those stairs. The ones I had walked up a million times before. Yet this time, I entered the apartment across the hall from my parents' place. As I unlocked the door, the most delicious smell of home cooking invaded my every pore, and the sounds of laughter came from the living room. I followed the sounds, and instead of finding the sisters, I found the television switched on. I sat down and watched for a few minutes, laughing at the silly man who pranced around like a complete idiot getting himself stuck in ridiculous situations. Watching until it finished, I discovered that he was called Mr Bean. It was then that I felt an overwhelming sense of guilt for doing something I was never permitted to do. I peered over my shoulder guiltily before getting up and walking into the kitchen.

"Oh, hello, dear. You're just in time for dinner. Come in. Don't just hover by the door. I hope you had a good day at school. I've made us a Shepherd's Pie. I hope you like that," said Dorothy as she gently pushed her white-blonde curls behind her ears before spooning the food onto a plate for me.

I had no idea what a Shepherd's Pie was, but I nodded enthusiastically nonetheless. It was easily the most delicious meal I had ever had. At home, everything came straight from a tin. Tinned spaghetti, tinned beans, tinned peas, tinned mince, tinned potatoes, tinned soup, and so on. And most of it was given to me cold. Stone cold. I only knew it was all tinned food because of the time I had sneaked in when she wasn't looking and had opened the cupboards to find a lifetime's supply of the stuff.

I had never been allowed to spend any length of time in our kitchen, other than to quickly eat, so I had no idea how to prepare food. I guess back then I had assumed that everybody ate that kind of stuff.

"Did this come out of a tin, Dorothy?" I asked.

"Oh my dear!" she said, "Of course not. We cook everything fresh in this house. Did your mother never prepare you a home-cooked meal?"

I shook my head and told her about the kinds of things I had eaten, and she looked shocked, as did June.

"I take it that means she never taught you to how to cook?"

I shook my head again and told them I wasn't allowed in the kitchen other than to quickly eat.

"Well, while you're staying with us, we'll just have to change that, won't we? We'll show you everything you need to know. But first, eat up and enjoy dear. We'll start to teach the basics tomorrow after school," Dorothy smiled kindly as she patted my hand.

As I enjoyed those wonderful mashed potatoes with the tasty meat beneath, I felt another pang of guilt. Guilt that my parents had vanished and there I was, stuffing myself like some sort of famished orphan. But then, perhaps that's what I had become. An orphan. And I was hungry. Very hungry.

That evening, the guilt continued to consume me. So much so that I felt the need to do something about it. Something drastic. And there was only one thing that I could do. I secretly borrowed a pair of scissors from the kitchen and sneaked into the bathroom. After locking the door, I stood looking at my reflection in the mirror, and before I could talk myself out of it, I took those scissors to my hair and hacked it all off. As I stared at myself, I wished for that guilt to disappear. It didn't. I needed to do more. Searching through the sisters' belongings in the cupboard, I came across a box with a picture of a woman with the same coloured hair as Dorothy. Without giving it a second thought, I opened the box, emptied the contents on the floor and sat on the bath mat as I read everything on the leaflet inside the box. As instructed, I mixed the contents of the bottles together and began covering my hair with the cream. The strong odour made my eyes water as I slowly began to bleach out the black from my hair.

Over an hour later, I stood staring at my reflection, a mountain of long black hair covered the floor by my feet. I inched closer to the mirror and stared into my eyes. Their usual shade of vivid green seemed flat and lifeless. Murky. I wished the guilt would disappear. I wished for tears to come. I wished for the return of my parents. But it was no good. There was no one to make my wishes come true.

I crept back into the spare bedroom and pulled out all of my awful yellow clothes. Spreading them on the soft pink carpet, I used the same pair of scissors to cut them and rip them so that they didn't hang loosely from my body any more. Just for a moment, I forgot my circumstances and enjoyed the creativity. What I was left with, however, wasn't what I had intended. They were still a mess, and they were all still yellow. I didn't want to wear yellow any more. I didn't want to be the Mellow Yellow girl.

I walked into the living room where Dorothy and June sat glued to the television, and I stopped in the doorway to watch the screen for a few moments. I listened as a middle-aged man talked about a recent spate of mysterious attacks on horses that had taken place within the London area.

A minute later, the cat jumped off the sofa and started making a fuss of me. The two women noticed and turned to see what she was so interested in. Dorothy let out a cry when she saw me. June gave me a hug. She just seemed to understand why I had done it. I sat down in between them both on the sofa and told them what I had done to all my clothes. Their look of sadness didn't go unnoticed by me, and I felt bad for making them feel that way.

As the cat rubbed itself against my bare legs, Dorothy suddenly stood up and smiled with a twinkle in her.

"I have an idea," she said, "come on."

June stood up too and laughed, "Of course."

"We always wondered why your mother dressed you in yellow, dear. It's really not a flattering colour for you at all. I know we're just a couple of old spinsters, but we've still got our clothes from when we were younger. We just might have some things that will fit you. Let's go and have a look," added June.

I followed the sisters into a fourth bedroom, a room without a bed, instead filled with hangers and hangers of clothes. I had never seen so many bright and beautiful things. It wasn't just the colours that were so beautiful to me, it was the feel of the clothes, soft and silky. So unlike the hard and scratchy fabrics I had always worn.

However, as much as they tried to give me colourful skirts and blouses, I found myself drawn to black. With my newly-dyed white hair, I told them I just wanted to wear black. Deep down, I felt unworthy somehow of wearing anything else. Eventually, they conceded and pulled out everything they had in black. There wasn't much, but it was a far cry from Mellow Yellow. That night, the sisters' sewing machine went into overdrive – making all my new clothes to fit my small frame.

Walking through the school gates the following day, I held my head up high and let them point and stare. There were whispers, but there were also wolf whistles from the heartless boys that didn't care for my emotions. But I couldn't care less. Nobody called me Mellow Yellow after that. I was finally just Lilly.

"Your hair!" were the first words from December's mouth. "As much as I loved the black hair, I do love the white, although I'm not so keen on the hacked look," she giggled. December was always good at making me feel better with a well-timed, and much-needed joke. She didn't mention my missing parents or the lack of yellow. She didn't need to. She was just there, and that was all that mattered.

As the weeks went by without any sign of my parents, true to their word, Dorothy and June began to demonstrate how to cook all kinds of simple recipes. They tried to keep me busy. The police concluded that the blood they had found was my father's, but they neglected to tell me what was in the other vial. However, as they had made no further discoveries, it looked as though the case may well be shelved, unsolved. An X file. I didn't know what to think. A vial of my father's blood? Did that mean he was injured? Or worse? I tried not to let my imagination run wild.

From conversations with the Social Services, the authorities and Dorothy and June, I knew I would have to move to Canada. My grand-father telephoned me and told me that all the arrangements had been made. We didn't have much to say to each other. Not just because I didn't know the man, but also because I simply wasn't used to talking on the telephone.

In just a few short weeks, I would no longer live in England. A sense of sadness overcame me, but still, the tears did not come. I was upset that I was leaving my parents behind... wherever they were. But it was the fact that my life had actually improved since they'd disappeared that made me feel guilty. The guilt turned to sadness, and the sadness turned to guilt, like an unstoppable swinging pendulum.

4

One night as I lay on my bed drifting off to sleep, there was a tapping sound on the window. Opening my eyes, I saw two blackbirds sitting on the windowsill, staring solemnly in at me. Having never taken any notice of local birds before, I wanted to know what they were, so I trundled out of bed and tiptoed into the living room where the sisters kept all their books. There I found an encyclopaedia from which I managed to identify them as ravens. After watching them for a few more minutes, they flew away. Exhaustion soon set in and it didn't take long for me to forget all about them and fall asleep.

But the following night, they re-appeared. There was a tap on the window, and as I looked up from the book I was reading, I saw them both sitting in the same spot looking in at me again.

This happened every night until my move to Canada. Why they visited me there, I had no idea. But there they were, every night, sitting on my windowsill as if protecting me from something.

The way they perched there and repeatedly cocked their heads from one side to the other made me giggle, but they also frightened me somewhat, and so I soon stopped. I dared not open the window. I never closed the curtains because, although I was fearful, I was also comforted by them. They became a constant in my strange, lonesome life.

I almost wished they could go with me to Canada, a country that I had few expectations of. I hadn't always known that my grand-father Gabriel was Canadian. In fact, I hadn't even known of his existence until my thirteenth birthday, nearly a year earlier. I had bumped into the postman at the bottom of the stairs, and so I had taken our mail directly from him, instead of letting him place it in our post box as usual. I hadn't intended to look through it, but a Canadian postmark had caught my attention, and it was addressed... to me.

So I sat down on the edge of the step and had almost torn the envelope apart to get to the letter. I started to read it...

MY DEAREST LILLIAN

It is thirteen years since you were born and you are missed terribly.

I have written to you before, but I can only imagine the letters have not reached you. I wish I could see you again, Lillian. I am your paternal grand-father after all...

BUT BEFORE I HAD THE CHANCE TO READ ON, THE LETTER WAS cruelly ripped from my hands and torn into shreds by my mother. She had been so angry that I had opened that letter. More so when I told her it was addressed to me. I tried to ask her about my grandfather, but she refused to say a word. So all I knew was that I had a Canadian grand-father yet I longed to know more about him. I couldn't ask my father because, on the rare occasion that I did see him, he was never alone. My mother never seemed to allow us to be together, just the two of us.

All I knew about my grandfather was that he was Canadian. I didn't know what to feel. There was a sadness there. A numbness too. I missed my parents so much that I had a deep ache in my stomach. Yet during those weeks, I didn't miss the life that we'd had at all. But that didn't detract from the fact that they were my parents and I needed to know where they were. Even though I had December, Dorothy and June – and their beautiful cat Iris – I still felt lonely, as if a huge piece of me was missing.

As I boarded the plane to Canada, I knew I had been completely left in the dark and that my life was about to change, possibly forever. I wished to know what I was going to... and to whom. If my parents had filled me in on their backgrounds, their childhoods, perhaps I would know where I was heading. My only knowledge was that I was boarding a flight to Vancouver and that someone was collecting me. On the brief telephone call with my grand-father Gabriel, he had told me that he was unable to come and collect me but that a 'very close family friend' would be picking me up. That friend was called Ben. I didn't even know where I was going after Vancouver.

The airport was hugely confusing to me. Dorothy and June had wanted to come with me, but I confidently told them that I'd be okay. That I'd manage. They were old ladies, they didn't need the hassle. Eventually, they agreed to let me go alone and had arranged it with the airline, and as we said our goodbyes, I thanked them for everything. I promised I would stay in touch and let them know how everything was going. They cried as I waved to them from the back of the taxi cab and secretly, so did I. I waited until they could no longer see me and then the tears that I had managed to keep at bay for so long, began to stream down my face. I don't know how I'd managed to keep from crying for so many weeks, but I felt as though the tears had been building up as I sobbed and sobbed in the back of that car, as I drove away from the only life I'd ever known.

I cried not only for my missing parents and for leaving my home behind, but because I would desperately miss those two ladies who had become like family to me. I would miss them, and I would miss December.

I didn't know how I would live without her, but she had promised to keep in touch. "Lilly Taylor, you're my best friend in the whole world. I can't imagine life without you, but we'll manage... for now. It won't be too long until we're together again. We'll see each other soon," she'd said the day before as we'd hugged goodbye. It had sounded so rehearsed, but I figured it needed to be; otherwise, we would have just been in floods of tears. She was the brightest star in my life, and I couldn't imagine being without her.

The airport was bigger and brighter than I imagined it to be. It seemed to go on for miles, but after reading my ticket, and with a little help from the taxi driver, we figured out where I was supposed to go. I felt like a very tiny fish in a vast sea, but as soon as I had checked in and asked a few questions, I was told that the airline staff would make sure I was in the right place at the right time.

The next few hours were spent watching people coming and going before I finally climbed aboard the plane that would take me to my new home. Excitement, as well as panic, flowed through me.

Soon after take-off, darkness clung to me, and I felt cold. I shivered.

As I sat there alone, cold and dazed, a friendly flight attendant approached me with a warm blanket and a pillow.

"I couldn't help noticing you shivering," she said warmly as she handed them to me.

I took them gratefully and wrapped myself up tightly.

"Would you like some hot tea or hot chocolate?" she asked. I opted for some hot chocolate, and she smiled and turned away.

I was pleased the flight was quiet. I had the back row to myself, so I put up all the armrests and stretched my legs out as I watched her walk towards me, bearing the hot drink a few minutes later.

She looked a little like me. At least like me, when my hair had been its natural colour. Jet black hair, bright eyes that were wide apart, pale skin and of delicate build. Her face was pretty and friendly, and I was glad of the attention. It was as if she was taking extra special care of me.

The hours soon passed by and it seemed like no time at all when the pilot announced to the crew that they should prepare the cabin for landing. I must have looked frightened as the kind attendant came over to reassure me.

"Don't worry. You're almost home now," she whispered.

I smiled and nodded. Perhaps she was just kind. Although I couldn't shake the feeling that she knew of my fate.

So I had landed in Canada. I guessed this was my home now. But for how long? When my parents returned, would I go back to London? What if they were never found? What then?

At least for now, Canada was my home.

As I stepped off that plane, I felt helpless. I felt as if I had no control over my life. Perhaps I no longer did.

❧   5   ❧

I didn't have to wait. The moment I stepped out into the arrivals hall with my luggage, I heard someone calling out my name. My eyes searched the crowd until they stopped on a young man who waved avidly at me. I tried to smile but probably failed.

"Lillian? Is that you? I wasn't sure if I'd recognise you from the photo... you look very different! It's the hair, I guess. Although you're a lot younger in the photo. Anyway, Gabriel - I mean your grand-father - couldn't make it as you know and so he asked me to pick you up. I'm Benjamin. It's great to finally meet you," he gushed.

"Hi," was all I could muster as he delved into his pocket and pulled out a photo of what looked a little (and I mean a little) like me from when I was just a baby. He turned the image to show me, and I laughed at the sheer ridiculousness of it.

"Er... I'd like to think I've changed a lot. I'm amazed you recog-nised me at all," I said, starting to feel comfortable with the stranger, but wondering where the photo had come from. It wasn't one I was familiar with. That said, no picture would be one I was familiar with. We didn't have any family photos at all.

Together we laughed as Benjamin quickly lifted my bag from the luggage trolley and asked me to follow him. I stumbled behind him, not sure what to say as we walked through the car park until we stopped in front of a large dark green, slightly rusty pick-up truck.

Luckily Benjamin was the chatty type, so I needn't have worried. All I had to do was listen and give the occasional reply.

"I hope you don't get travel sickness as we've quite a long drive ahead of us," he said as we climbed into the pick-up and he started the engine.

"I don't think so... I was okay in the taxi and on the plane, so I guess not."

"You mean that's the only time you've ever travelled anywhere?" he asked, surprised, as I nodded in response.

"Well then, sit back and enjoy the trip. I'm sure you'll be impressed by what you see. Canada, especially this part of the country, is pretty awesome. There's lots to see."

I made myself as comfortable as possible as he made small talk as we drove out of the airport towards our destination. I listened while I looked out the window at the dramatic ocean views, enjoying the moment until he broached the subject I had been dreading: my parents.

"So, Lillian..." it was coming.

"Please, Benjamin... call me Lilly. Nobody has called me Lillian since, since, well probably since that photo was taken."

He laughed and nodded, "Okay, Lilly, but only if you call me Ben."

We smiled and were both silent for a moment, but I knew he was going to try and ask me again.

"Lilly. I just wanted to say how sorry I am about your parents going missing. I can't imagine what you must be going through. It must be absolutely awful..."

I didn't really know how to respond. So I chose not to.

"It's okay. I get it. If you don't want to talk about it, that is. You barely know me after all," he said with a sad smile as he pulled onto a busy motorway.

Feeling a little guilty, I nodded, "Why don't you tell me about you, then?"

"Not a heck of a lot to say, really," he took a breath before continuing, "my name you now know. I'm twenty-seven years old. I've lived in the same town pretty much all my life. I've recently opened a vet practice on the outskirts of town. Yes, I'm the local vet, in case you were wondering why the truck is covered in dog hair. What else would you like to know?"

"Brothers, sisters?" I queried.

"Oh, yeah. I have a younger brother, Oliver, who'll be seventeen," Ben looked at his watch, "in about thirty-six hours," he laughed. "I think your grandfather is hoping you'll join the party the day after tomorrow. Nothing grand. Just family and a few friends. I guess he's hoping you'll make some friends of your own."

I cringed slightly, and Ben noticed. "Sorry, too soon, I guess. You know, everyone will completely understand if you'd rather not join in. You need some time to settle in and chill out and... er... never mind."

I nodded. I didn't think Ben had the slightest clue how grateful I was. At the same time, I wondered who he meant by 'everyone', but I didn't ask. I thought about what he said about making some new friends, and I sighed quietly, remembering my sheltered life in England with so few friends. What if people didn't like me? Having never made any other friends, it was hard for me to imagine meeting people and being all... well... friendly. But then this life was going to be completely different from my old life. Perhaps I'd fit in perfectly. Maybe I could change. I struggled with the thought.

It was just after midday and the sky started to cloud over. I hadn't noticed how cold it was. I shivered.

Ben immediately whacked up the heat without saying a word.

We drove in silence for quite a while until I noticed we were approaching a ferry terminal. It dawned on me then that I had barely asked any questions, not even the most important one.

"You know, Ben, I haven't got the faintest idea where we're going."

"I love your accent, Lilly. It's so damn cute... just give me a sec while I sort out the ferry ticket," he wound down his window and while he chatted to the friendly lady with a big grin in the ticket booth and paid for our crossing, I read the signs around us and concluded we were going to a place called Langdale.

"Is that where you live? Where I'll be living? Langdale?" I asked as he wound the window back up again.

"No, we need to get a second ferry afterwards up to Powell River – that's where we're going."

I felt like such a child asking silly questions. I wish I had known more about this journey before it had begun.

"Sorry, I just haven't got a clue," I choked, as I felt as if those tears might emerge again.

Luckily I managed to hold them at bay and offer what was probably my most pathetic smile yet.

"Don't be sorry, Lilly. It's not your fault that nobody shared any of this with you. It's such a shame, really. It would have been great for you and your grand-father if you'd been able to meet each other before... and under better circumstances."

Ben was so kind. Just from this short trip, I knew that we would become friends. My first Canadian friend. I also got the impression that he understood me. More than anybody had understood me since the vanishing. Probably more than anybody had understood me at all. Ever. In my life. Why he could possibly understand what I was going through was beyond me, though. But I just had the feeling that he did, probably more than December had done over the past few weeks.

I hoped that I would find everyone in Powell River as understanding and kind as him. If they were, I would have no problem making those friends I was so worried about.

$\maltese$ 6 $\maltese$

It wasn't until the following day when some home truths finally started to trickle into my head. It turned out that my father and my grandfather hadn't spoken to each other for years. This explained why we never had anything to do with Canada or why my parents never even spoke of it.

"You need to sit down and have a proper talk with Lilly, Gabriel. She is totally in the dark. She's been through enough recently. Don't you think she deserves to hear the truth?"

I could hear the voices through the thin walls. I guessed that both Ben and my grand-father assumed I was still jet-lagged. Actually, I had barely slept a wink. I had found it difficult to fall asleep with no noise surrounding me. The silence had kept me awake for hours.

"There is a reason why things happen in this life, Benjamin, and my son must have had a reason not to have told his daughter about our life here. I do not feel that I should break his silence," replied my grandfather.

"But she's nearly fourteen years old, Gabriel. What if Jack never comes back?"

"Don't you say that Ben... don't even think it."

When Ben and I had returned from our five-hour journey the previous day, I felt so nervous about meeting my grandfather for the first time. But I was in for a huge surprise... there was much more to my family than just a grand-father. In fact, I soon found out that I had a much larger family than I could ever have dreamed of.

I needn't have been nervous, of course. I was treated like the long lost granddaughter, cousin and niece that I was.

As soon as we pulled into the long gravel driveway, a group of people bundled out of the house and stood on the porch, awaiting my arrival. All looked more nervous than me if that was possible.

"Don't worry, Lilly. This is your family. They won't bite. Come on. Come and meet them," said Ben with a smile and a gentle pat on my shoulder.

Tentatively, I climbed out of the truck. Ben collected my bags while I walked up to these strangers who suddenly burst into smiles and rushed over to me and began hugging me enthusiastically. I noticed that one person remained behind them all and stayed quiet while they all made their noisy introductions.

"Hi, Lillian. I'm your Aunt Meredith," said a rather short cuddly middle-aged lady with long black hair, and a tear in her eye.

"And I'm your cousin, Cormac. Meredith is my mum," said a shy chubby, spotty boy in his mid-teens.

"Hello, Lillian. I'm John. I'm Meredith's husband. It's a pleasure to finally meet you," said a tall, grey-haired man with glasses as he shook my hand energetically. "We have two other sons, Shayne and Bailey, but both are away studying at the moment and couldn't be here, I'm afraid," he added.

An attractive man with an uncanny resemblance to my father stepped forward next. He had long black hair tied at the nape of his neck and was probably in his early forties. He patted me gently on the back and said, "Lillian. I wish this had been under other circumstances, but it is a great pleasure to see you at last. I wish that you had been able to visit us long before now. I am your father's brother, Wyatt. This is my wife, Sonya." A beautiful slim woman with long bright white hair took my hand in hers and smiled kindly.

"I am so happy to meet you, Lillian. I believe we will be friends," she whispered in the most angelic voice. Instantly, I felt the same way. We would be friends.

"I would like you to meet our daughter, your cousin Josephine."

"Mum... please don't call me that! Hi Lillian, you can call me Jo. All my friends do," said a girl a little older than me with a scowl at her mother. The scowl was given with a laugh, so it was easy to see that this mother and daughter shared a close bond.

Jo was the image of her mother. Beautiful with long hair that was as black as her mothers was white. Both of them carried themselves with confidence, yet neither seemed aware of the incredible beauty that emanated from them.

"And this old boy here is your grand-father, Gabriel," said Ben with a smile. As he said the words, the group parted to reveal a broad old man with short greying hair waiting patiently to be introduced.

"Grandfather," I said, approaching him slowly.

He nodded and took both my hands in his, "We have waited for many moons for this day to come. Lillian Tulugaq, welcome home. Welcome home," he said, pulling me towards him. He hugged me tightly just for a moment before we all bundled indoors out of the cold. My hands and feet were freezing.

As Ben talked to my grand-father the following morning, I jumped out of bed and rushed into the kitchen where they stood, eager for them to see that I was not asleep and that I had heard every word they'd said.

"Oh... you're awake, Lilly. I'm sorry if we woke you," said Ben, blushing slightly.

Gabriel just shook his head as if to say, 'Well, now look what you've done.'

"I just popped in to have a quick word with Gabriel about... er... Oliver's party. Yes. Well, I'd better be going now. I hope to see you tomorrow, Lilly," he said as he put on his thick coat and gloves, adding with a wink, "but I completely understand if you'd rather give it a miss." And he was gone, leaving the two of us standing silently in the kitchen.

"Lillian..." said Gabriel. I waited.

"This is your home now. You must treat it as your home. Everything that is here is now yours."

I waited for the crunch, but it didn't come.

"Grandfather?"

"Lillian?"

"Please call me Lilly. Nobody has called me Lillian since... since before I can remember. But last night you called me something else, after my name. I didn't understand. My surname is Taylor... isn't it?"

Shaking his head, he said, "Tulugaq is the name of our forefathers, Lilly. It is your name, it is my name. It is your father's name as well as his brother's and sister's. It is in you. It is in here," he said, placing his hand over his heart. "It would do you well to remember this. This is where you come from, Lilly."

"But what does it mean?"

"Tulugaq?" he asked, and I nodded.

"It is the great blackbird of the sky. The Raven."

"It means raven?" I gasped.

"You are surprised, child?" asked Gabriel.

Unsure whether to tell him or not, while at the same time a little irritated at being called child, I walked over to boil some water to bide my time. Maybe he'll think I'm totally mad, I thought. Although I got a strange impression that nothing would shock him. I decided to fill him in on what happened on those lonely nights in England.

"Just before I came here I was... visited... by two big black ravens. They appeared at my window every night and frightened me a little bit. It wasn't just because they were there, it's because they knocked at the glass and looked at me. Really looked at me, you know. Almost as if they knew me. As if they were trying to tell me something. I don't know. I can't really explain it... I know it sounds totally crazy..."

But it turned out that I was right, he was not easily surprised.

"The ravens in London were our ancestors looking out for you in your hour of need, my dear child. There was no need to fear them. They were simply there to watch over you. To protect you. Fear not. They are a part of us."

It was difficult for me to know how to react to that. Clearly, I couldn't believe that my ancestors had come back from the dead, in the form of ravens, no less, to watch over me. Why would they watch over me? Why was I so special? Surely, if anybody needed to be watched over, it was my parents. Certainly not me. But ravens? Ancestors? Please.

My grandfather took my reaction rather well, actually. I guess he knew that I wouldn't, couldn't, believe something like that. Me, a teenager who had lived her entire life cooped up in a tiny room within an apartment block in a big city on the other side of the world. Nothing out of the ordinary had ever happened to me.

"My dear Lilly... must you keep your hair this way? Black is the colour of magical power. It is not something you should change unless nature requires it to be changed. You are beautiful. You look very much like my son. Your father. Embrace it. Do not hide from it."

"Oh, and another thing... Lilly.... you can call me Gabriel. Everybody else does." He smiled then and placed his hand on my shoulder before leaving me alone in the kitchen to my thoughts.

I had hoped that he would have told me whatever it was that was being hidden from me, but he didn't. I would have to wait.

$$\approx \quad 7 \quad \approx$$

Later, I felt the need to get out of the house and have a look around. Gabriel had told me not to wander too far and, above all, he warned, "Do not venture into the forest."

I had no idea why I was to avoid the forest, but I did as he said and instead took the gravel pathway towards the water. I didn't have to go far.

As I wandered along the edge of the ice-cold blue waters of the Pacific Ocean, I tried not to dwell on the fact that there was still no trace of my parents. Even after all these weeks, there was still nothing. We had been in touch with the British authorities, but it was looking more and more like this case would be shelved. It would continue to be unexplained. An unsolved mystery.

Instead of dwelling on recent life-changing events, I attempted to fill my head with the beauty that surrounded me. From the deep blue ocean to the bright blue of the cloudless sky and the star-tlingly beautiful green islands off in the distance, I was left genuinely breathless by its utter magnitude. Having little chance to appreciate it before now, I thought of how narrow-minded I must have been while living within London. Why my mother and father had never told me of the awe-inspiring landscapes to be found here, I will never know. It was like stepping foot inside the most magnificent giant oil painting – a true masterpiece that no artist could ever imitate.

Had I grown up here, I would never have wanted to leave, and everyone I knew would have been told of its breathtaking magnificence.

Suddenly something jumped high out of the water and back again with a loud plop. I was startled but curious. I searched for more movement, but there was nothing other than the gentle lolling of the soft waves lapping against the shore.

Finding a huge piece of driftwood on the little beach, I sat and waited patiently for it to happen again. I was determined to see what was capable of jumping right out of the water before my eyes.

I didn't have to wait long. Another splash and a plop, and a large fish revealed itself to me. Having little experience of such things, I had no idea what type of fish jumped like this – actually, I had no experience of fish at all – not to eat, nor to catch or even to look at, other than in school books.

I had never been in the ocean, nor had I even been on a boat before my arrival in Canada. Narrow-minded, lacking in experience of all kinds and naïve is probably how the people here must see me, I thought, sighing. If only my parents knew what I was going through. I didn't blame them, of course, I didn't. I just wished they had been more forthcoming with so many things. And now... perhaps they would never get the chance.

On the other hand, had they not disappeared, I would have continued on that same path. The same boring road with no twists or turns. The only 'fun' I had ever had was with December, and even then that was only ever at school. There had never been any excitement unless you counted the day when some kids had tried to blow up a school toilet. That was the extent of the drama in my world. Until now.

Not even the stories from the fairy tales I was so fond of could match the magic that could be found here in British Columbia. Even though I'd only been here a day or so, I hadn't even realised I was in British Columbia. I had noticed it on the licence plates of some of the cars in the area... 'Beautiful British Columbia'.

So I'd found an atlas in Gabriel's huge book collection and pinpointed Canada and discovered how vast a country it was. A country that was divided into several different provinces. British Columbia was the one the furthest to the west of the country and Powell River, I discovered is right on the west coast, right by the Pacific Ocean. I was also amazed by how close it seemed to Asia and how far from England.

Clearly, had I known when I was younger, I would have taken a lot more notice in my geography class. Now though, I would simply have to learn myself. I decided that I would start with Gabriel's ample book collection, once I had settled in.

As I admired the giant oil painting that surrounded me, I took a deep breath, breathing in that lovely scent of the fresh country air, the ocean and the pebbles around my feet. I could hear the faint squawks of birds in the distance where they flew from treetop to treetop and then soared overhead, eye-balling the fish below. But the breathtaking scenery could not stop my thoughts from once again returning to my parents, and I felt a little pang of guilt. Guilt for enjoying myself.

Shivering, I stood up, intent on walking a little more to warm myself up. I continued along the same stretch, carefully climbing over gigantic pieces of driftwood, clueless as to how such immense logs of wood could find themselves washed up here. Where had they come from? Had they drifted for hundreds of miles, thousands of miles? Or had they just come from around the corner? Probably the sort of question that every Canadian would know the answer to.

Canadian. That was me now. Actually, that had always been me. My father was Canadian, I didn't know about my mother. I was just born in the UK, wasn't I? Suddenly I had doubts about everything. I remembered that photo Ben had shown me at the airport. I was just a baby. I had never seen it before, and if I recalled correctly, the background certainly didn't appear to be London. Could I have been to Canada before? Could I have been born here? These were questions that needed answering.

Yes, I had an English accent that everybody absolutely loved here (they couldn't get enough of it, which was difficult for me, being such a quiet girl) but I was Canadian.

Another splash revealed yet another jumping fish to my side as I turned away from the water and headed towards a dirt track that

I presumed would take me back to the main road to lead me back home. Home. Weird that it didn't feel wrong to call it that after so little time.

I was just a few metres down the track when a grey cat suddenly appeared from nowhere. It approached me and began to purr gently at my side. I bent down to stroke it, and it stayed put for just a moment while it stretched regally before it began walking away from me, towards the sound of some softly playing music that took me by surprise as I hadn't noticed any houses nearby. Although the music sounded foreign, it was beautiful. Slightly eerie.

I approached, tiptoeing towards the sounds. Leaning against a huge tree almost twice the width of me, I carefully peered around it to get a better view of the property. The cat had left me alone and had wandered up towards the house.

Even though it was the chilliest day since my arrival, on account of the cloudless sky, I guessed, I saw an older lady standing outdoors with her back to me. She was painting. What she was painting, I couldn't quite see. She was humming loudly to the music as the cat positioned itself at her side.

Her grey and white hair was tied up in a bun, revealing an elegant long neck. She wore a woolly grey poncho that ended in a point just below her bottom. She was slim and sleek, and as she moved, she did so gracefully.

"Come on over, child. I won't bite or scratch you," she yelled above the sound of the music. She didn't turn; instead, she continued to sing and paint as if I wasn't there.

I came out of my hiding place and slowly walked towards her, wondering why she would say that she won't bite or scratch me.

As I approached, she finally turned to reveal perhaps one of the most beautiful faces I have ever seen on a lady of her age. But even with such beauty, I was startled by her apparent feline appearance. The way the colours in her hair intertwined with each other reminded me of the cat that had led me there. Her ears, although small, appeared to have a slight pointedness to them. And she had the brightest of light blue eyes. As she looked at me, she smiled a big hearty smile.

"I'm guessing you're Lilly?" she said with a voice that could melt chocolate. She must have every man in Powell River after her, I thought.

Nodding, I held out my hand, "How do you know?" I asked.

"You look just like your grandmother when she was young," she said as she took my hand, kindly holding it in one and stroking it with the other. "Plus... you have the same scent," she added, smiling. "She, however, didn't have dyed hair!" she said with a laugh. "I'm Rose. I know your family well."

Rose. It suited her.

"Plus, not a lot happens around here without me hearing about it. I do like a bit of gossip, and you've been the talk of the town for some time. People have been gossiping ever since your parents disappeared. Now, I understand that you probably don't want to talk about it, but I just want you to know that when you do feel like talking, my door is always open to any of the Tulugaq clan," she said matter-of-factly.

"Tulugaq" I repeated, "my grandfather told me what it meant this morning. I had no idea. I've always been known as Lilly Taylor, so it's going to take me some time to get used to it," I replied.

She looked shocked. "You didn't know what it means? And you didn't know that you are a Tulugaq?" she asked, clearly not expecting an answer.

Shaking her head, she gently pulled me by the hand and led me indoors. "Boy have you been kept in the dark."

We walked in through the back door that led into a cosy country kitchen, and she suggested I sit down at her breakfast bar while she placed a pan of water to boil on the hob and prepared a cup of tea for us both.

"I understand from Gabriel that your father changed your surname when you left the country. I'm sure it was because Tulugaq is not the easiest of names to pronounce. Especially for those English folk over there," she added, smiling.

"The word itself, Tulugaq, as you now know, means raven and it has been your family's name for many generations. There is much more for you to know, but perhaps you are not ready for that yet."

"Can you tell me what you mean?" I asked curiously.

Stopping what she was doing for a second, she turned and smiled, "Now that wouldn't be right. It is Gabriel who will tell you, but he will only do so when you are ready. Now, would you like sugar in your tea?"

I nodded as she dropped a heaped teaspoonful into the hot tea and swiftly stirred it before handing it to me.

"Rose?"

"Yes, dear?"

"Did you know my parents? I mean, before they moved to England?"

"I knew your father, Jack, well, but not... not your... your mother. She wasn't from around here. I believe she was a city girl," she sighed, "I am astounded that you know so little about your parents, your family and your ancestry. We are proud of our heritage here. I do know why you have been kept in the dark, but like I said... that's a conversation Gabriel will have with you when you are ready."

More like when he's ready, I thought.

Changing the subject altogether, Rose led me into the living room, where I noticed about six cats laying in various places - a sofa, a soft rug, on top of a cabinet. Any nook and cranny seemed to have a cat curled up tightly inside it. The sound of soft, gentle purring floated into my ears. It was so calming that I could easily have curled up with them for a nap.

"These are my babies," pointed Rose, "I won't bore you with all their names. There are 11 of them altogether... for now anyway."

We sat where there was a free space, and immediately three cats jumped onto her lap, and another two rubbed themselves against her legs, purring even louder than before.

I looked around and noticed that almost every painting on the wall was of some kind of feline animal. A wild mountain lion, a domestic siamese, a ginger tom, a black puma, a lynx. The most beautiful image was of a white tiger – the animal seemed ready to jump out of the frame and into the living room. I stood up to take a closer look and saw that they were all painted by a person called Rosa Lima.

"Did you do these, Rose?" I asked. "They're absolutely amazing. So lifelike."

"Why thank you, dear, that's very kind of you. They are all mine. Rosa Lima is my real name. It's Portuguese actually. My great-great-grand-father was originally from Portugal, and he married a local girl so you could say I have Portuguese blood." As she answered me, it was then that I noticed her eyes appeared to have changed colour. No longer were they bright blue, but so dark that they reminded me of treacle. I had never seen anything like it. Or was I mistaken? Perhaps it was merely a trick of the light?

"Is that what language the music was earlier, Portuguese?" I queried, recalling that lovely music with the foreign words that, along with the cat, had enticed me towards Rose's house.

"Why, yes, that's right. It's my favourite song. Canção do Mar – Song of the Sea. It's traditional Portuguese music called Fado. Do you like it?" Rose asked me.

Nodding, "I love it," I answered, and she stood up and went to her stereo and pressed play again before returning to her soft brown leather armchair with slightly ripped arms.

Together we sat in silence and listened to the beautiful sounds of Rose's favourite song.

素 8 ⅍

The following day I discovered that the birthday party for Ben's brother was to be held at Gabriel's house... my house. My home. And as I looked forward to the company of my new family, I got stuck in and helped wherever I could.

Meredith and Sonya turned up early in the day to give the place a good clean. I used a vacuum cleaner for the first time ever to clean all the floors while the two of them dusted the wooden surfaces and washed the kitchen from top to bottom before we started preparing the food. Both women were completely taken aback at discovering that I had never cooked anything in my life before staying with Dorothy and June. In fact, they were even more upset when I told them everything I had ever eaten had come out of a tin.

"Goodness, it's amazing that you still look relatively healthy. A little pale, perhaps, and certainly very thin. You could obviously use some good home cooking and some fresh vegetables," said Meredith as she turned me around to take a good look at me.

"I think we need to teach you how to cook, too," said Sonya. "It would be nice for Gabriel if you were able to help him cook a nice dinner every now and then," she added. I agreed, excited at the prospect of spending some more time in the kitchen to learn a new skill, after my kind old neighbours had taught me the basics.

If only my mother had been more like them. Meredith patted me on the shoulder and gave my hand a squeeze as if I'd spoken aloud.

For the first time in weeks, I actually felt safe and more importantly... loved. It was strange being rallied around by fellow family members when all I'd ever known were my parents, and they had never rallied around me for anything. There had never been anyone else.

As the two women laughed and joked with me, I smiled a sad smile. It would have been wonderful to have grown up like this, in this environment, I thought. In fact, it would have been wonderful to have been able to share some moments like those with my parents. What I wouldn't have given to have them there with me then, all of us laughing and joking together. But they were not there. They were still missing. I felt a tugging in my chest, and just for a second, I thought my eyes might well up with tears.

Sonya looked at me, and I just knew that she understood what I had been thinking. She reached over and squeezed my hand and smiled.

I returned her smile, and my tears retreated as I tried to change the subject on my mind.

"So how come Oliver's birthday party is being held here?" I asked, trying hard to think of other things.

"I guess Ben didn't tell you that both his parents died quite a few years ago," said Meredith as she kneaded the dough that would later become the most delicious homemade bread rolls.

I was shocked and surprised that he hadn't mentioned it in the car on the way from the airport. In hindsight, though, he probably didn't tell me because he didn't want to upset me.

"What happened to them?" I asked, thinking they can't have been very old at all.

"They were out together one day, taking a long trek when they came across an injured mountain lion. His mother was such a softy when it came to animals, and she insisted they try to help it. But it wasn't alone, and its mate attacked them. It wasn't to know they were trying to help. It was so tragic. Eleanor's wounds were so severe that she died almost instantly, but Jonathan carried her body all the way back to the main road where he managed to find help.

He later died in hospital. Ben was 12 years old. Oliver was barely two," she said.

Sonya explained that Gabriel insisted on bringing the children up himself, as Jonathan had been like another son to him. They had no other family, so it seemed like the natural thing to do.

As I took everything in, I began to understand my grandfather a little more. He was clearly a loving man that cared a great deal for his family and friends, which confused me as to why my own father, his own son, had fallen out with him. Why had they not spoken for so many years? It angered me a little, knowing that I could have experienced this wonderful way of life as opposed to that miserable life I had known in England.

Presumably, this had all happened a few years before I was born. I wondered where my father was during that time. Was it around that time that he had left with my mother? Or had they moved later after I was born? I was making so many assumptions. I needed to know the truth. Someone would tell me... eventually.

As the afternoon wore on, people started to arrive for the party. A few of them had clearly just come to get a good look at me. But they were all friendly and many offered words of reassurance and kindness.

I still had not met Oliver. I assumed he would be the last to arrive. Like a surprise party that wasn't really a surprise.

Ben had arrived and had sought me out before doing anything else. He wanted to apologise for butting in the day before. He'd known that I'd heard what had been said. I laughed as he said it, though, understanding that it was his way of showing that he cared... about my grand-father and about me. It was reassuring.

"I know something is being kept from me and I will find out what it is. Gabriel will tell me, but I do understand that he will only do so when we are both ready, so don't worry Ben, I won't be in the dark for much longer," I said, thinking of Rose's words. And as I thought of what she'd said to me, I could see her approaching the house. I hadn't realised she would be attending the party, but I was delighted she was.

"Hello, dear Lilly," she said as she entered without knocking, "hello ladies... you're all hard at work, I see," she smiled as she handed them a large basket. "I thought I'd better do my bit, so I made some scones with fresh cream. I know how the boys love them. And where are all the boys?" she asked, looking around.

"They'll be along in a little while, but Ben is here already... somewhere," answered Meredith.

He suddenly appeared, "Hi Rose," he said as he walked over to give her a hug and a gentle kiss on her cheek. They stood together, whispering quietly, casually glancing in my direction.

Giving them some privacy, I said I needed a little time to be alone and headed to my room where I sat on the bed for a while, staring out of the window into the green foliage of the dark forest beyond.

After a few minutes, I began to feel like it was calling out to me. I stood up and moved closer to the glass which steamed up as I breathed against it. I thought I saw something white move within the trees, but as I wiped the glass with my sleeve, there was nothing there.

I sat back on the bed again and lay down. I closed my eyes and thought of the past couple of days, of the wonderful welcome I had received and of all the lovely people I had met.

As I lay there, I heard a gentle tapping on the window. Before I opened my eyes, I imagined myself back in London with the two ravens who visited every night. It was the same tapping sound, and as I let my imagination run wild, there it was again. Tap tap.

I opened my eyes, and sure enough, there were two ravens at my window. I watched them as they tapped twice with their beaks against the glass, heads cocking from one side to the other. They looked at me for a few minutes and then flew away. I wasn't frightened, in fact, they made me smile. Then I heard my name. It was very faint, but it sounded like someone was calling me. The sound didn't come from the house... but from further away. I wondered if it was coming from the forest. I sat up and looked out the window again. Nothing. As I strained to listen for it again, there was a knock on my door, and Rose appeared.

"Are you all right, my dear?" she asked, smiling.

I nodded, but I could tell from her expression that she didn't believe me.

"Are you ready to come back out? Almost everyone is here – including Oliver."

I nodded and followed her towards the door.

Pleased that I had decided to join the party, I came to the conclusion that I needed to make more of an effort to make friends. I wanted my new life to be full of people. As I walked into the living room, all the guests were already mingling and milling around. Although I was dreading being the object of everybody's attention, I needn't have been concerned as it seemed that a lot of people were more interested in the birthday boy himself. And everyone else was talking and laughing among themselves. If only December were there.

But before I had a chance to dwell on that thought, Ben made a beeline for me and took my hand in his. "Hey, Lilly. Let me introduce you to Oliver." He gently led me to the centre of the attention where a group of people ranging in age from 16 to their mid-twenties appeared to be listening intently to a story being told by the tall young man in the centre, with his back towards me. They were clearly enraptured by his funny tale, which was about were-wolves and vampires.

After he'd given his punchline, the group burst out laughing and began talking among themselves. Ben tapped the young man on the shoulder to get his attention.

"Oli... there's someone here you should meet."

I wasn't prepared for what happened next. As he turned, I let out an involuntary gasp. I tried to make it sound like a cough. I failed, totally embarrassed.

Oliver was, without doubt, the most beautiful boy I had ever seen... but it was his eyes that I couldn't pull mine away from. They were so deep and dark, almost jet black. I could quite easily have sunk into them. It was quite extraordinary, actually. I had never seen anything quite like them. And I liked the feeling. I liked the feeling a lot.

Even though he was 10 years younger, Oliver was taller than Ben and was as blonde as Ben was dark with strong features, a slightly pointy nose and a chiselled chin.

"Hi. You must be Lilly. It's great to finally meet you after all this time," he said with a smooth voice that belied his young years.

It was the first time that the sight and sound of anyone had taken my breath away, and I didn't know what to do. I didn't know what to say either, so I quickly mumbled 'hi'. With my cheeks burning, and before I could make even more of a fool of myself, I turned around and walked as fast as I could, away from him. I didn't even give him a chance to reply. I just carried on walking, without a backward glance. Away from the other guests. Away from the party. I rushed back into my room and sat on my bed for a few minutes, trying to catch my breath. But it wasn't enough. I needed to get out. I needed some fresh air. So I grabbed my coat and, careful not to be seen, opened the front door and ran away from the party.

❈ 9 ❈

I felt like such a fool. An idiot. I hoped that nobody had noticed me, but I was sure that Oliver's first opinion of me was not a particularly good one. How could it possibly be? I was rude, and then I ran away. If I'm lucky, I thought, perhaps everybody would just think it's too much for me to cope with. All those people. Yes, it is a lot to deal with in such a short amount of time.

Before I knew it, I had run to the edge of the tall, dark trees. The forest Gabriel had told me not to enter. I turned briefly to see if anyone had noticed. I appeared to be alone. What the hell? I thought. What have I got to lose? So I walked beyond the trees as I zipped up my coat and put on my warm gloves.

Adrenaline coursed through my body, just as it had when I'd chopped off all my lovely long hair and bleached it. It was the first time I had gone against someone's wishes. Although I did feel guilty, I couldn't shake the fact that I was being kept in the dark about something important, and it wasn't fair. It was my life, and I deserved to know. And so I felt free taking those steps into the unknown. If they don't tell me what I have a right to know, then I won't go along with their wishes, I thought.

I started to walk a little faster, breaking out into a run and as I approached each tree, the branches seemed to welcome me in. As my breathing quickened, my face began to become gently scratched by the foliage around me.

I stopped to catch my breath and to look around. I was surrounded by beautiful tall green trees and wide thick tree trunks but no footpath. What did drift into my ears, though, was the sound of trickling water. I strained to hear where it was coming from and followed the gentle, soothing tones.

Moments later, the trees gave way to a large open expanse, and I stood beside a gently flowing river. The water was crystal clear and revealed pebbles and stones of all shapes and sizes laying on its bed. I sat on a huge smooth boulder and enjoyed the moment, leaning back so that I was flat on my back. I looked up into the blue sky and noticed some dark clouds rolling in, but I didn't care. In fact, for the first time in a long time, I didn't give a damn.

The sounds of the forest and the water beside me gently lulled me, and so I closed my eyes, feeling restful, wondering why on earth my grandfather had tried to stop me from walking into the forest. There was nothing but beauty and peace. I felt myself slowly dropping off to sleep, and even though my fingers and toes tingled in the cold, I drifted and drifted until sleep overcame me.

A WOMAN DRESSED IN WHITE APPEARS FROM NOWHERE IN FRONT OF me. She is very pretty with long black hair down her back. Her smile lights up her face, and she sits by my side. She says nothing while we sit in silence. Suddenly she lifts her arm and a raven lands on her hand. She looks at me and nods. She's trying to tell me something. I try to ask her what it is, but nothing comes out of my mouth. I try to speak again, but there are no words. I begin to feel a little frustrated. Why can't I speak? Suddenly the woman disappears, and a large cat is sitting by my side, with the raven perched on its back. It opens its beak, "Lilly... Lilly," it says. I'm frightened. The raven speaks? "Lilly... Lilly." It becomes louder and louder, and suddenly it is shaking me.

10

"Lilly!"

I woke up and noticed Jo standing beside me, gently nudging me and calling my name, "Lilly, wake up."

"You had me worried for a little while, then," she said. "I saw you lying here and, well, I didn't really know what to think."

"Sorry... I just had to get out of the house, and I guess I was much more exhausted than I thought. The sound of the water must've sent me to sleep," I answered guiltily with a yawn.

"How you can sleep in this cold, I've no idea," she laughed, "You know, Gabriel would be so disappointed to know that you came here... but don't worry, I won't tell him. After all, I come walking in the forest all the time, and I know he'd go nuts at me too," she added with a guilty giggle.

A feeling of relief flooded through my veins. Earlier, I had been intent on rebellion but thinking about it now, I didn't want to hurt my family.

"I haven't been gone very long, have I?" I asked.

Jo reassured me that my nap was only a short one and she had, in fact, watched me leave the house and had followed me ten minutes later to make sure I was okay.

Sitting down beside me, I noticed she had a small rucksack on her back, which she took off as she smiled at me. "I figured we might need sustenance, so I grabbed a few bits before coming after you." She opened the bag, revealing scones, sandwiches, fruit and cans of what she called 'soda'.

My stomach rumbled in response.

"I guess I was right," she said as we delved in and enjoyed our own mini banquet out in the cold as we listened to the peaceful sounds of the river.

As we ate and drank and got to know each other a bit better, we knew that we would become good friends. Jo was a few years older than me and would be celebrating her eighteenth birthday in a few months.

"I'm so glad you came out to find me, Jo. My life has been so weird over the past few months, and so it's good to have someone to confide in."

Cocking her head to one side just like the ravens on my windowsill, Jo smiled inquisitively, and I continued, "After my parents vanished, I felt like I didn't belong anywhere, you know? Actually, come to think of it, I guess I've never felt like I belonged. But coming here... and meeting all of you guys, it's just incredible. I can't describe it, really. Well, it's like, like I've finally come home, you know?"

She nodded sadly.

"But I feel guilty about it. How can I feel like that when my parents are gone?" Tears threatened to erupt down my cheeks.

"You have nothing to feel guilty about, Lilly. You have come home. You clearly belong here. It's not your fault your parents disappeared. We will find them. I'm sure they're okay. Why don't you tell me all about your life in England? I'd love to know more!" she said in an attempt to cheer me up. I knew she would be horrified when she learnt the truth, but she insisted on hearing about it.

So I told her how I had grown up. In a strange and lonely world, trapped in a home with no love, no joy.

"Lilly, that is so sad. All of this proves that you really have nothing to feel guilty about. You deserve some happiness now. I wish you had grown up here with us, though. We would probably have been the best of friends from the day you were born. You know, for someone that never had a loving family, you're very grounded. If I had to guess, I would have said that you grew up happy and loved, judging by your personality."

Jo's upbringing couldn't have been more different from my own. She had always been surrounded by the most loving family, the Tulugaqs, and it showed. She was happy and delightful to be around.

"If you had grown up in Powell River, you'd know that it is wonderful here. Of course, there's always going to be your typical neighbourhood gossip, but everyone always rallies round and makes it the most wonderful place to be. But at least you're here now. We can enjoy it together from now on."

I was so touched that I hugged her before she asked me a little more about England.

After telling her of the little I knew of the country that had been my home, I expressed how upset I was to be kept in the dark about something within the family, about something that I believed I had a right to know.

"I do understand, Lilly, but Gabriel never does anything without giving it a lot of thought first. He must have a very good reason not to tell you... yet, anyway. I'm sure he will tell you soon enough."

"Don't you know anything, Jo? Is there something you can tell me?" I asked, hoping that she would at least be able to give me just a hint of something... anything to put my mind at ease.

She looked away then and sighed, and I knew I was wrong to ask her. She was obviously torn between her love for her family and her newfound friendship with me.

I decided not to push it. It wouldn't be fair. So as she looked back at me, I smiled and changed the subject.

"Tell me about the school, Jo... I guess I'll be attending the same school as you. Can you give me an idea of what to expect?"

Relieved to have a change of subject, she smiled at me with thanks and told me all about the local high school, how it was like any other American or Canadian high school – with popular kids and geeks and football and cheerleading. She told me I shouldn't worry, though. She knew I would fit in well. I certainly hoped so. I just hoped that I was at the same level as the other kids in my class; it would be so embarrassing to be behind them. Jo just had one school year left, whereas I still had a few to go. I wished we were the same age so I would have at least one person to go to class with. But she reassured me that I would get on with everyone. There weren't really any awful kids there, she'd said.

Didn't every school have their fair share of awful kids?

"Come on, Lilly. We ought to make a move and get back to the party. Everyone will be wondering where we are. We don't want them to worry. Plus, Oliver was asking after you."

Jo could tell I was mortified, so I explained my reaction to him, and she smiled. "Well, he seemed interested to know more about you so I wouldn't worry if I were you."

I told her that I'd rather give the party a miss altogether and she suggested we at least go back and show our faces. We could always sneak off somewhere else if we felt like it.

Reluctantly, I joined her, and she led the way back through the forest until we reached the footpath I had walked on earlier.

It was then that I realised I could have so easily become lost within those trees and so I was genuinely grateful to Jo for following me. After voicing my thanks, she became a little more serious... "If I'm totally honest with you, Lilly, it was Rose that saw you leave. She asked me to make sure you were okay, and it was her that gave me the bag with the food. Of course, I would have followed you had I known you'd ventured out into the forest alone, but I hadn't actually noticed."

"Well, I am grateful to you both," I said, gently punching her on her shoulder as we approached the log home that was full of the sounds of music, voices and laughing.

Although gratitude enveloped me, I knew it wouldn't be the last time I ventured out into those woods. Although I knew I could easily get lost in there, deep down I had the feeling that the forest held the key to this secret and if nobody would tell me, I would have to find out for myself.

That night after everybody had gone home and I lay there in the darkness, I thought about Oliver and how stupid I must have looked on our first encounter. Fortunately, Jo had assured me that Oliver wasn't the type of person to think of anyone as stupid. Apparently, he was a great guy, loved by all, and she was sure my initial reaction had just left him curious to find out more about me.

When we'd returned to the party, albeit briefly, I'd scanned the crowd for him, and he'd looked up and seen me. I blushed like an idiot, but he waved and flashed those beautiful white teeth at me in what can only be described as the most stunning smile... ever. My stomach had flipped before I'd disappeared back into my bedroom.

I was fully aware that I was beginning to look like a lovesick puppy, and I felt stupid. Although I had never had a boyfriend, I'd had my share of crushes at school. None of them was like this though. Perhaps it was just an aftereffect of losing my parents, and I was looking for someone to love and to love me back.

Before I closed my eyes that night, I took one last look towards the forest – I'd purposefully left the blinds open, so I could see outside. But there was nothing but pitch black all around, the only lights were those coming from the sky above, where a million glittering stars squinted brightly. The night sky in this part of the world was amazing. But just as I admired them, the pitch-black reminded me once more about something Gabriel had said before, that black was the colour of magic. I wondered then if there was, in fact, magic around me as I dozed off to sleep.

I found myself back in the forest, surrounded by the sounds of running water and hundreds of birds twittering away. I was standing in the same spot where I had stood earlier, and so I decided to do a bit of investigating. I climbed down the smooth rocks towards the water. It was icy blue and sparkling so bright that I had to shield my eyes.

As I bent down to touch it, a raven flew down and stood to my left, followed by another one to my right. They pointed with their wings to the opposite side of the river bank. I looked up and saw two cats – one pure black and one pure white. Their eyes as black as night. They sat and watched my every move. Even when the ravens took to the sky, they didn't take their eyes off me. I looked upwards and saw them flying high above me, watching me from above, and I felt as though I was being pulled between the birds and the cats. I couldn't understand, but it was as though I needed to follow them... but did I cross the river to be with the cats or did I go upwards to be with the ravens? I looked up again, and in a matter of seconds, I was up there with them, flying in the sky looking down on the two majestic creatures below. Yet I felt a pull between them but for now, the feeling of freedom, of flying, was just too good and so I remained with my two friends as we glided effortlessly above the trees. As I swooped down towards the water, I saw three birds below. Three black ravens, graceful and serene. Then I realised what I saw was a reflection in the water. I was a bird. I was no longer a teenage girl. I had become a raven. The shock of the realisation temporarily stunned me, and I had no control over my body. I fell towards the water.

I awoke with a thud... I'd fallen out of bed.

"Lilly... are you all right, my dear?" said a concerned voice as the light was flicked on and my grandfather rushed in towards me.

"I heard you scream and then there was a bang," he said worryingly.

I explained I'd just had a strange dream and it had made me fall out of bed. "I'm fine. No need to worry," I said. But I couldn't help but notice that he looked a little preoccupied.

"A strange dream?" he'd asked.

"Just a dream, Gabriel. People have strange dreams all the time," I laughed. "It's okay, I'm fine, go back to bed. I'll see you in the morning."

He said nothing more, except to wish me a good night and he switched the light back off as he left me to think about the ravens and the cats and that exhilarating feeling of flying.

few days had passed since Oliver's party, and the Tulugaq
family had made me feel like I was part of their clan. I
truly felt like I was one of them, even though I often
thought about my parents. I had also started school. And although
it was excruciatingly embarrassing having to stand in front of my
new classmates as I was introduced, strangely enough, I was
welcomed with open arms by everybody.

I did have a feeling that being Jo's cousin had a lot to do with it.
That, and the fact that I have 'such a cute English accent,' they
said.

The most surprising part about my going back to school was
that I discovered that my love of reading had stood me in good
stead and I was more advanced than everybody else in my year, so I
had managed to skip a year... which had taken me by complete
surprise.

During a few lunchtimes with Jo, I noticed she was the focus of
many admiring glances, from boys and girls alike. She was one of
the most popular girls in school, and it wasn't just because she was
beautiful or because she had an aura about her. It was because she
was caring and friendly and was just really well-liked by all...
teachers and students alike.

As we sat and ate our sandwiches, Jo introduced me to some of
her friends, but none of them stayed to eat with us. She said she

had something important to discuss with me alone and so her many friends happily went and sat elsewhere.

"Gabriel called me this morning Lilly and told me you had a strange dream the other night. Do you want to talk about it?"

She wanted to talk about a dream? I was surprised that such a big deal would be made from a bunch of way-out thoughts that were going through my head in my sleep.

"Dreams are our unconscious mind trying to tell us something. It could be something important. It could be a memory from childhood that you're blocking, maybe…?"

I laughed, "I don't think so, somehow, Jo. I dreamed I was flying. If I was ever able to fly, I'm sure I'd remember."

She laughed too, and we continued to eat in silence for a moment, but I could sense there was something she wasn't saying.

"How come Gabriel is asking you about this, anyway?"

"I guess he thinks I'm the best person to speak to you about anything… and everything. He can see we're becoming close and I guess he wants to take advantage," she laughed again.

"So you're like his spy or something?" I laughed.

"Yeah, I guess you could say that. But don't worry, I won't tell him anything you don't want me to tell him."

Why was it such an issue? They were just dreams. Dreams weren't important. Not to me, anyway.

"Well, if you really need to know – and I don't mind you telling him – in that dream, I turned into a raven. I doubt that's an early repressed childhood memory though," I said smiling, as I suddenly recalled another dream I'd had. "Remember when I went into the woods alone and fell asleep by the river? Well, I dreamed of a woman and a raven then too. There's something about these ravens here, isn't there?" I laughed.

Jo looked at me in a way she hadn't looked at me before. Almost as if she was looking at someone else. "Jo?" I whispered.

Her expression softened, and she smiled, and then the bell went, signalling the end of lunch break. "Saved by the bell, eh Jo?" I joked as she told me she'd see me later before I headed in the opposite direction to my next class.

All afternoon I couldn't shake the feeling that something strange was about to happen. It was Jo's expression that had started it all off. That feeling that she was looking at someone else even though she was looking right at me.

When I got back from school that afternoon, Meredith greeted me.

"Hi, sweetie! How was your day?" she asked, giving me a quick hug as I dropped my bag on the kitchen floor and flopped down onto one of Gabriel's handmade wooden chairs.

"It was okay, thanks. Where's Gabriel?" I asked, eager to sit down with him and have a proper chat to find out, finally, just what was going on.

"I'm afraid he's had to leave town for a day or two... which is why I'm here. I'll be staying with you until he gets back."

I tried to hide my disappointment. I loved being with Meredith, but I had been hoping to finally get some answers. And why hadn't he told me he was going away? Why was everything so secretive? Life seemed even weirder all of a sudden. Instead of getting the answers I craved, the questions were just piling up, and I was becoming increasingly frustrated.

Early that evening, however, something happened to take my mind off things. Oliver came round to see me. Yes... to see me!

Meredith and I had just finished eating dinner, followed by a dessert totally new to me: pumpkin pie. I'd only ever read that pumpkins were for Halloween, after seeing pictures of them carved out to make creepy lanterns. I had no idea something so delicious could be made from them. So there I was, totally stuffed with the top button of my new black jeans undone, the jeans that Jo had given me when she'd seen my wardrobe – or lack of it. So I was lazing on the sofa when the doorbell rang. I assumed it would be for Meredith, so I stayed put, eagerly reading the first Harry Potter book which I had found on the bookshelf when in walked Oliver. Blood rushed to my cheeks as I saw him standing there.

"Hi Lilly," he said as I struggled to get up from the sofa and do up my button at the same time.

"Er... Hi! What are you doing here?" I asked, hoping that I could make a better impression this time.

"Well... I was kind of in the area and thought I'd pop by and say hello... so hello," he laughed as he fidgeted with a pair of gloves in his hands.

"He..llo." God I felt stupid. Why couldn't I utter more than a few syllables to this boy?

He stood and looked around awkwardly.

"Er... why don't you sit down." He sat.

And then silence again.

"Can I get you a drink?" I asked.

"Sure. A Coke would be great. Thanks."

I rushed into the kitchen, via my bedroom where I brushed my hair and put on a little lip gloss (another gift donated by Jo), picked up two cans of coke and walked back into the living room. He stood as I entered the room and sat when I sat.

"So... Lilly. How are you settling in?"

"Okay, I guess. Pretty well under the circumstances," I said without even thinking.

"I'm so sorry about your parents."

"I'm sorry about yours too."

"Kindred spirits," he said.

"Sorry?"

"I guess we're like kindred spirits. You and me," he said with a sad smile.

I warmed to him even more than before, and all I could think was that I just wanted to know everything about him.

"I'm sorry about the other day at your party. I didn't mean to be rude."

"I didn't think you were rude at all. I thought you were... kind of cute, actually. Okay maybe a bit weird too," he laughed.

He thought I was cute!

"I was disappointed that you left so abruptly, though. It would have been a great party... if you'd stayed."

"Sorry," I managed to mumble.

"That's okay. I understand that being thrown into a party after everything you've been through was probably a little tough. All those people and stuff. I was very tempted to come after you, but I didn't want you to feel uncomfortable."

"Are you always this quiet?" he asked as he turned to look me in the eyes.

I looked at him and shook my head, "No... not really. It must just be you."

"Oh." He looked disappointed.

"No... I don't mean that in a bad sense. I mean, it's like at the party. I just couldn't talk. I wanted to say so many things. I just couldn't. And now, I don't know where to start."

"So it's not because you don't like me, then," he asked, smiling.

"Oh, no! Absolutely not. You're great. I guess I just get a little shy around you."

He laughed.

"Why don't we start like this: I'll ask you some questions about yourself, and you answer?"

I agreed. "So, do you miss England?"

"That's a difficult one because if I say no, that's almost like saying I don't miss my parents. But I honestly really don't miss England. I never felt particularly alive there, if you know what I mean. Here it's so different. I feel like I belong here. I never felt that over there."

"I don't think it means you don't miss your parents. Of course, you miss them. I still miss mine, and they died a long time ago."

I smiled sadly, "Ask me another."

After a few moments, he asked, "What do you think of the Canadian hospitality?"

I laughed, "That's a funny question! But now that you ask, I never realised people could be so nice. I haven't met a single person here who has been unfriendly or rude. Everyone I've met – even just briefly – has been wonderful. That's probably another reason why I'm falling for Canada."

He smiled again and was silent for a few moments while he came up with another question.

"How are you enjoying school here?"

"Honestly? I love it. I always liked school because it was so good to get out of our flat... I mean apartment. I didn't feel as restricted there, and here... well it's a whole new ball game. For the first time in my life, I have more than one friend at school. Respect from everybody, if you know what I mean," I said as I looked at Oliver's confused expression.

"You don't really understand what I'm talking about, do you?" He shook his head.

"Let's just say I lived a very lonely life in England. I was naïve. I didn't know anything about life. Yes, I learned a lot in school, but school doesn't necessarily teach you about life, it just teaches you facts about life. I'm sorry, I'm rambling now."

"Don't be sorry, Lilly. I think I understand what you mean. I'm just sorry that you had such a lonely upbringing. If you had grown up here, it wouldn't have been like that at all. I would have made sure of that," he added shyly, "I would have liked to have known you before now," he said, colour creeping up to his cheeks.

"I'd better go," he said suddenly as he stood up. "Thanks for the Coke. Maybe we can see each other again soon?"

I nodded and smiled, and before I knew it, he was gone.

As I went to sleep that night, I still had butterflies. Oliver liked me. And he thought I was cute!

❧ 12 ❧

The following evening, Oliver unexpectedly turned up again. It was almost a re-enactment of the previous night. I was sitting on the couch comfortably reading a book, full from eating a hearty dinner when in walked Oliver wearing a shy grin.

"Hey, Lilly. I hope you don't mind me popping in to say hi again."

"Of course not," I answered, as I made a mental note to make more of an effort with myself in future.

I offered him a Coke, and he said yes. I ran into the kitchen, via the bedroom again, brushed my hair and put on some lip gloss before rushing back in.

But this time, as I handed him the can and we both sat down, he said, "You know what. Why don't we take a walk instead?" Standing up, he placed the can on the coffee table almost as soon as he'd sat down.

Relieved to have something else to do, I jumped up and grabbed my coat, gloves, hat and scarf.

He laughed at me as I wrapped myself up and we stepped outdoors after I yelled to Meredith that we were going for a walk. She appeared briefly with a cheeky smile and winked at me before closing the front door.

"So..." I said.

"So…"

"Here, we are again."

"Yup," he answered as we strolled down the road.

I waited for him to say something to break the ice. We walked for a few minutes until he finally said, "Lilly?"

"Yes?" I answered, hopefully.

"Last night when we spoke, you mentioned that you were falling for Canada… well, I wanted to ask you if… if it is just Canada that you're falling for? Or whether there might be something, or someone, that you're falling for too," he asked. But before I could answer, he blushed and added, "Sorry, you don't have to answer that if you don't want to."

I wanted to answer his question; after all, I knew the answer. I was falling for him, without a doubt. I felt like we had a connection.

"Can I ask you a question?" I asked hesitantly.

"Shoot."

"Why did you really come to see me tonight?" I asked bravely.

This time, his face turned pink before he replied.

"Honestly… I was hooked the second I laid eyes on you, Lilly. It's weird really, because I've always hung out with girls my age, but I almost feel like you've put a spell on me. Not that I'm calling you a witch or anything," he laughed, "but I've never been bewitched before."

During the silence that followed, I swear I could hear his, and my own, hearts beating.

I was so glad that I'd wrapped my scarf around my face… because I was blushing so much and grinning like a Cheshire Cat.

"And even though I barely even know you, I feel like I've always known you," he laughed, breaking the silence, "and I can't believe I'm actually saying all this. Out loud. To you."

"Well, I'm kind of glad that you are saying it out loud. To me. I know how you feel, Oliver. I like being around you. It just feels… right. But I guess we'll just have to get to know each other better won't we?" I replied happily, "but now… it's so freezing. Why don't you walk me back home?"

As we turned to walk back towards the house, I looked up at him and smiled. He caught me watching, and he laughed.

"In answer to your question... Canada isn't the only thing I'm falling for," and I laughed cheekily as he took my gloved hand in his.

As we approached the front door, Oliver asked me out on a date, "a proper date," he said, the following Friday night. I happily accepted, and he leaned in and gently kissed me on the cheek. My first kiss!

"I'll pick you up at seven," he said, and then he was gone.

That night I drifted off to sleep happier than I had done for a long time. But my dreams were strange and vivid once again.

I found myself flying freely with the ravens while I was looking down at the cats below. Only this time they weren't small cats, one was a white mountain lion and the other a black panther.

They were stalking something. I couldn't quite see what it was, but as I flew closer, I saw that they were stalking Oliver. I tried to get his attention, but he couldn't see me, he could only see and hear ravens squawking at him from above. "Oliver, Oliver, watch out!" I yelled, but as hard as I tried to get him to understand me, I knew that all he could hear were the incomprehensible noises of a bird.

I tried to reach him in time, but it was no good, the cats had already pounced, and as I landed nearby, I saw that he was covered in blood. As I approached the bloody scene, the cats seemed to bow down to me and skulked away as I picked him up with ease and carried him to the waterside to try and clean his wounds, but as I looked down into the water, my reflection wasn't that of a raven or a girl... it was that of a mountain lion. I screamed.

I awoke with a start. My face was soaked from tears streaming down my cheeks.

"Lilly, goodness me," said Meredith as she rushed into my room and switched on the light. Sitting down on the bed, she cradled me in her arms. "It's all right. It was just a bad dream. Just a dream. Shhhh. It's over. It's over."

The tears wouldn't stop as I tried to tell her that Oliver was in danger. "The cats, the cats," I sobbed.

"No, it was just a dream, sweetie. Oliver is fine. Calm down." Eventually, I realised that it had been nothing but a nightmare – triggered by the memory of the words I had learnt just days before... that Oliver and Ben's parents had been killed by wild mountain lions. It was nothing more than my subconscious mind playing horrible tricks on me.

Meredith had been kind, assuring me that all was well. She even made me a cup of sweet cocoa to help soothe me back to sleep. The rest of the night went by quietly.

❦ 13 ❦

The following day I was awoken by the gentle sound of Gabriel's voice.

"Another dream, Meredith? I guess I have no choice now but to tell her the truth. I had hoped the dreams wouldn't have started until she was at least eighteen. I understand now that it is a sign. She must be told. It's such a shame that this is all happening now. She is so young," he'd said.

I could hear the sadness in the way Gabriel spoke, and that made me feel sad, too, even though I had no idea what he had to tell me. I finally felt relief. Relief that, at last, I would know the truth. But along with the relief came the dread. After all, it must be bad for there to have been so much secrecy in the first place.

Now that I knew he planned to tell me, I waited for him to broach the subject, so that day I just acted as normal, I went to school and completed my homework before dinner. It was after we'd eaten and washed the dishes that something finally happened.

He had summoned my father's brother and sister, Wyatt and Meredith, who had arrived just as we had finished washing the dishes.

"Lilly. It is time," said Gabriel, as Meredith took my hand and led me into the living room where we all sat in silence before Gabriel produced an old battered shoe box and took off the lid. In it were photos and letters. He handed me a picture of a very beautiful young woman with long black hair. There was something vaguely familiar about her. In her arms was a tiny newborn baby. Clearly, the photo had been taken in a hospital immediately after the baby had been born.

"Who is this?" I asked.

"Her name was Serena," answered Meredith with a sad smile, "Lilly. This is your mother."

I gasped and shook my head.

"No, my mother is Vivian. This isn't Vivian."

"No, Lilly. Vivian isn't your mother. Serena is. And this little child is your sister, Neleh," said Gabriel as he passed a number of different photos to me. All were the same little girl at different ages. One was the photo Ben had taken to the airport to identify me with. Gabriel told me it was the closest image he had of me. "You two looked so alike when you were babies."

In another, the little girl was about four and was being cuddled by my father on a beach on a lovely sunny day. He looked like a completely different person, so happy. I had never seen him happy before. Another pictured her aged around 10, posing happily for the camera in this very living room with Gabriel laughing to her side. The most poignant image was that of her as a teenager pictured with Serena and my father. The image of a very happy family – it was then that I noticed Serena was pregnant."

Wyatt spoke. "She was carrying you in this picture, Lilly."

I shook my head, but deep down, I knew. It was obvious to see. I looked very much like Neleh and Serena. And as I looked at the photos, I realised that Serena was the woman from my dream. I didn't know what to think. For so many years, I had grown up believing Vivian was my mother, yet I had never felt any kind of bond with her. She had always made it blatantly obvious that she didn't care for me. It made sense. I felt my eyes welling up, so I blinked hard to try and get rid of the tears before they spilt down my face.

"Lilly," said Gabriel, "this is just the beginning. There are things we need to tell you that you are going to find hard to believe."

I nodded, unable to say a word.

"Just after you were born, Neleh was killed," said Wyatt.

I gasped and gulped back the tears as it hit me that I'd once had a sister, but now she was dead.

"And shortly afterwards... Serena died too. I'm so sorry, Lilly," he said sadly.

"What? But how? Why?" I cried, looking down at the picture of the happy family, ripped apart by two deaths.

"Nobody knows exactly what happened, dear. All we know is that Neleh was murdered in the forest. By who or what we don't know for sure – although there were suspicions at the time," said Meredith as she held my hand tightly in hers.

"Suspicions?" I asked.

Gabriel looked so angry, but before he could speak, he was interrupted by Wyatt, "Lilly there is a man in that forest who is believed to have been responsible for Neleh's death. His name is Sammy Morton."

Gabriel gave me another photo showing Neleh probably a couple of years older than me, pictured with a handsome young man with olive skin and black hair and even darker eyes. They looked so happy together.

"Is that him?" I asked.

Meredith nodded.

"But they looked so happy. Why would he kill her? I don't understand."

"Nobody understands. But he hasn't been seen since. There was a lot of talk. But we can't be sure," added Meredith.

The angry look on Gabriel's face suggested he thought Sammy was guilty.

"But what about Serena? What about my mother?" I asked.

"Your mother killed herself, Lilly," said Wyatt, quietly.

"How could she do that? How could she just leave me, her baby. Her own daughter?" I cried.

"Again, Lilly dear, we do not understand that either. Grief is a funny thing. People react to it in such unusual ways. She must have been so heartbroken, and she just couldn't believe that her eldest daughter was dead. That combined with postnatal hormones. We simply don't know. We wish we knew what had been happening. Perhaps we could have stopped her from doing what she did.

Serena was my best friend, Lilly. It was tough to understand for me too," said Meredith as she choked back the tears.

"Tell me," I asked slowly, "tell me how she did it. How did my mother kill herself?"

Gabriel stood up abruptly then and turned his back towards me as if he was still struggling to come to terms with what had happened all those years ago. He spoke slowly and quietly, "She just walked out of the hospital in the middle of the night and continued walking until she reached the highest point in the forest and she threw herself into the river. She must have half frozen to death before she even got there. All she had on was a hospital gown. She didn't even have any shoes on. It was December. It was freezing."

I could barely breathe. My mother. My true flesh and blood. The woman who had carried me for nine months and had given birth to me had killed herself just after I was born. I could picture her walking through the snow, barefoot – yet she was probably barely even aware of the cold. Clearly, all she could think of was the death of her precious daughter. My sister. Both were dead. Tears rolled down from the corners of my eyes. I couldn't stop them. Soon my face was completely wet.

Gabriel approached me and crouched down in front of me. He placed his hand on my shoulder and patted me. Looking me deep in the eyes, he said, "I didn't just lose my grandchild and my daughter-in-law that night, Lilly. I lost your father, and I lost you too." He held me close to him then, just for a moment.

There was a knock on the door. "That'll be Rose," he said as he stood up.

"I'll get it," said Wyatt as he stood and went to open the door. "Hi, Rose. Thanks for coming," I heard him say. She whispered something, and I heard him respond, "yes, she knows everything up until Serena's death."

"Oh, the poor dear," I heard her say.

Rose walked in then, removing her warm fur coat and throwing it accurately on the coat hook on the wall. "Darling, Lilly," she said as Gabriel and Meredith gave her room to embrace me tightly.

She said nothing for a few minutes. We just sat in silence while the tragic news sank in, making my heart feel so heavy. The sound of the kitchen clock could be heard ticking, almost in time to the beating of my heart. To the beating of all our hearts.

Rose looked at me then. She really looked at me as if she was looking deep into my soul.

"You are my sister's daughter," she said nodding. "Yes, Serena was my darling little sister. She was the most wonderful person, Lilly. Everybody loved her. When she was born, she was a little miracle. That's what my parents and I had called her. 'Our little miracle'. My parents were getting on, you see. They never thought they'd have another child so when she appeared, it was a huge shock... a wonderful shock, of course, but a shock nonetheless," she said smiling.

Gabriel laughed then, and I thought what a lovely face he had when he laughed. I hadn't seen much laughter in him since my arrival.

"It was a shock to the whole community," he said. "Your mother was nearly seventy," he chuckled as he spoke to Rose and they shared a smile together.

I was amazed too. A woman of nearly seventy had given birth, naturally, to a healthy baby girl. Not something you heard much of these days, I thought.

"She was embraced by everyone here," said Rose, "and I raised her as my own after mother and father passed away nearly ten years later. I was happy to do it though, with the... absence of children of my own. Serena wasn't your average ten-year-old. She was so mature and bright. She and Jack were the best of friends from a very early age. We all knew that they were soul mates, so when they told us they wanted to get married, we were overjoyed. It was the most natural thing in the world for them both. She was nearly sixteen, and Jack was nineteen."

"She became pregnant with Neleh almost immediately, and they loved that child. They doted on her. Neleh was exactly like her mother... your mother..." she said, nodding at me, "she was head-strong, beautiful and intelligent. Everybody loved her. So when the cycle started to repeat itself again, nobody was worried. Neleh and Sammy seemed like soul mates too. They had wanted to get married themselves and start a family at a very early age. We didn't worry. We thought it was the most natural thing in the world –

Neleh following in your mother's footsteps," she stopped then and asked Meredith for a glass of water, who quickly poured her a drink and passed it to her before she continued.

"Sammy Morton was a very well-liked boy here. He was an orphan, raised by a foster family in town. We really thought he and Neleh were well suited. What went wrong between them, we don't know, but that day when he carried her lifeless body back into town, he just looked different. He didn't look like the same person. He looked crazed somehow. And everybody just started believing that he had murdered her. He disappeared that day, and nobody has ever seen him since. Some people say he still lives in the forest, some people say he is dead and haunts the forest. Whatever happened, he disappeared within that forest, Lilly, which is one of the reasons Gabriel doesn't want you to ever go in there."

"But what happened to his foster parents? Didn't they want to find him?" I asked.

"They couldn't accept what had happened and so they left Powell River a few weeks later."

I found it hard to believe that his foster parents would just up and leave like that unless they thought he was guilty too.

It was so much to take in that my head began pounding harder and harder, and the sound of blood pulsing through my veins became louder and louder until I could barely hear myself think. I felt hot and uncomfortable, and I just needed a moment to myself. I excused myself for a couple of minutes and went and splashed my face with cold water in the bathroom.

As I stood there, I looked at myself in the mirror, but I couldn't see myself. All I could see were the morphing faces of Neleh and my mother.

Again, I recalled the dream I'd had in the forest. The woman that had tried to speak to me in my dream had been Serena. Had my mother been trying to tell me something? I suddenly remembered Gabriel's words to Meredith that morning: 'I guess I have no choice now but to tell her the truth. I had hoped the dreams wouldn't have started until she was at least eighteen. I understand now that it is a sign. She must be told'.

Were my dreams real signs? I thought of Oliver, and the feral cats and a cold shiver ran down my spine.

As I returned to my family, they were whispering among themselves. They quietened down as I approached them and sat down.

"I know there is more... so please go on," I said bravely, although I didn't feel so brave.

This time, Meredith spoke. "Lilly, what we are going to tell you now might sound fantastical and surreal, but we need you to keep an open mind, okay?"

I nodded.

"When your father left us and took you away to live in England, we believe that he did so against his own will. We believe that a witch cast a spell on him," she said nervously.

It was like an epiphany to me, and it was then that I knew they were talking about Vivian.

"Vivian was a witch. Yes, it makes sense to me now," I whispered.

I could feel a weight being lifted not only from my shoulders but from those around me too. I could hear sighs of relief. I thought once again to that strange black room and Gabriel's words: black was a magical colour.

"Lilly... why does this make sense to you? Did she ever do anything to you? Did she ever hurt you?" asked Gabriel.

"She never laid a finger on me, but she did hurt me in other ways. She stopped my father from spending any time with me. She tried to stop him from loving me. Although he withdrew from me, he would never have stopped loving me, would he?" I said. A few more tears fell down my cheeks as I began to see Vivian in a totally new light. The truth hurt.

"Of course not, Lilly. You mean the world to him. I'm sure of that," said Meredith.

"How did you know that Vivian is a witch? What did she do?" I asked, wondering how it had all begun.

Between them, they explained how my father had met Vivian at the hospital when I was born and that she had not left his side after my mother had died. My father, apparently, had changed instantly and it wasn't the kind of change that happens after the death of a loved one. It was an inexplicable change. A change that could have only occurred through some kind of skulduggery. In this case, they believed that skulduggery to be witchcraft. And the person responsible was, undoubtedly, Vivian.

"She somehow stopped us from seeing you, and Jack," said Wyatt. "We did everything we could to see you both, but there was some kind of physical force preventing us from doing so."

"We spent a lot of time at Serena's graveside, hoping that we would see him there but he never appeared. Not once. That wasn't the Jack we knew. And before we knew it, we found out that Vivian was taking you both to England. When we confronted her, she became so angry, she threatened us. She said if we ever tried to come after her, she would... she would hurt you," said Meredith.

"That's why we've never been able to see you or why we never tried to call you, sweetie. God knows we wanted to. We desperately wanted to, but we couldn't risk it. We couldn't risk losing you for good. We managed to track down your address and wrote to you, but we're sure that Vivian disposed of the letters before you ever saw them."

"So you've not seen my father since my mother died?" I asked.

They shook their heads.

"That must have been so awful for you all... and now we don't know if we'll ever see him again," I cried.

"We have no idea what has happened to him... or to Vivian, but I sincerely believe that they are both still alive. The fact that they vanished without a trace suggests more witchcraft though. We have been doing everything we can to find Jack, and we have reason to believe that they are somewhere in Canada," Gabriel said.

I asked him what they have been doing to try and track them down and why he felt they were still alive, but before I could get an answer from him, Rose spoke instead, and I certainly wasn't prepared for what she was about to tell me.

"Lilly, dear, for us to answer that question, you need to learn the truth about who you are."

Confused, I nodded.

The truth turned out to completely change my view of the world.

❧ 14 ❧

The things that I had only read about in fairy tales turned out to be far from fantasy. According to Gabriel, these things were very real, indeed... a secret world that I had no clue really existed until my family began to unfold the truth...

Werewolves, werecats, vampires, witches, ghosts... you name it, it existed within this world. A world that seemed so alien to me that would soon become my everyday life.

I was told all about my father's side of the family, that they were descendants of ravens and actually could morph into the bird. Not just that, but my mother's side of the family could morph into cats.

"Okay... this is just sounding ridiculous... how is this possible? Surely you're joking with me now? How can a human being become an animal? It's impossible."

Rose shook her head slowly and told me that it was very possible. She said that it was very real and that there was a strong possibility that I had the gift myself.

"W...what gift?" I asked gingerly, afraid of what they might say.

Gabriel and Rose both glanced at each other sideways, before telling me that it was possible that I had the ability to change into either a cat or a raven... or even both.

Clearly, the idea was absurd to me, and I told them so as I

stood up abruptly and paced up and down the room shaking my head.

"Lilly, these dreams you've been having are the strongest indication so far that you can change into both animals. Remember you told me you changed into a mountain lion and a raven? Well, it appears that may be true. Your subconscious has been telling you so," said Gabriel softly.

"Well, can you change, Gabriel? Can you?" I asked, defensively.

"And what about you, Wyatt? Meredith? Rose? We're all related... surely you can all change too?" I said, my body shaking as I spoke.

There was silence for a moment before Rose stood and took both my cold hands in hers. "I can, Lilly. I can change into a lynx. Your mother wasn't able to, and sadly we never knew if Neleh had the ability as she died before she became of age," she said softly.

I could tell she was telling me the truth by her eyes, those black eyes that became the brightest blue in different lights. I remembered the day that I'd met her. She'd known I was there without even looking, her sense of smell and her sense of hearing were both incredible, just like a cat. I'd even thought she'd looked feline-like at the time. Her home was full of cats and they'd all gravitated towards her as if she was one of them.

It all made sense. What didn't make sense was the fact that I was one too. Could I really be? Could I really be able to change into a cat or into a raven? I felt as if I was dreaming. I even pinched myself to see if I would wake up. I didn't.

"What about the ravens? Which of you can change into a raven?"

"None of us here can, sweetheart. Your great-grand-father could though. He was a great man and a great raven," said Meredith.

"What about my father... could he?" I asked suddenly thinking that perhaps that's what happened. He escaped Vivian by changing into a bird, but apparently, I was wrong because according to Gabriel, he was never able to either.

"We usually find out around the age of seventeen or eighteen. If it hasn't happened by the time we're twenty, it tends to mean that it's not going to," said Wyatt.

I wondered if it had happened to Jo, but they told me she was still 'innocent' as they put it. However, she was fully aware that it could, and she has had some dreams to indicate that she may well have the raven 'gene'. And Cormac? At fourteen, he too was still too young, apparently.

"But we're practically the same age," I stuttered.

"With you, dear, it just seems to be happening sooner rather than later," said Rose.

"After all, you have already demonstrated an intelligence beyond your years, according to the high school that is," smiled Gabriel.

"Does the rest of the family know about all of this?" I asked. The answer was yes, it was our family secret that had to remain a secret in order to protect us all.

"To protect us from what... or who?"

It was then that I found out about the predators and other creatures.

"In the past, the werecats and the ravens were enemies, but over the years they have formed a strong bond – mainly due to the friendship between Rose and me. However, elsewhere in the world, they continued to hold a strong dislike for one another," said Gabriel.

This sounded quite natural to me.

"So what does this make me," I thought aloud, "if I have the genes of both within me?" I asked as I struggled to understand what this could mean.

"Honestly, we don't know. You appear to be the first of your kind Lilly. Well... the second after Neleh but we don't believe she ever changed," said Gabriel.

Sitting down, I took a deep breath before my imagination began to run riot.

"So what other predators do we have?"

It turned out that werewolves were not particularly fond of ravens or cats. Generally speaking, though, we didn't have a problem with the vampires as they tended to lust after pure human blood. There have been times far in the past when we were the victims of the bloodsuckers, as Wyatt described them, but they were not too fond of the way we tasted, apparently. Well, that was positive, I supposed.

I laughed aloud as it sounded so ludicrous. The others laughed with me momentarily, but it didn't last long. Again there was silence as I tried to take in all these bizarre stories.

I took a moment again to think of my father and Vivian and, as if reading my mind, Meredith crouched down to the tin of photos and rummaged through them, clearly looking for something in particular. She found what she was looking for. It was a picture of Serena and me at the hospital and to one side, was Vivian.

"This is the only photograph we have of Vivian, and the only photo we have of you," she said as she passed it to me.

Vivian looked much the same as the last time I'd seen her. The only real difference was that she had a long deep gash on her cheek. It looked fresh. I'd never noticed a scar, though.

Up until a few months ago, the last day I'd seen her, she had kept her hair the same way – a blunt bob in a deep red colour with never a single hair out of place. Her piercing blue eyes stood out menacingly, belying the innocent, sweet smile that curled from her lips. It was the only time I'd ever seen her smile.

It was the first time that I could see her for what she really was. Pure evil. If only I'd known before. Perhaps I could have done something. Perhaps I could have stopped the spell she maintained over my father.

As if reading my mind, Meredith spoke up, "There's no point in thinking about what could have been, Lilly."

"How do you always seem to know what I'm thinking," I asked, surprised.

"Just one of my special talents," she said with a wink, before changing the subject to Vivian again.

"When Vivian first met your mother, she was the sweetest person. Obviously, we found out later that it had all been an act. She was after your father the whole time. She was weaving her way in. And when Serena died, it was her perfect opportunity to pounce, and that's exactly what she did. She needed to get to know your father before she could cast her spell. Sadly we weren't quick enough to prevent it from happening because we had no idea what she really was."

"She was obviously a very good actress," added Rose.

"But how did you know that she wasn't who she said she was?"

Vivian had managed to get a job as a nurse at the hospital, whether she was qualified or not wasn't clear. Not that it mattered... she was a witch, after all. My family believed that was where she first saw my father and there that she decided she must have him. She didn't care that he was madly in love with Serena and that his second daughter was about to come into the world. All she cared about was having him for herself.

"It was when your father acted like we were strangers, and then Vivian threatening us – and you – that we started to suspect that there was something darker going on, so we started to try to find out more about her. It took us a long time, but we managed to find out that she wasn't just a normal woman," said Wyatt.

The real 'being' behind the 'perfect' Vivian was a far cry from the beautifully manicured and perfectly made-up woman I had thought I knew. An evil monster was a better way to describe her. Although her look said she was an attractive mother in her 30s, the truth was frightening.

Gabriel had tracked down a coven of white witches in north-western Canada who knew exactly who she was.

Vivian was just one of many aliases she had used over time. And she had existed in this world for many hundreds of years. In order for her to continue to be young and beautiful, she needed a man. But not just any man.

She needed a man who possessed unusual powers like were-wolves, werecats, ravens, halflings, changelings, and so on. Which is why it was strange that she latched onto my father, apparently, because he had never shown to possess any such powers. He had never been able to change into a raven, so why choose him? It was a question neither Gabriel nor the witches could answer.

Could she have mistaken him for someone else? Could she have wrongly thought he had the powers? Could he really have had the powers but not told anyone? Not even his closest family members? Although unlikely, it was a possibility.

I tried to stifle a long yawn, but Meredith noticed and said, "It's getting very late. We should all get some sleep, especially you Lilly. We know this has been very hard for you to take in – especially all in one evening. Why don't you go to bed now and we'll continue our talk in the morning?"

The thought of my comfortable, warm bed was appealing, even though I had a feeling that my sleep would be particularly fitful that night. Now that I knew the truth about myself and my family, my subconscious would undoubtedly go into overdrive.

"Don't worry, Lilly, we'll be here for you all night. We'll know if the dreams start. Try and get some rest," she added as if she had read my mind again.

All four of my family members gave me long, hard hugs before I headed to my room. I knew they would continue talking well into the night.

As I tried to sleep, things started dawning on me about Vivian. Now that I knew she was truly evil, so much more started making sense.

I remembered the many times that she had prevented me from being alone with my father. Come to think of it, as long as I could remember, I had never had any time with him at all. Vivian had always ensured that she was there... always. It had never occurred to me to be a problem because I honestly thought she was my mother.

For a long time, I'd thought all mothers treated their children the way she had treated me. Up until I had met December, I had nothing to compare it with. Of course now, when I see the way Meredith is with Cormac and the way Sonya is with Jo, I knew that she was about as far away from a real mother than anyone could possibly be.

She had not once praised me for doing anything right. She had scolded me for the slightest thing, and she would lock me away in that tiny little room called my bedroom for hours and hours on end. The real reason I had spent so many years with no friends, the real reason I never watched any television, the real reason for my lonely existence was entirely the fault of Vivian. How could I have not seen it before? I could have rebelled. Why didn't I rebel? I honestly didn't know. Maybe deep down I knew there was something evil about her. Perhaps deep down, I knew that either me or my father would end up getting hurt or worse.

There was something niggling me as I forced my eyes closed and I couldn't quite put my finger on it. It was something about my father. I knew there was something hidden in my subconscious that might help me understand, but it just wouldn't come to the surface of my mind. As I eventually slept, my dreams were more like repressed childhood memories than real dreams, but they were obviously things that I needed to remember to help me move forward.

I was a little girl, perhaps six or seven, locked in my bedroom. I heard gentle footsteps outside the door... someone was tiptoeing. The handle turned slowly, and the door was pushed open before my father appeared silently as always. He was acting like he didn't want to be heard, and he kept looking behind him to make sure he was alone. He put his finger to his mouth to stop me from speaking and then he produced a large hardback book which he handed to me, again placing a finger on his lips. I knew he wanted me to keep it a secret, so I hid it immediately. I put it under the bed until later that night when I knew they would both be sleeping. When I looked up, he was gone.

I later remembered that this wasn't just a single memory. This had happened many times over the years. Each time, he crept in silently and stealthily, handed me a book and then disappeared. The books were always similar. They were all either fairy tales or books with supernatural themes.

When I woke up the following morning, I knew what it was that had been niggling me.

My father had been trying to tell me that I was in the middle of my very own supernatural fairy tale. He was trying to say to me that he was trapped, that Vivian was the evil stepmother and that there was danger. Everything now fell into place. Everything I had been told by my family the previous night had been true. I had just needed my father to confirm it, and he had in a way by allowing all those memories to flood back in a dream.

I felt more alive than I ever had, and I was ready to face the world. More importantly, though, that morning, I had the overwhelming sensation that my father was still alive, and I wanted to do everything possible to find... and help him.

I had obviously slept for quite some time because after I had showered and dressed and walked into the kitchen, everyone looked as though they had been waiting for me for a while. Clearly, they were unsure as to how I would be after all the news of the previous night had sunk in, but they smiled when they saw that I looked positively happy and refreshed.

"So, when are you going to show me how to change into a raven... or a cat?" I said, breaking the ice with a smile.

Gabriel smiled and said, "Now Lilly is truly home."

I felt more at home then than I ever had, and it felt so good to be surrounded by such loving family members. Real family. I had a real family. A family who had finally revealed the truth about who I am. No more secrets. No more lies. This was the truth, and I was accepting it.

I wondered who else knew of our secret... whether it was a curse or a gift I didn't know but I would in time. Was it just my immediate family or did friends know who we truly were too? It would have been wonderful for me to be able to confide in my dear friend, December, in England, but I feared I could not. My mind then drifted to Oliver and Ben. Would I have to hide my true self from the boy I had fallen for? The boy that made my heart leap just at the mention of his name?

I asked my family, and I was told exactly what I didn't want to hear. Neither Oliver nor Ben knew the truth, and it was better to keep it that way, especially in light of the fact that their parents were killed by mountain lions. After all, we did not know yet what kind of cat I would have the ability to transform into. It would be heartbreaking for them to know.

I felt heavy-hearted. Would this mean the end of our relationship before it had even begun? I was saddened because I had felt such a connection to Oliver and was developing such a close friendship with Ben. I certainly didn't want to lose what we had so I had no choice but to keep my secret closely guarded.

"It is for the best, at least for the moment, Lilly. We understand there is a connection between you and Oliver," said Gabriel and I gasped in embarrassment. They knew? I blushed.

Meredith smiled, as did Rose, who winked at the same time. "It's no secret. It was obvious the moment you laid eyes on each other that sparks were flying," she laughed.

I was so embarrassed that I had hoped the floor would open and gobble me up, but I was growing up. I had to act like a grown-up, not like a child.

"I hate to have secrets from him before we've even got to know each other. But I do understand. I won't say a word to him or to Ben."

As I thought about the fact that nobody else knew of our family's remarkable abilities, I was reminded of Vivian. How had she known that there was a raven gene if it was such a guarded secret?

I was told more about all the weird, wonderful and frankly terrifying things that really existed in our world. That it was a completely different world to that which most people know about. It was a world full of supernatural entities and people with super-human abilities. This was a world more like that of the fairy tales than the one I'd become accustomed to. I had to be careful who I trusted, and I had to watch out for things I wouldn't normally have to look out for...

A person's excessively beady and watchful eyes could indicate a changeling – a human that could morph into any number of other beings in the blink of an eye.

A person who avoided the sunlight with the palest of skin and a certain redness to their eyes could be a vampire, eager to feed on the blood of others.

I might notice someone with sharper-looking teeth than usual – this could potentially be a werewolf. Their teeth becoming fangs during the change, and contrary to popular belief they couldn't just change during a full moon, they could change at any time, anywhere.

These were just some of the beings that I might be able to identify, but the most dangerous ones were those that I would have no idea who or what they were. Like me, for example. Nobody would ever think that I was capable of changing into an alternate being (neither did I, for that matter, at that stage) so I had to be ultra-careful around everybody, at all times.

Some of these others could be everywhere and anywhere, including people that could change into a variety of beasts. Gabriel mentioned some of the animals that he knew about, but he was certain there are more.

Bears, already known as one of the most dangerous animals in the world – imagine one with the intelligence of a human and no way of knowing who could change into one.

Sharks – provided I steered clear of the ocean I wouldn't have to worry about these, as long as I took note of anyone who had an unusual love of the ocean.

What he told me next really gave me the creeps. I've never liked the idea of any form of reptiles so to hear that there were people out there that could change into large slithering serpents, that just freaked me out. Give me a bear any day.

There were also mountain goats, elk and coyotes in these parts too.

Gabriel described how he had heard of a man who could change into a crocodile, although he'd never seen it with his own eyes. Apparently, this man was originally from Africa, where crocodiles are common. He told me that I should note that these beasts were only the ones he had heard of in Canada and the United States – there would undoubtedly be hundreds more across the world. And in this day and age, with global travel at its peak, they could be anywhere.

I was astonished that we were constantly surrounded by so much danger, and yet millions and millions of people had no idea. There were many myths and legends in all corners of the world but to know that they were probably true was shocking, almost beyond belief.

"The only way you can prepare yourself for any of these beasts, Lilly, is to start doing a lot more reading. Not just the supernatural stuff your father gave you, but you need to understand everything you can about these deadly animals. What makes them tick. At least then, in the unlikely event that you should ever come across any in a dangerous situation, you'll at least have some semblance of preparation on how to deal with them," said Wyatt.

I agreed that knowledge was important. I also thought that I could learn a lot from Ben, being a vet. I knew then that he would be an asset, as well as a friend.

As if reading my mind again, Meredith mentioned that Ben was looking for a trainee assistant. She was sure that he would be delighted if I applied for the position. She said I could continue with school and work with him at weekends and then take up the job when I'd completed my studies in a few years. It sounded like a great plan. Something to work towards. I liked the idea.

The others approved too. I would have a word with him later to see if he would be interested, but I had to make it clear that I didn't want to be a charity case, just because we're friends... practically family.

As lunchtime approached, I suddenly realised it was Friday, and

I hadn't gone to school. I voiced my thoughts aloud and was reassured to hear that Gabriel had phoned the school that morning and told them I was unable to attend, for personal reasons. He told me I shouldn't worry because, under the circumstances, they were very understanding.

It also dawned on me that Friday was when I had a date with Oliver. I blushed at the thought. Meredith smiled. She knew what was going through my mind.

"I think perhaps we've put rather a lot on poor Lilly since last night. We should all go home and leave her to think about everything. After all, it is a lot to take in," she said, standing, "plus, John will be coming home for lunch, so I'd better go and get him some food ready."

She kissed me on the top of my head, kissed everyone else before putting on her warm green coat and walked out the front door without a backwards glance.

The others stood and said similar things before they prepared themselves for the cold weather outside with coats, scarves and gloves before following along behind her.

As Rose stood up, she took my hand and offered to make me some lunch at her house if I wanted to walk her home. As Gabriel had also gone out, I locked up and wrapped up warm as we headed off in the direction of her home. Instead of walking along the roadside, we chose to take the scenic route, the way I had walked when I had first come across the lovely Portuguese music.

I thought back to that day, to my first impression of Rose and wondered if I looked anything like a cat... or a raven for that matter, but I couldn't see it in myself. Perhaps others saw me that way. Although I hoped that the dangerous ones couldn't tell, I certainly wouldn't want them to know.

As we wandered along the shoreline, I heard the plops again of the fish jumping out of the water and back again, wondering if they were simply fish or fish that had another secret side to them. A human side.

They looked pretty harmless, so I assumed, and hoped, that they were of the simple fish variety. They were small creatures, so it was hard to imagine them changing into human form. But then, so were ravens and cats. I wished I knew how the change took place. I didn't feel the need to change myself, but I would have liked to witness someone else changing – perhaps then I would feel better prepared for what was to come in my own life.

Just 24 hours ago I would have walked down there by the sea, and I wouldn't have had a care in the world (other than that of my missing 'mother' and father). I would have seen everything in a completely different light. Innocent and naïve to the real world. That was me... yesterday.

How things can change in less than a day. Now everything I looked at appeared different. Everything that once would have taken my breath away because of its natural beauty would be scrutinised in a way I never dreamed possible. Even the other birds that sat innocently in the trees above us could be more than just birds. Were they really birds? Or were they humans that could change? As they watched us, what were they seeing? Did they see innocent bystanders to the world? Or did they see us as threats? Particularly Rose with her catlike appearance? Could they sense the cats in us?

The world was a completely different place to what it was yesterday.

As we wandered through those immensely tall cedar trees and I noticed glimpses of the bright blue sky between the branches, Rose stopped and turned to face me.

"I'm sorry that I couldn't tell you the truth when we first met, my dear. I do hope you understand that I had to wait for your grand-father to speak first. It was between him and you."

I told her that I did understand the reasons behind the decisions, and I didn't hold it against her. It was irritating at first but not any more.

"I so wanted to tell you about your mother."

"You can now, though," I responded hopefully as we wandered through the trees along a winding pathway that had probably been created by my family over the years.

It was what she wanted to hear, and so she began to tell me what my mother was truly like. Beautiful, honest and playful. From childhood until her early death, she was the same. Devoted was another word she used. "Devoted to me. To our parents. To Neleh. She was devoted to you the whole nine months she carried you, too, Lilly. You mustn't forget that. Although you didn't have the chance to know her, you two developed a bond during that time, and that's a bond that can never be broken. I think this is why she is able to get through to you so strongly in your dreams. You need that bond to be able to do that."

That simple sentence meant the world to me. Even though I had never had the opportunity to know this remarkable woman, I did have an unbreakable bond with her. She was my mother. She gave birth to me. She loved me, and she would never forget me. Not even in death.

"I was always very envious of her thick dark hair. She only ever had it trimmed – so it grew very long over the years, and she didn't have a single grey hair!" Rose reminisced. "Whereas I had grey hair from my early twenties," she laughed.

"But isn't that because of the cat... business?" I asked.

"That's a good way to put it, dear. Cat business," she laughed out loud again, a graceful deep sound that matched her own grace and beauty.

"I guess you're right. It must be the siamese in me," she chuckled as she unlocked the white wooden back door of her house. Four of the cats were already with us, they had joined us in the forest a good few hundred metres away. The others gathered in the kitchen as we walked in. When they had first seen me, they hadn't appeared interested at all. Now, they all made a point of brushing up against my legs, purring loudly. It was as if they were welcoming me.

"I told them about you, dear. They know you're a part of this family now."

I stuttered, thinking of something to say in response but I honestly couldn't think of anything suitable. Nothing that made much sense anyway.

Clearly, being part cat, part human had its advantages when you wanted to communicate with your fellow felines.

"In time, you'll be able to speak with them too. For now, though, they'll be happy with a stroke and a nice warm lap to sit on," she said, suggesting I sit down in the only well-worn comfy armchair next to the breakfast bar.

I did as I was told and immediately a cat that was so black he almost looked blue jumped up onto my lap. He stood there for a few moments looking deep into my eyes, before hopping onto the armrest and curling up. I patted him gently on his back before a second one leapt onto my knees too. This was the one that resembled Rose and was the one that had greeted me when I had first laid eyes on her. She was an off-white colour with a faint grey pattern all over her. The best way to describe her was that she looked like she'd been run over by a car and had a tyre print across her back. Her eyes, like Rose's, were so dark, yet as I had seen outdoors in the sunlight, were bright blue.

She did as the black cat had, stood and stared into my eyes. Her head dropped slightly to the side as if she was really looking into the depths of my soul as if she was reaching inside of me to see what was really there. Once she had come to some sort of conclusion, she began to purr. It was as if a smile crossed her face. It was hard to describe but not only did she remind me of Rose, but she reminded me of... me. I liked her, and she clearly liked me too, judging by the way she curled up on my lap and began to pummel me with her paws.

"She's happy," said Rose, "she's very fond of you. Her name is Scully."

"As in the X Files?"

She nodded, and I remembered the book my father had given me once. It was a book from the TV series, hence me knowing the name. Having never watched television, I wouldn't have otherwise known.

"Why did you call her Scully?"

"It wasn't my idea. Ben came up with it actually, and I liked it so it just kind of stuck."

Scully had been found wandering the streets of Vancouver when she was just a few months old. Someone had rescued her and taken her to the local vets – it just happened to be the vets where Ben was training at the time.

"You're a lucky cat, Scully, to have found a home here of all places."

I probably imagined it, but she appeared to nod at me as if she was perfectly aware of how lucky she was.

"I believe they all came here because they were meant to come here. Some divine force brought them to me. I'm quite a strong believer in that," said Rose, as she put the finishing touches to two tuna sandwiches and two glasses of milk. Leftover tuna was placed into a large bowl on the floor to where all the other cats rushed to get in on the action.

Scully remained comfortably seated on my knee, so I had little choice but to eat my lunch where I sat.

🌿 16 🌿

Rose began to tell me more about my mother. Even though she had Neleh at an early age, Serena never dropped out of school – continuing until she graduated before getting a part-time job at a local museum.

"She loved that place. She felt like she really belonged there. You should go and have a look around it one of these days. It may also help you understand a bit more about Canadian culture."

Apparently, the museum was almost exactly the same as to the day she died, so it would be nice for me to see what the place was like where she spent quite a lot of her time.

Wondering what her life must have been like before I was born, I asked Rose where she, my father and Neleh had lived. Was it nearby?

"They actually lived with Gabriel for a few years before renting a small cottage on the outskirts of town. A few years before she died, Jack bought a plot of land. It took him a long time to save up enough money to build a house on it, but he had scraped enough together and was planning to start construction just before you were born. Sadly it was never built because of what happened."

"But he had started to build it?" I asked curiously.

There wasn't much to it apparently. Just a concrete base and some wood had been delivered. Rose told me that nothing had been touched since Vivian took us away. Keen to see the house where I could have spent my childhood, I asked Rose if she could give me directions so I could go and find it myself. After we'd eaten our lunch, she drew a rough map to help me get there. She did offer to take me herself but understood when I said it was something I felt I should do alone.

I heard more about my mother as we sat amidst the cats that afternoon. Rose told me some funny stories of how naughty Serena could be when she was a child and how she had made their parents feel young again. Theirs truly was a happy family and even when their parents died within a short time of each other, the mourning period didn't last so long because they both believed that their parents continued to be together, soul mates forevermore. It was the stuff of fairy tales with happy endings, until of course that terrible day when Neleh had been killed. A tragedy which led to such heartbreak for everyone... except Vivian.

"Is there any way of finding out more about Vivian? Is there nothing we can do to try and find her? I feel certain that my father is still alive, and I wish I could do something to help him," I asked.

Rose explained that Gabriel was currently doing everything in his power to do just that. He had found out a few things about her, and he hoped to be able to inform the family more about her when he had gathered sufficient relevant information.

"But in the meantime, you shouldn't worry about any of that. You're still only thirteen, Lilly – nearly fourteen, I know! You should be enjoying your life as much as you can. I understand that it is difficult to do so when there is so much tragedy surrounding you, now and in the past. I also understand that you have been told such overwhelming news since this time yesterday, so you need to just take some time to let it sink in. You must come to terms with it before you throw yourself in at the deep end, my dear. You've got nearly fourteen years worth of fun to catch up on. And besides... I understand you've got a date tonight. You should be preparing for that," she laughed.

Meredith had obviously told her... and probably the rest of the family too, but I didn't mind. It was wonderful having people actually caring about me.

"Perhaps you ought to do something with your hair," she half-joked. She did have a point.

I left Rose's house soon afterwards so that I could have some time alone before my date with Oliver. I'd never been on a date before and wanted to look as good as possible. This was something that was a bit difficult considering I had chopped my lovely hair off and dyed it peroxide blonde.

It was a while ago now, and my hair grew fast. My black roots and white ends were not a pretty sight. How Oliver had found me cute with a hairstyle like that, I've no idea. I decided my best option was to get some hair dye and change it back to the way it was meant to be. Black. Like Gabriel said to me when I'd first arrived – I'm naturally dark-haired like the rest of my family and should be proud of it.

It was particularly chilly as I walked along the roadside into town and so I wrapped my knee length-parka tightly around my body and pulled my black beanie further down my face in an effort to warm up, but I needn't have worried too much because I was soon offered a ride by Ben who was on his way back from treating an injured horse.

"Hey, Lilly. What are you doing here? How come you're not in school? Can I give you a lift?"

I hopped into the passenger seat with the eagerness of a person about to pass out from hypothermia, and he laughed and turned up the heat to help warm me up.

To keep up the charade that Gabriel had begun with the school, I explained I'd not been feeling so great emotionally and needed some time alone. But I told him I was feeling better now and was glad of his company.

He told me about his latest patient. It was a horse that had a mysterious injury to his leg and that his owner couldn't understand how it had happened, especially since the animal had been locked in his stable overnight, and had been perfectly all right the previous evening. He had called Ben immediately to attend to the bloody mess, but he could offer no explanation either.

"I mean, this poor horse had looked as if it had been attacked by a wild animal. Yet there was no way he could get out of his stable and no way any animal large enough to do the damage could get in," he said with a creased brow as if he was still trying to fathom the mystery out.

I knew that it was quite possible that the horse had fought with something. Something dark and unnatural, probably.

My gut feeling was that the horse wasn't just a horse. Maybe it had the power of transformation and had let itself out into the darkness. Or some kind of beast had unlocked the stable, crept in and made a frenzied attack on the horse... why, I had no idea. There were so many bizarre theories going around in my head, and I couldn't suggest a single one to Ben, which I hated. Being a vet, I believed that it could have been really useful for him to know. But I had been advised not to tell a soul, and it was of the utmost importance that I kept this secret, for my family's sake.

I mentioned that I had heard he was looking for a part-time trainee assistant. After he nodded, I suggested myself as a possible candidate. Surprisingly, he was thrilled that I would be interested in the position.

"Are you kidding? That would be terrific, Lilly! It would almost be like keeping it in the family. That's great... really great!"

"Really? I don't want you to hire me just because we're practically family though, Ben."

"Don't be silly. It's perfect. I'd love you to come and work with me. Great!"

"Unfortunately, I still have a few years to go at high school; otherwise I could start full-time work straight away."

We agreed that I would begin training with him every Saturday and would do the occasional stint after school. During the holidays I would work three days a week. I was excited at the prospect of having something important to do, working with animals. And at the same time, I would learn everything that I needed to know.

When he asked why I was heading into town, I blushed and told him I was so embarrassed about the state of my hair, I was going to buy a do-at-home hair dye to sort it out.

He laughed "I don't think a simple hair dye will do the trick, Lilly!"

"Thanks, Ben!" but I laughed too, knowing only too well that my haircut left a lot to be desired.

"Look, a really good friend of mine is a hairdresser in town, and she owes me a favour. Why don't we pop into her salon and we'll see what she can do?"

Although I was embarrassed that he would be willing to use his favour on me, I agreed that my appearance was in desperate need of an overhaul and so I nodded in agreement.

"Thank you," I whispered shyly, and he looked over at me and winked.

It turned out that his good friend was actually more of a girl-friend, judging by the smouldering looks that passed between them when we arrived. I was lucky that she was between appointments, and she was delighted to help. Her name was Crystal.

Unlike most of the girls I had met so far in Powell River who had long flowing locks, Crystal's cropped elfin-like hair made her beautiful African-American features more pronounced. She was a beauty, there was no doubt about that, and on top of that, she had a beautiful soul. Her naturally black afro hair had been dyed a golden brown, which made her eyes appear to have so much depth that you could almost sink into them. They reminded me of Scully's eyes, deep, dark and soulful.

Ben only stayed for a couple of minutes, as there were clients waiting back at the practice so he left me there, before assuring me that I was in the best of hands and that I would leave feeling a million dollars.

"Enjoy your date tonight," he yelled with a wink as he closed the door without giving me the chance to respond.

Did everyone know? I thought, as I followed Crystal to the chair in front of the mirror and sat down while she inspected my hair carefully and thoughtfully before smiling brightly at me.

"So... I'm guessing you hacked at your hair yourself?"

She clearly knew my answer before carrying on, "And I'm guessing you bleached it yourself too. Well, the hair is in surprisingly good condition, but it is in some serious need of shape. Do you want the colour back to its natural shade?"

I nodded, and she agreed it was the best choice for my colouring.

And so as she went about returning my hair back to some kind of normality, I relaxed and enjoyed the pampering while thinking about the journey my life had begun to take. It was one that I would never have imagined, not in a million years.

Growing up the way I had, trapped within what appeared to be a loveless family, not able to go out and meet people, not even able to see the world through the television. My only glimmer of the world out there was through the eyes of authors like the Grimms Brothers and Hans Christian Andersen. When I read those magical tales, I'd had no idea that their worlds had existed, yet here I was with the knowledge that they did exist, yet within a veil of secrecy.

A secret world. And I knew about it. I was part of it. I shivered.

"Sorry, Lilly. Is the water too cold?" asked Crystal.

I assured her it was fine. The cold came from within. Within the knowledge that I couldn't share. Not even with Oliver – the boy that gave me goosebumps just by looking at him. And he felt the same way that I did. His heart skipped a beat when he was with me too. It was hard for me to fathom anybody could have feelings for me in that way.

I was young, I had never had a boyfriend. I had never been kissed. I didn't know the meaning of love, other than the new love I felt for my newfound family members. I had never even felt love for my father because I had always had the impression that he didn't love me. Not really. A feeling of shame enveloped me. All this time, of course, he had loved me. His only way of sharing that love was to sneak those books to me. And I had never shown him that he meant everything to me. Of course, it was easy for me to say that now. Now that I knew the truth. He was under a spell. Pure and simple.

It didn't take Crystal long to return me to my 'natural' beauty as she put it and when I left over an hour later, Ben had been right, I did feel like a million dollars. I felt pretty, and I hadn't felt pretty in a long, long time. In fact, I had never felt pretty because I'd never been told I was pretty.

Crystal had worked wonders, and my new short crop was surprisingly a great shape for my face. I was astounded how much it suited me, considering what a mess I had looked before. As much as I wanted to show the world my new style, I had no choice but to cover it up the second I stepped outside because of the cold, so on went the beanie once again.

As I glanced back through the window, I waved goodbye to Crystal as she waved back happily before attending to the other young woman who had entered just five minutes before. I hadn't taken much notice of the salon's entrance as we'd arrived, so I looked up at her sign. Crystal's salon was in big, bold black lettering on an orange background with a catchy logo featuring a cat with big eyes and long hair. It made me chuckle to myself as it matched her personality perfectly.

I put my hands in my pocket and felt a piece of paper. It was the map to my father's land that Rose had drawn for me. I checked my watch and figured I had plenty of time, so I headed in that direction.

As I walked through town, a number of familiar faces smiled at me and said their hellos before hurrying out of the cold. It was still so alien to me to be known by so many people. In London, I knew the faces of the kids at school. I knew the faces of the many teachers. I knew the face of the postman, but I didn't know anybody but December, my secret best friend. Vivian had never allowed me to get to know anyone at all. I couldn't even say hello to the neighbours without fear of being grabbed and pulled away by her. Yet here I was surrounded by friendly people that I could get to know if I wanted to. And who wanted to get to know me.

Some even stopped me in the street and made small talk, asking how I was doing, if I was settling in okay and so on. It was rather nice actually. It made me smile, and again, I felt liked. I felt loved. It was a feeling I would cherish.

Heading out of town, I smiled to myself happily and checked the map again before taking a turning off the main road. There was tarmac for a hundred or so metres, and then I had to take a left down a small and winding dirt track. The track became even longer and narrower then, giving an almost funnel effect.

I continued walking until I eventually came upon a wide-open space. In the middle was a large concrete base. I had found it. This should have been the place that I grew up. The happy years that we could have all spent together. Should have spent together. Serena, my father, Neleh... and me. How different my life could have been, I thought as I walked slowly towards what would have been our home.

I looked around and noticed that it was surrounded by trees, hidden away from any kind of prying eyes, perhaps that was the reason my father had chosen it. He knew the family secret, and he knew the importance of keeping it just that: a secret. It was perfect, and it was peaceful. I understood perfectly why my father had chosen this plot of land. Not only was it well hidden, but it also had a great feeling to it. I tried to picture what the house could have looked like. A large log home a bit like Gabriel's perhaps? No, this would have been quite a bit smaller and even cosier. It was perfect.

As I wandered around the base, I noticed a large pallet of logs which had become ruined from years of neglect in the outdoors. I felt sad as I approached them and gently rubbed my hand along one of the logs.

I had been so focused on what could have been that I didn't even notice that it had started raining. I looked up as the storm clouds collected overhead. I pulled my beanie down further over my face, and as I turned away from the logs, I heard a tear and then a click before an almighty crash.

A searing pain went through my leg as I fell to the ground with a thud. A log had come loose and had landed on top of me. I barely remember anything, except that I screamed out in pain. I felt nauseous all of a sudden and, barely conscious, I tried to shout for help, yet I knew nobody would hear me. As I had noted before, the house was perfectly well hidden, after all. I could just about feel my face becoming wet from the rain when I heard a loud of clap of thunder.

I felt trapped in a nightmare. One where I couldn't move. The more I struggled, the worse it became. The log was too heavy, and I was too injured to move a muscle.

I've no idea how long I was there.

Just as I felt like giving up all hope, drifting in and out of consciousness, I saw movement from beyond the trees and then before I knew it, I heard the voice of an angel. "Don't worry, Lilly. You're going to be all right. I'll make sure of that."

I must have been hallucinating as I remember being lifted higher and higher into the sky before completely losing consciousness.

❧ 17 ☙

When I came to, I noticed a pale green ceiling and green walls. A distinctive smell hovered in the air. It smelled... clinical. Hearing people moving around beyond my room, I realised I was in the hospital. I had absolutely no idea what had happened to me.

"Lilly?" said a deep voice to the side of the bed.

I turned my head and saw Ben sitting patiently by my side, waiting for me to wake up.

"What happened?" I asked.

Apparently, it was a mystery to him too. After he had treated his patients, he had been working alone on some paperwork in his practice, when there had been a knock on the door, and when he opened it, he found me lying on the floor unconscious.

"I had absolutely no idea what had happened. At first, I assumed you had knocked on the door and then collapsed, but when I tried to pick you up, I noticed someone had roughly wrapped your leg with these huge leaves. Someone had clearly helped you and then left you there. Do you have any idea what happened?" he asked.

I shook my head, which ached a little, and I asked for Gabriel.

"Don't worry, he's here. He's just having a word with the doctor. Rose is here too, and Sonya and Meredith are on their way."

"They don't need to come. I'm okay... aren't I?" I asked, unsure whether I was or not.

"You've broken your leg, and you've got a few bruises, but other than that I think you're okay so don't worry. Your hair looks great, by the way," he said, trying to make light of the situation.

Gabriel walked into the room and thanked Ben profusely for bringing me to the hospital so quickly. "If you need to get back to work, Ben, go ahead. I'll take over for now," he said.

As Ben nodded, he picked up his coat, leaned over and kissed my forehead. "You had me scared for a while there, Lilly. I'm glad you're okay. You call me if you need anything, okay?"

I nodded as best as I could without my head throbbing and smiled back.

"Thank you, Ben."

The moment he left, Gabriel closed the door behind him.

"Oh Lilly... what on earth happened? Did you go into the forest?" Gabriel asked.

I explained everything that I could remember, which wasn't much. Just that I had gone to find the land that belonged to my father. I remembered finding it, but I couldn't recall much more than that.

"But how did you get to Ben's?"

"I really don't know, Gabriel. But I wish I did."

I was uncomfortable lying flat on my back, so I asked him if he would help me sit up a little, and as I did so, I noticed I was clenching something in my hand. I opened it and found a single black feather. Strange, I thought, I don't recall picking up a feather, and why would I still have it in my hand?

Gabriel saw the look on my face and followed my gaze.

"I must have found it there and picked it up, for some reason," I said innocently as Rose opened the door with a cup of coffee that she handed to Gabriel.

"Hello, dear. Are you feeling all right? I've been worried out of my mind," she said as she tiptoed over to me and leaned over to peck me on my cheek. She hovered for a moment, and I could have sworn she sniffed at me a couple of times. As she straightened up, she turned to Gabriel and they shared a quizzical look.

She walked over to my coat and picked it up. As she did so, another black feather, a much larger one, fell to the ground.

This time it was my turn to gasp as she crouched down to pick it up.

Gabriel took it from her and held it up to the light.

"This is the feather of a raven," he whispered.

"But it is too large, Gabriel," Rose whispered in reply.

He nodded, and they both turned to look at me.

"Lilly, it's very important that you recall what happened to you this afternoon. Is there anything, anything at all that you remember? The slightest thing could make all the difference," Gabriel said hopefully.

I closed my eyes and thought back to when I left Crystal's, looking up at the sign and smiling, then I'd walked through town and had spoken to a few people, and then I'd followed Rose's map to find the land belonging to my father. I remember the dirt track that had started off winding and then had straightened out, giving that funnel effect.

As I walked in my mind, I walked into the clearing where the concrete base was situated. I remember feeling sad. My eyes settled on the logs where I had gently caressed the wood that would have made a house for my family and me. As I explained all of this, Gabriel nodded, waiting to hear more.

"My coat got caught on something, and then the log fell on my leg... I remember being trapped and there was so much pain," I said, flinching at the memory.

"That's obviously how your leg was broken, my dear. It has broken in two places. But if you were trapped, how did you get out? And how on earth did you get to Ben's?" asked Rose.

I tried hard to remember again, but there was nothing. I had no memory after that. I was so frustrated. But then as I looked at that huge feather, something was triggered in my subconscious.

"There was a man's voice," I gasped, "'don't worry, Lilly. You're going to be all right. I'll make sure of that'. That's what he said, but I don't know what happened after that."

"Well, whoever he was, he must have been the one that took you to Ben's practice. We just have to try and find out who he was. We'll ask around and see if anybody saw anything strange this afternoon. There's a lot more to this. I can feel it," said Gabriel as he drank the last of his coffee and threw the polystyrene cup into the rubbish bin.

"Whoever he was, I'm eternally grateful to him, that's for sure. I don't even care to imagine what might have happened had he not been there," said Rose as Gabriel nodded in agreement.

"Can I come home with you, Gabriel?" I asked, hopefully. I didn't want to stay there in that hospital bed. I was reminded of how my mother had died, and I felt physically sick to the stomach at the thought of having to remain there.

Gabriel checked with the doctor who said it shouldn't be a problem for me to go home, as long as I stayed horizontal and was well looked after. The doctor had known the Tulugaqs for many years and therefore knew that we were a strong family who cared for each other deeply. He was confident that I would get even better care than at the hospital itself, so he discharged me immediately.

Using his cell phone, Gabriel called both Meredith and Sonya and told them to go straight home instead of coming to the hospital. Then, for the first time, I was driven by Gabriel. He and Rose had struggled to get me into the back seat with my broken leg in plaster but eventually, they managed, and we were on our way.

As I lay there, barely able to move, I tried so hard to remember what had happened that afternoon, but the memory could not be tempted out of my subconscious mind. It was deep in there somewhere, and I knew it would eventually come out... most likely during my sleep.

Laying on the sofa later, I felt awful that I would miss out on my very first date with Oliver. Why couldn't I have just walked straight home? Why couldn't I have gone to see my father's house another time? Instead, I had completely messed up my chances with Oliver.

As if on cue, there was a knock on the front door. Sonya stood up and went to see who was there. At the same time, Meredith smiled at me and made a quick exit into the kitchen. Clearly, she knew who it was.

Oliver rushed into the living room and sat by my side immediately, "Lilly, are you all right? I was really freaked out when I heard what happened. What were you thinking going out alone like that?"

His reaction actually made me laugh out loud, and he suddenly stopped talking, and he looked at me before laughing too. "Sorry, I guess I sound like Gabriel. I was just worried," he said.

The fact that he was there with me helped ease the pain tremendously, and I felt utter relief that he cared that much for me already. And we hadn't even had our date yet.

"I'm glad you're here, Oliver. Thank you for coming," I said shyly, nervously running my hand through my hair, which I had completely forgotten actually looked good.

"Wow... I've only just had the chance to really look at you. You look amazing. I love the new hairstyle. You certainly don't look like someone who has just had a near-death experience."

I felt myself blush. "It was hardly a brush with death. I just had a log fall on me, that's all."

"Are you kidding? Do you know how much those logs weigh?" he joked.

We sat together for a few minutes in silence, enjoying each other's company when Sonya and Meredith walked in, carrying two big plates of food for us.

"We figured you'd both be hungry and seeing as you aren't able to actually go out, we thought we'd bring the restaurant to you... oh and we brought you a few movies too, just in case."

"Aww, thanks," said Oliver.

"We both have to get home now so we'll leave you to it. Gabriel is over at Rose's house. He said if you need anything just buzz him on his cell and he'll come right over. You look after our patient, Oliver," said Meredith with a wink and then they were gone.

They were well aware that I was supposed to be having a date with Oliver that night, so it was very sweet that they had all left and allowed the 'date' to happen at home instead.

"So how did you know about my little accident?" I asked.

"Actually I had a few phone calls," he laughed, "first Ben rang me as soon as he'd got you to the hospital. Unfortunately, I couldn't get out of work otherwise I would have come straight over. And then Meredith called me to let me know and then Rose did too! It appears everyone knows that we're close now," he added, with a cheeky smirk.

To hear him say that we were close, out loud, was just amazing – it really made my heart leap and certainly helped take my mind off the bad day I'd had.

As we sat there on the sofa, me with my leg stretched out in front of me and my dinner on my lap and Oliver sitting so close to me with his dinner on his lap, we looked a right pair.

"So what are these movies that Meredith mentioned?" I asked as I ate a mouthful of pasta.

Oliver leaned forward to pick up the DVDs that had been left on the coffee table and laughed, "Well, I don't quite know if they're your sort of thing, but there's Twilight, Van Helsing or League of Extraordinary Gentleman. Not really date movies but if you're into supernatural stuff..."

I laughed at the choices. Clearly, Meredith or Gabriel had been responsible for them, but I appreciated the thought all the same. It was just a shame I couldn't share the joke with Oliver.

I opted for Twilight, at least there was a little romance in with the vampires – it seemed more appropriate than the others, and at least it had a bit of action for Oliver too.

He stood up to put the film on and then sat back down so we could finish dinner together. Although the film played on in the background, there was too much to say to each other to really take any notice of it. We had a lifetime of experiences to share with each other. Well, Oliver had a lifetime of experience to tell me about. I, on the other hand, was a little embarrassed that I didn't have an awful lot to tell him about me.

He told me about his parents' death but that he was too young to really understand what had happened, and he admitted to not being able to remember them, sadly. He still liked to look at their photos, but the memories just weren't there. "But I still miss them, if that makes sense?" he asked, and I nodded with a mouthful of pasta.

He talked a little about his brother, whom he was clearly incredibly proud of. "To become a vet because of what happened to our parents is just awesome," he said and to which I wholeheartedly agreed, "and I think it's fantastic that you're going to be working with him," he added happily.

I raised my eyebrows, and he laughed, "Ben told me when he phoned me earlier... he's really thrilled and wanted to share it with me."

"Do you realise that you still haven't told me what you do for a living?" I asked, eager to know everything about him.

He looked surprised, and I felt a momentary stab of guilt for not asking anybody else. Ben could have told me. I felt a bit silly, but still, I guess it had just never come up in conversation.

Oliver explained that when he had left high school, he hadn't got a clue what to do with his life. He wasn't like Ben, who had known from a young age what he wanted to do.

"All I did know was that I didn't really want to go to college. I was never very academic; I was more of a hands-on sort of guy. Gabriel had always said I was good with my hands, and I ought to do something creative instead, so I ended up working for a construction company where I am currently learning the tricks of the trade. My favourite part of it so far is building log homes like this one. So my long term plan is to start my own wooden home building company," he said energetically as if it meant the world to him. It was exciting to see him so enthusiastic about his career, especially since he wasn't interested in college like so many other kids these days.

I told him I was impressed. He was even cuter when he blushed.

Having grown up in this house and raised by Gabriel since he was just a boy, I wondered why he no longer lived here.

"There is no real reason except for the fact that I like my independence and so I rent a small lodge on John and Meredith's land. It's like a separate little house, an annexe, I guess," he answered. "It's a great little place. Great for my life at the moment anyway. Eventually, I'd like to build my own place. A log home, of course," he grinned.

For some reason, his words took me back to earlier in the day when I had accidentally found myself underneath a very heavy log. The memory had an instant effect on my stomach, and I felt a strong urge to throw up.

Oliver immediately stood up and helped me sit upright as I fought the urge.

"Are you okay? You looked a bit pale for a second there," he whispered.

I shook my head, and he rushed into the kitchen to get me a glass of cold water. As he returned and stood above me, his movement triggered another memory, and I heard that voice again: 'don't worry, Lilly. You're going to be all right. I'll make sure of that', and then I felt as though I was flying.

Unfortunately, the whole thing caused me to vomit suddenly with little warning.

Again, Oliver rushed to the kitchen to get some kitchen paper, a bowl and a damp flannel.

When he returned he handed me a few sheets of the paper for me to clean myself with, he swiftly cleaned up the mess and then sat by my side as he very gently mopped my forehead with the flannel.

I felt very sorry for myself and stupid at the same time.

"I'm so sorry, Oliver," I said, feeling like such a child.

"Don't be silly... it's only natural that this would happen. You had quite a day today. You're on some heavy-duty painkillers, and here I am keeping you awake and talking when you should be completely resting. I'm the one who should be sorry. Not you," he smiled as he patted my forehead again.

"I'll wait for Gabriel to come back and then I'll leave you to get some sleep. Do you want me to help you to your bedroom? Or would you rather I brought you an extra blanket in here?"

I opted for the blanket, knowing that trying to move too much might make me sick again and I was already so embarrassed at having thrown up in front of him.

Oliver came back from my bedroom with my duvet cover and another pillow. He then went into the bathroom and returned with my toothbrush, toothpaste, a glass of water and a bowl.

"I figured you might want to brush your teeth. It might make you feel better," he said, handing everything to me like a father would probably treat a sick child.

I told him I was grateful even though my mouth was

completely full of frothed up toothpaste. I grinned in an effort to make him laugh. It worked, as he shook his head, chuckling at me.

Just as I spat out the water, we heard the door open, and Gabriel announced he had returned home. He greeted Oliver like a son and looked at me with concern.

Oliver explained that I'd been sick and so Gabriel reassured him that he would look after me, giving Oliver his cue to go home.

"Well, I'd better go now, Lilly, but I'll be back in the morning... if that's okay with you Gabriel?"

Gabriel smiled and said "Yes, of course, provided Lilly wants you to come back, that is," he chuckled.

"I certainly do," I answered as he leaned down and gently brushed my cheeks with his lips.

"Try and get some sleep. See you in the morning. Goodnight Gabriel," he said as he wrapped up for the cold.

"Goodnight!" he yelled again before the front door shut behind him.

A minute later I heard the revving of his car, and then there was silence. Just the sound of my breathing, before Gabriel came and sat down opposite me and then I could hear his gentle breath too. He didn't say anything. He just let me fall asleep in peace.

❧ 18 ☙

I slept right through the night. Not a single dream managed to wake me from my stupor. The shock of the previous day's events must have taken its toll and pretty much knocked me out. That and the fact that Oliver had come over to have our date at home. Snuggling under the duvet, I slowly forced my eyes open to see rays of sunlight through the window. It soon dawned on me that Gabriel had left me to sleep in the living room. My leg throbbed beneath the covers, and as I turned to try and manoeuvre myself off the sofa, I heard voices coming from the kitchen. Gabriel was not alone.

I could easily identify the voices of Gabriel, Meredith, Wyatt and Rose. I came to the conclusion that they had joined forces once again to talk about my father or me. Either that or they were waiting for me to wake to talk further about the news they'd hit me with a few days earlier.

Or were they eager to find out who had rescued me from my close call yesterday?

As I tried to stand up, I managed to knock over a bottle of water with my leg. It crashed to the floor.

Hurrying in, they all made a fuss of me. Meredith offered assistance where I needed it the most. Having a shower with a broken leg isn't the easiest thing to do, so she ran me a bath and helped me in. I was grateful. Although I felt such a nuisance and a hindrance, I also felt a massive sense of gratitude for having such caring people around me. It would have been a very different story had I been in England with Vivian and my father. Goodness only knew how I would have managed.

After I'd struggled to get dressed, Meredith helped me back to the sofa where I lay down, exhausted. Barely a minute went by before Rose whizzed in with my breakfast on a tray. A lovely hot cup of tea and a plate full of eggs and bacon. I was thoroughly spoilt, and I relished it.

The others joined me while I ate and we chatted about general things like the weather, friends and neighbours as well as our plans for Thanksgiving and Christmas which were fast approaching.

But ultimately, I knew the conversation would move on to more pressing matters. The unusually large raven's feather was cause for some concern, as Gabriel explained to me. When our ancestors had first changed, they morphed almost magically into the bird's actual size. He had never seen or even heard of anybody having the ability to change into a raven the size of a human. Yet there we were presented with evidence to suggest it was possible. What we didn't know was who in our community possessed the ability to change and why wasn't Gabriel aware of it?

It troubled him as he knew all of the members within the Tulugaq clan and was on friendly terms with pretty much all of the residents of Powell River. It was possible that whoever had saved me came from further afield, but why not show themselves?

Gabriel was desperate that I recall exactly what had happened. I wished I could remember but having fallen unconscious made it considerably more difficult.

"I believe the only way to tap into your unconscious mind and find out the truth, Lilly, is to take you on a journey to meet some very unique and special people. But it will be quite a long journey, and much of it needs to be taken on foot, and you are certainly not able at the moment. Your leg must heal first, and then we will travel to the mountains to see the elders. We will do so in the spring. Until then, we must not worry about any of this. We must continue life as usual. Although we do not know who this person, or creature, is, we do know one thing. He saved you, Lilly. So clearly he wishes you no harm. You must not dwell on your father's disappearance, either. The elders are aware of what has been happening within our family, and they are keeping eyes and ears open for any news," he said while the others nodded solemnly behind him.

"He's right, dear. You haven't been here all that long and look what's happened to you already. You must completely settle into life in Powell River. When you've recovered, and the weather starts to get warmer, you and Gabriel will go and visit the elders. But until then... just concentrate on your studies and making friends. Okay?" Rose said with her eyebrows raised, waiting for my reply. I nodded reluctantly. They all meant well.

But that didn't mean I had to agree with them. Of course, I couldn't. My father was out there somewhere, and he might be in danger. I didn't want to wait until the spring. But I had no choice. I could do nothing alone, especially with a broken leg. I couldn't even start my part-time job.

There was still a possibility that my memory might be triggered during one of my dreams, but until that happened, I imagined the next few months would include an awful lot of reading and very little else.

Later that morning after everyone, except Gabriel, had left and I'd spent hours with my head in a book, Jo arrived.

As she walked in, her brow was furrowed so deep with worry that she made me laugh. "I'm okay, I'm okay," I said to her with my hands held up, before she'd even opened her mouth.

"I was so worried for you. Especially seeing as you didn't turn up for school. I've obviously heard from the others, but I want to hear from you. What on earth happened, Lilly?"

I told her all about the previous day, and she was relieved that we could finally open up to each other about our family's secret.

"I'm so sorry I couldn't tell you anything before, but I was literally sworn to secrecy by the whole family. I really wanted to. It was killing me. I have to admit, finally having a friend, a girl, to be able to talk to about all of this crazy stuff is brilliant. Sometimes it really eats you up when the only people you can talk with are parents, grandparents, uncles and aunts," she said, barely taking a breath.

I totally understood. Even though I'd only known the truth for a short time, I did feel the need to have a close friend to confide in.

She told me about the time she'd had the 'family of ravens' talk with the rest of the family and, although it came as a bit of a shock, she'd always known our family was special. It was just a feeling she'd had.

"But you've never transformed, have you?" I asked, eager to know more about the physical change.

She shook her head, "No, not yet, but I've had all the weird dreams too so we're just waiting for it to hit me one of these days. I have no idea when it will happen, though. It's a bit scary, isn't it? Not knowing how we turn. I worry that it will be painful," she said, twirling her long hair around her fingers nervously. "But Rose told me that provided you relax completely and just let your body change of its own accord, the pain should be controllable. She said it's all mind over matter. I've been doing meditation and yoga ever since!" she laughed.

"Seriously?" I asked, wondering if she was joking or not.

She nodded enthusiastically and jumped up from the armchair, demonstrating a few awkward-looking poses. "The yoga poses are easy once you've done them for a while. When I first started, my muscles were so stiff, I struggled even with the simplest moves. I'll teach them to you, and we can do it together," she said eagerly.

Looking down at my leg and back up at her comically, she burst into a fit of giggles. "Okay, I'll teach you in a few months when you can actually get your backside off the sofa!" She sat back down on the chair and curled her shoeless feet underneath her bottom.

"So, you didn't see who rescued you yesterday, then?"

Shaking my head and raising my eyebrows, I wished there was something exciting I could tell her. The only way I would be able to identify him would be by his voice, I told her, but I explained that I didn't recognise it. It wasn't a voice I'd heard before.

"You don't think it was your dad, do you?" she almost whispered.

It had crossed my mind, but as I explained, even though I'd barely ever heard my father speak, I didn't feel like it was him. Surely I would have felt something. And if it had been him, wouldn't he have stayed? He wouldn't have just dumped me on someone's doorstep. And why would he vanish afterwards?

"It just didn't feel like him, you know," I added.

She nodded, clearly understanding what I meant. We sat in silence for a while, each lost in our own thoughts about the man who had saved my life. Had I been left there, under that log in the storm, I could have frozen to death. I could have bled to death for all I knew. The thought made me shiver. There were many ifs in this world. I was just grateful to whoever he was.

"So, did I miss much at school yesterday?"

"Not a great deal, unless you count poor Jemima falling flat on her face in front of the basketball team in cheerleading practice. She had a bloody nose and everything. Poor thing. Oh, and Mrs Ormond seemed interested to know why you weren't there yesterday. A little too interested really. There's something odd about that woman, but I can't quite put my finger on it," she laughed.

She asked how my date had gone with Oliver. Sonya had told her that he'd come over and that we'd had dinner prepared for us.

My instant grin answered her question. "That well, huh?" she laughed and as if on cue, Oliver arrived bearing a box of chocolates for his "patient". It was good to see him.

"Hey Oliver, good to see you," Jo said as she stood up, put on her shoes and started doing up her shoelaces.

They exchanged a few words before she decided to leave us alone.

"I'll call you later," she said with a wink, before shouting "Bye Gabriel," and closing the front door on her way out.

"Ben sends his love and hopes you're feeling better today," Oliver said as he bent to kiss me on the cheek. As usual, I blushed and smiled as he handed me the pretty black box with a pink ribbon.

"Awww thanks, Oliver... that's really sweet. But you didn't have to."

"I was going to go and start my training with Ben today... so much for that," I said, as I rolled my eyes and lifted my leg.

He smiled and told me that Ben had said for me not to worry about it. He wasn't overly busy at the moment anyway so it could wait a few more weeks until I was ready.

"How are you feeling?" he asked as he sat down and watched me rip off the ribbon and delve inside the box to discover which chocolate was which. He laughed at my enthusiasm.

"I'm good thanks. I woke up feeling a bit groggy, but I feel much better now."

"I guess I was right to bring chocolates rather than flowers."

I nodded with a mouth full before realising I wasn't very polite, so I offered them to him.

Chocolate wasn't something I was used to eating, but they were delicious. They didn't last long though as we spent the next few hours chatting whilst we savoured them. Occasionally Gabriel would pop his head round the door to make sure we were okay, but he figured I was fine whenever I was with Oliver, so he ended up leaving us alone for a few hours.

Oliver stayed with me the entire day.

"I feel bad about keeping you cooped up indoors for so long."

"That's okay. You're not exactly in any state to do anything else, are you? But maybe tomorrow we could try and go for a short walk? What did the doctor say about walking?" he asked.

I honestly didn't have a clue. I had been so keen to get out of the hospital that I hadn't even asked any questions. I was sure Gabriel would know, though, so I promised to ask him.

Oliver scolded me for not talking to the medical staff, and he shook his head as if I was in big trouble, but he couldn't keep a straight face and ended up laughing.

"Well, I'll come over tomorrow whether we can go for a walk or not," he promised as he prepared to leave. "Call me if you need anything?" he said as he kissed me gently on the lips. It was my first real kiss, and it felt like I'd been given an electric shock. Not the kind that hurts, but a wonderful, sweet, electric shock. I smiled and touched my lips with my fingers.

As I slowly opened my eyes, I saw that he was smiling too. And then before I knew it, he was gone.

❧ 19 ❧

I had to wear my cast for nearly two months, and they were, without a doubt, the best two months of my life so far. Even the pain and awkwardness of a broken leg couldn't dull my happiness.

I'd dreaded being unable to do anything, especially after Rose and Gabriel said I should avoid agonising over recent events and should just concentrate on getting my life back together. That is exactly what I did, and admittedly, it was the best thing for me.

It was January, it was absolutely freezing, yet I had become accustomed to the colder weather in Canada. I had actually begun to love waking up on a chilly morning and opening my bedroom window to take a few breaths of crisp cold air. It was the perfect way to wake myself up, followed by a hot bath, which I had finally mastered getting into without the help of either Meredith, Sonya or Jo who had all taken it in turns to pop round first thing to help. But still, I couldn't wait to get the cast off.

Thanksgiving had been an eye-opener for me. It was time for family, pure and simple. And although my family had a lot to be thankful for, it was a sad occasion because we missed my father terribly.

Much of the day was spent talking about old times, the times I had missed – either because I had not yet been born to this world, or I was being kept holed up in a London apartment. I heard stories about my father and his brother and sister when they were children. The fun they'd had growing up in this fantastic part of the world. The mischief they had created and the love that had bound them together.

With Ben, Crystal and Oliver with us for much of the day, we were unable to talk about the unusual circumstances that surrounded our lives and, in a way, it was nice to just be normal. It was also wonderful to be able to spend time with my family as well as my boyfriend. There had never been any need to hide the fact that we were together, as everyone had accepted us immediately.

But it was my first real Christmas that was particularly memorable. It was unlike anything I had ever experienced. It was the first time I had ever had the opportunity to celebrate it, and so I immersed myself into the festive spirit.

While living in London, I had overheard wonderful stories at school about what the other kids had been up to during the holidays, and I had envied them tremendously. For me though, Christmas was simply any other day in the calendar. No gifts, no decorations but more importantly, no loving family, no joy.

Yet in Canada, we had experienced all of this and much more. The whole family, as well as Oliver, Ben and Crystal again, came to our house to celebrate Christmas day. Everybody helped prepare the most sumptuous feast I had ever laid my eyes on and then we had all exchanged gifts.

I was given clothes by everyone. My family were clearly sick of seeing me wearing nothing but black, and so they had all produced a new wardrobe. They had planned everything together, and I assumed that Jo was responsible for doing most of the shopping. When I asked her, she nodded, "With the help of my mom, of course!"

"You're such a great person, Lilly, we want to see you in colours that match your personality," Sonya had said, speaking for them all later on. I was touched. After thirteen years of yellow and months of black, the time had finally come for the rainbow.

The day was glorious. My biggest regret was that my father was not there. I would have given anything to have him spend that day with us. It would have meant so much, not just to me but to the rest of the family, especially Gabriel who had lost his son so many years before. But as we had spent most of Thanksgiving thinking about him and what had become of him, we refused to be sad on December 25th too.

Everybody knew that Christmas was totally new to me and I got the impression that they'd made more of an occasion out of it than they would normally have done.

I believe they were making up for all those years of my 'living' in a room with little contact with the outside world. I told them they needn't have made so much effort. I'd have been equally as happy to put up a Christmas tree and have a normal dinner with everyone. But I understood that they were showing me how much they loved me and how much they'd missed me over the years. The feeling was completely mutual.

Between Christmas and New Year I had received another huge surprise – a birthday party.

It was December 28th and, although I was aware that it was the date I was born, it never even occurred to me that anyone else would take much notice. After all, nobody ever had. The other thing that had been on my mind was the fact that not only was it my birthday, it was also the date I had lost my sister. The date of Neleh's death. And it was very close to the anniversary of my mother's death too.

How could I celebrate when something so horrific had happened on that very day fourteen years earlier? It was difficult, but having never had the opportunity to meet my mother or my sister, my sorrow could not equal the sorrow that perhaps Rose was feeling. Or Gabriel. Or any of my family for that matter.

I refused to dwell on the sad facts of that day, remembering instead that it was my birthday. I was a year older, and I was excited at turning fourteen. On the outside, I didn't look any different, but on the inside, I felt like I was becoming a completely different person. Comparing me to the person I was just a year earlier, I could barely recognise myself.

In England, while living under the roof of that witch, it was as if she had reached down into my soul and sucked my true personality and character right out of me. I had been a simple and insanely naïve girl who had truly believed that my life had been normal. How wrong could I have been?

A year on and the real me was finally emerging from my shell. I felt like I was becoming a young woman. A strong, independent young woman and I finally felt good about myself. I finally felt like I could face the world head-on.

The day had passed much like any other. Gabriel had rushed out of the house and yelled that he would see me later. He didn't mention what day it was, so neither did I. Ben had come by the house to collect me first thing that morning, and we had gone straight to the practice where I had started training a few weeks before. It was a bit of a struggle at first, moving around with my crutches clumsily getting in the way of everything. I hadn't been able to physically handle any of the animals as we were waiting for my cast to be removed first. But I learned a lot just by watching Ben carefully, answering telephone calls and speaking to the locals about their pet's problems. It had opened a whole new world to me, and I was becoming even more confident in myself. I wouldn't shy away from anything like I would have done just a few months previously.

Ben had even taken me out on occasion when he had horses to treat. Although I could do very little, I was fascinated by these regal creatures. There was always a part of me that wondered who they really were though. Twice we had been called out to injured horses – just like the injuries Ben had treated on the day of my accident. He concluded that whatever had attacked them had managed to remove some of the sinew from the inside of their legs. It was a mystery to him. To me, however, it was slightly less mysterious. I knew the crimes had probably been committed by a changeling, a vampire perhaps? A witch, even? But, as usual, I had to keep my thoughts to myself.

On my birthday, after a few hours of work (it was particularly busy that Christmas), we had made sure everything was cleaned up before we locked up the clinic before heading back in Ben's truck.

I had noticed Ben's sideways glances at me a couple of times throughout the day but had assumed it was because he was checking how I was doing. However, as we arrived home, I soon figured out that hadn't been the reason at all.

"Happy Birthday, Lilly!" shouted a house full of family and

friends as I gingerly pushed open the front door with one of my crutches.

Shock rippled through me, and my initial reaction was to cry. I was totally overwhelmed. It hit me even more than Christmas day had. A birthday party. For me. I was completely speechless as everybody laughed and rushed over to hug and kiss me. Sonya was a little concerned why tears were falling down my face, but I reassured her that they were most certainly tears of happiness.

There was even a big banner with the words 'Happy Birthday Lilly' hung loosely across the top of the dining table which was covered in a mass of food, the likes of which I'd never seen before.

There were miniature sausages, boiled eggs that had been cut in half and the hard yolks mixed with mayonnaise, little pastries in all shapes and sizes, pieces of cheese on sticks with pineapple and ham, my favourite crisps and nuts and they were just the things to nibble on. Another table that I hadn't noticed at first was covered in salads and cooked meats, full-size sausages and burgers and more. Lastly, though, there was a huge variety of cute little cupcakes all with little wings on them. It was an amazing spread, and I couldn't believe it had all been done under a cloud of secrecy. I had no idea that it was being planned at all.

I saw that Oliver was standing back, patiently waiting for me to speak to everyone else first. And then when there was a gap, he approached me and put his arms around me and gave me a big hug, "Happy birthday, babe. You're catching me up," he whispered in my ear.

I pulled back and looked at him and smiled before he leaned forward and kissed me briefly on the lips. I knew he was a little shy about kissing me in front of my family, so a bear bug was his way of showing how much he cared.

As he loosened his grip, I turned to have another look at the scene before me and shook my head in disbelief. I still couldn't believe that they had all gone to such effort for me.

Oliver went to get us some drinks while I was dragged away by Jo, who was clearly dying to give me her gift. She pulled me away from the crowd and into my bedroom, where she handed me a beautifully wrapped box and sat cross-legged on my bed.

"I've been dying to come and see you all day but I couldn't, of course. I couldn't spoil the surprise," she laughed.

As I tried to remove the paper carefully without ripping it, Jo laughed at me and grabbed at the box, "Oh... just rip it," she said.

I pulled the box back from her and did as I was told, ripping the shiny pink paper away from the present underneath. I opened the lid and found a little gadget and some headphones.

"It's an MP3 player!" squealed Jo as she jumped up from the bed, "here, let me show you," and she demonstrated how it worked and how I could now listen to music wherever and whenever I wanted.

I was so touched. Even though we hadn't spoken very much about music, she had obviously picked up on the one thing that I loved. It had been another thing forbidden by Vivian so to actually own my own music player was amazing, and I told Jo so while giving her a big hug.

"I've taken the liberty of putting some of my favourite songs on there, just to get you started. There's some Taylor Swift, Kelly Clarkson, Lady Antebellum, Raintown, Sugarland, Rascal Flatts and a few others that I'm sure you'll love. Now I know you haven't got a computer yet, but you can always come round to my house to download some more, okay?" she said happily, with a smirk on her face.

I nodded while I put the headphones in my ears and switched it on. The sounds that floated into my ears was like heaven, and I couldn't thank her enough. I stood listening for a few minutes while she watched me, giggling before grabbing my arm and pulling me back into the party, nearly knocking me over.

"Oops... sorry, I keep forgetting about your leg. Come on... there's probably lots more presents to open," she said, my bedroom door closing behind us.

"There you are. I was looking for you," said Oliver with a glass of orange juice in his hand. His other hand was sneakily hidden behind his back. He smirked as he handed me the juice and waited a few moments as I took a few gulps and then put the glass down before he gave me my birthday present. It was a very small gift, wrapped haphazardly, for which he apologised, laughing. "Wrapping gifts isn't one of my strong points," he joked.

I looked around to make sure I wasn't being watched by anyone else, as I was still a little embarrassed at being given things. I had never been given very much before so I wasn't used to it – not even after all the wonderful things that had been lovingly given to me on Christmas day.

As I unwrapped the purple and silver paper, I found a circular box, and when I opened it, I saw two beautiful little crystals in the shape of angels.

"It's to hang from the window in your bedroom. When I saw them I thought of you," he said, adding "and your mother and sister," he shrugged shyly, embarrassed.

"I know that today is the day Neleh died, and I just thought, well, I just thought you could hang them up today, and they would be like guardian angels or something. It's silly, really," he said shrugging again, as his cheeks turned a little pink.

I hugged him tightly and grabbed his hand and pulled him towards my room, "Oliver, they are absolutely beautiful," I said, trying hard not to shed a tear. "This is the best gift I've ever had. Thank you."

With the bedroom door closed behind us, I leaned up to him and kissed him gently while he wrapped his arms around me tightly.

"I'm so lucky to have you, you know that?" I asked him as I snuggled into his shoulder, and he laughed.

"I'm the lucky one," he said.

The crystal angels were even more stunning when hung on either side of my window. The way the sun caught them made shafts of glimmering light shoot across the room, creating miniature rainbows all over the place. It was beautiful.

But we couldn't lounge around alone for much longer as I was soon called back into the party as there were lots more gifts to open and partying to do. My final birthday present was a joint gift from Gabriel, Rose, Meredith and Wyatt. They had waited for everybody to leave before giving it to me... it was my very own computer.

They explained that even though they had split the cost between them, they had only been able to afford a second-hand laptop, but it was in excellent order, Wyatt had said as he showed me how to work it.

"It wouldn't matter if it were out of the ark, it's fantastic," I told them as they laughed.

"We know you've only ever used computers at school, and we know most kids have them these days and felt that you should no longer have to miss out on anything," said Rose.

"Plus, it'll come in very handy for your research," added Meredith.

No matter how hard I tried at that moment, I could not stop the tears from flowing down my cheeks.

I gave each one a big hug and thanked them from the bottom of my heart, knowing that I would use my new computer more than they could have imagined. There was now a whole world at the end of my fingertips, and I was determined to discover it.

After the others had all gone home, I rang Jo to tell her the good news but, naturally, she'd already known and said that she'd had difficulty not saying something when she'd given me my MP3 player. We laughed and chatted for a little while before she told me that we could now chat online whenever we wanted to... as Gabriel had also organised for me to be hooked up to the internet.

"Which also means that you can finally keep in touch with your friend, December," added Jo. She was right, of course; the last letter I had received from my only friend in England had included her email address.

In fact, that night before I went to bed, I created my own email address and promptly sent December a message telling her all about Thanksgiving, Christmas and my birthday. I knew she would be delighted.

Again, my life was changing dramatically, and I loved every second of it. I still thought about my father every day but was beginning to realise there was little I could do to find him on my own. I would need my family's help and to be able to get that, I had to wait until the spring. Until then, I would continue to read books and articles online.

And that's what I did over the course of the next month. When I wasn't at school, working with Ben, hanging out with Oliver, or chatting to December or Jo online, I would devour as much information as possible. I didn't just read about all the animals that might appear in my path but also about myths, legends and tales about the so-called supernatural world. I read about beings that were only supposed to exist in storybooks, but I knew different, and I also knew that I needed to learn as much about them as possible. Naturally, much of what I read wasn't exactly strong factual information, but beliefs and, in some cases, pure fiction. Nevertheless, every little scrap of detail was devoured. The more I knew, whether it was entirely true or not, made me a stronger person. Or should I say a stronger raven or a stronger cat... which, I still didn't know.

I was fortunate that Oliver was interested in the same things as me. We spent much of our time watching spooky TV shows and movies, before discussing them in-depth. Oliver, assuming that we just shared a common thrill for the supernatural, when I knew that the majority of what we saw was, more than likely, true.

$\maltese$ 20 $\maltese$

As the end of January drew near, so my dreams began again. It had seemed like so many weeks since I'd had such vivid experiences during my sleeping hours that I had almost forgotten about them.

As the dreams intensified, one night, I found they had an altogether different effect. I awoke to find myself sleepwalking through the house. Although it worried me a little, I decided against telling Gabriel. I didn't want to concern him, and the fact that I'd woken up while still within the house reassured me that I probably wasn't capable of opening the front door.

I was wrong.

Just a few nights later, I had one of the most vivid dreams to date...

Voices called to me from within the forest. Ethereal voices sang my name, beckoning me to follow.

Before I knew it, I found myself approaching the tall trees that swayed in the softly blowing wind. I couldn't stop myself from following the sounds. Peering through the trees, I tried to see who the voices belonged to. My vision seemed blurred, and I couldn't quite see, but I did catch sight of a figure dressed in white. I pushed through the long branches and gently tiptoed through the cold mossy ground beneath my bare feet.

It's strange that in dreams I could walk barefooted in the snow and I didn't feel the slightest bit cold. In fact, the snow felt more like soft balls of moist cotton wool, squelching underfoot. I looked ahead and saw the figure moving like an angel in front of me. Or a ghost. She was not stepping but gliding along, almost as if she was on roller skates being pulled along on a smooth surface.

She didn't turn, so I was still unable to identify her, yet the smooth tones of her voice continued to sing my name, beckoning me to follow.

"Lilly... Lilly... come Lilly."

The forest soon became darker as the trees thickened ahead, the path we walked upon disappeared completely and I was forced to climb over huge tree roots that exploded from the ground underneath my toes. In areas it was slippery, and I stumbled a few times but managed to stay upright.

Although I was vaguely aware that I was dreaming, I was conscious that the cast on my leg had only recently been removed, so I had to be extra careful on my delicate bones.

"Lilly... Lilly..." sang the voice. Soon I heard another voice, and she too sang out my name. I quickened my pace, feeling like I needed to know who was calling me, and why.

Just as I was close enough to see, I noticed that both women had long black hair. They turned, and I gasped. Serena and Neleh stood before me, reaching out to me. My mother and my sister had called me this far, but why? I tried to speak, but no words would come out of my mouth. At the same time, they put their fingers to their own mouths, indicating that I shouldn't make a sound. Then they pointed ahead of them, and as I tried to reach out to them again, I stumbled. But that time, I couldn't stop myself, and I fell to my knees.

The jolt woke me immediately, but I found myself not in my bed. Not even in my home. But in the forest. In precisely the position I had dreamt I was.

I shivered uncontrollably, and as I looked down, I saw why. I had sleepwalked out of the house and into the forest in nothing but a pair of thick cotton pyjamas.

I panicked, thinking if I stayed out there like that, I would surely die of hypothermia. I would find myself with the same fate as my mother. Looking around, I tried to see a way back home, but I was well and truly lost. Why would Serena do this to me? She wouldn't want me dead, so there must be a reason for her and Neleh to bring me here.

I recalled the dream and remembered that they had been

pointing in the opposite direction. I had no choice but to go where they had told me to go. After a minute of stumbling through the freezing cold, something caught my eye. A flicker of light. I quick-ened my pace. It wasn't just light, it was fire. Warmth.

I began to run, not caring about the scratches my poor feet and ankles were picking up as I went. The warmth was much more important to me at that point. As I approached, I could hear another voice. It was the voice of a man humming to himself, in perfect tune. Because it was a kind voice, I didn't feel afraid.

I approached him. He hadn't heard or seen me so when a few twigs broke underfoot, he jumped and hid immediately behind the large tree he had been leaning on.

"Who goes there?" he asked.

The moment the words escaped from his lips, I felt even more at ease, and so I rushed towards the fire and sat down, rubbing my poor feet and hands in an effort to warm up as quickly as possible.

"My name is Lilly Tulugaq," I responded.

"You shouldn't be here, Lilly Tulugaq", he said, "it is not safe for you here. You should be frightened."

"Why would I be frightened... of the man that saved my life?" I questioned, recalling that stormy day when I had become trapped beneath an oversized log. Someone had rescued me and carefully placed my unconscious body somewhere safe, where he knew I would get immediate attention. That person was the same person that hid behind the tree in front of me. I would have recognised that gentle voice anywhere.

As he stepped out from his hiding place, although the light did not allow me to see his face, I could see his silhouette, and I was not prepared for what I saw.

His profile was that of a fit man in his early 30s, but as he moved to the side, he had something else that should have terrified me. Two huge black wings jutted out from his shoulder blades.

"What are you?" I whispered, "Are you a raven?"

He laughed then and shook his head. "I wish I was. I am neither a raven nor a man. Not any more," he said sadly.

"I don't understand."

"I was once a man, but an evil woman cursed me with these wings, and now I am neither one thing nor another," he said, sitting opposite me. It was then that he noticed I was wearing only pyjamas and he stood abruptly, making me jump in the process.

"Lilly... you could freeze to death like that. What were you thinking of walking in the forest with hardly any clothes on? Not even any shoes? Are you insane?" he said as he rushed into what looked like a cave that was well hidden by the trees. Returning, he had old thick socks, walking boots that were several sizes too big and a large woolly blanket.

As he came closer to me, I caught a glimpse of his face and jumped backwards, suddenly very afraid.

"You... you're... Sammy Morton," I muttered, confused and frightened.

He nodded in response and placed his hand gently on mine.

"Please don't be afraid of me, Lilly. I am not the killer that some people think I am. Neleh was everything to me. I loved her more than anything in the world. Come, sit closer to the fire and get warm. I will explain. I will tell you the truth about what happened to your sister... and to your mother."

His voice was so gentle and soothing that I believed every word that he said and I instantly found it impossible to believe that someone like him could ever be thought of as a killer.

As I sat next to the fire, Sammy produced some hot tea for me, made, he said, from herbs he picked from around the forest. Over the years he'd had little choice but to learn to fend for himself – teaching himself all about the different plants and animals. He had to learn how to hide from prying eyes and to defend himself from predators.

"But before I tell you about any of that, how did you find me here?"

I explained how I had been led to him by Serena and Neleh. How they had come to me in a dream.

"I understand now that they led me to you. They want the truth to be known... as I do," I said, before letting him continue his story about how he ended up in the forest all alone.

"Neleh and I used to spend a lot of time here in this forest. Although we never dared come this far. Jack and Gabriel would have gone mad. We would just hang out... do what young lovers do," he said sadly, before going on, "we were going to get married you, know? Neleh and I. But then that awful day happened, and our dreams were snatched from us. From all of us. Not just from Neleh and me but from you, your father, Gabriel. All because of that evil witch."

Of course, that's when things started to click into place. That evil witch. He was talking about Vivian. She had been responsible for a lot more than we had initially thought, and I was about to find out just how evil she really was.

"She killed Neleh," he said, and then he stood in front of me, his wings spread out majestically to his sides.

I realised that he had probably never spoken about it before. In fact, it dawned on me then that I was probably the only person he had spoken to in fourteen years. Fourteen lonely years with no company except for the animals that lived within the trees surrounding us.

He had kept the heartbreak to himself for a long, long time and it would undoubtedly hurt him immeasurably just to say these words, but I didn't interrupt. I knew the benefit of talking about things. Hopefully, this would be the start of his healing process, if it was still so raw.

"I had never known that Neleh was... was different," he stuttered.

"Different?" I asked.

He looked at me, his wings finally slowly closing behind him, while he appeared to wrestle with something within his head. He nodded and asked me if I knew anything unusual about my family. A family secret, he asked.

It was then that I understood. Neleh had the gene. She could change – the family just hadn't realised because it hadn't happened before she died. At least if it had, she had never had the chance to tell anyone about it.

"Yes," I nodded. "I understand what you mean. Could... could Neleh change?"

"I never knew about it until that day. In fact, I'm not even sure that she knew herself. I'd heard tales of such creatures but believed them to be nothing but fairy tales. We'd ventured a little further into the forest. Neleh was so happy because you'd just been born – she'd always wanted a baby sister, and so we were just hanging out together, having fun on our own. We'd left the hospital because we thought Serena and Jack should spend some quality time with you. We had taken a different path than usual and decided to investigate the area a bit more. That's when we found the run-down old cottage, well hidden within the forest."

"Neleh was so excited, so we'd approached it, assuming it to be empty but it wasn't. When we got closer, we heard a woman's voice chanting. I remember Neleh saying the voice was familiar so we'd looked through the window and we'd seen that nurse from the hospital. Vivian. She was wearing a long black robe and was reading from a thick heavy book. It wasn't your average book, either. Some kind of spellbook, I'm guessing now," he said, sighing as he gently threw some more wood onto the fire.

"What was she saying, Sammy?" I asked.

"None of it made any sense to me. It sounded foreign. Latin, perhaps. We wouldn't have really thought that much about it, but then we saw the photos... all those photos," he cried. "They were all over the cottage. Photos of Jack, your father. She was clearly obsessed. Neleh became angry and wanted to confront her. I tried to stop her, but it was too late. She burst through the door and shouted at her. She was asking 'What the hell are you doing?' over and over. Vivian was taken aback, but she just laughed, saying 'He's mine'. Neleh shook her head and said, 'Never. He loves my mother. He'll never leave her'."

"What happened next?" I asked, afraid to hear the truth.

Sammy looked away from me for a moment and closed his eyes, shaking his head. I placed my hand on his shoulder to reassure him. He turned, smiled sadly and continued.

"Vivian's eyes. They ch... they changed – they became completely red, like the devil's and she just said, 'Well I'll just have to get rid of her... and you'. Vivian lunged forward and grabbed at Neleh's hair. She must have pulled out a handful of it because she yelled in pain. Vivian started laughing and laughing. This evil laugh. I'll never forget it. I tried to pull Neleh away, but she suddenly became really strong. Then she changed. Neleh changed right in front of my eyes. She became this... this... big cat. She swiped at Vivian and caught her face. But Vivian killed her. She threw something at her, uttered a few strange words and the cat, Neleh, she just fell to the ground. She was dead. As I picked her up, she suddenly changed back into human form. But she was dead. She was dead," he cried, devastated.

Tears slowly fell down my cheeks too as I realised that the woman I had thought was my own mother for years had actually been responsible for the brutal murder of my only sister.

"How did she do this to you? How did you get these wings?" I asked horrified.

"I don't remember exactly what she said to me, but I do recall her saying that she had something 'special' in store for me. She lunged at me and pulled at my hair. But I was so devastated about Neleh that I couldn't do anything. I didn't even try. I just picked up her body and walked out of that cottage. She didn't even try to stop me. I carried on walking until I got to Gabriel's house. When he opened the door and saw me there with her dead body, I know he thought it was me. I knew he thought I was responsible. I could tell from his eyes. I laid Neleh's body on the bed, and I left. Gabriel was crying by her side, and he didn't notice me go. That's when I decided to go back and see if I could catch her myself, but as I walked back through the forest, the most horrendous pain started in my back. It lasted for hours and hours, and I couldn't do a thing. I couldn't move. I've never experienced pain like it," he said.

"You were growing the wings," I added, and he nodded.

Sammy explained that he knew perfectly well that he could never return to the town, nor go anywhere near civilisation. Already people thought he was a killer, and if they saw his wings, it would have just made things even worse. They would see him as the devil himself.

"Sammy, I'm so sorry about what happened to you. But we must tell Gabriel the truth. He will believe you now."

"Perhaps he will, but I can't go near the town. Not like this."

"But you did when you rescued me," I said hopefully, "Why did you do that?" I asked, not having realised the implications before.

"I couldn't save Neleh, but I'll be damned if I let anything happen to her sister," he said, with a smile.

I leaned my head on his shoulder, "Thank you".

Sammy told me that occasionally he would fly or walk a little closer to town, keeping himself very well hidden where he would listen to the conversations of hikers, just to feel human again. One day he had heard two women talking about a young girl who had returned to live with her grandfather in Powell River. "When they mentioned Gabriel by name I knew it was you," he said.

"Sammy, did you know that my mother had died too?" I asked.

He nodded, "She was murdered too. I think that was the spell Vivian was casting that day. She was trying to get rid of your mother, and she succeeded. I'm so sorry, Lilly. If only I had managed to stop her."

I reassured him that it would have been impossible. Nothing could have stopped her. Nothing at all.

For the next few hours, Sammy and I talked about what life had been like for the two of us over the years... me growing up in a kind of prison but not realising it until recently and him living in his own prison, hiding in the forest. We felt like life would begin to change again for us both, now that we had found each other. He was an important part of my family, and I had to convince the rest of my family that this was so. But more importantly, I had to convince them that he was no killer. That Vivian was responsible for much more than just taking my father and me away from them.

But first, I had to get home.

"Hold on tight, Lilly," said Sammy as he put his arms carefully around me. His wings flared out to his sides, and with a simple jump, we moved skywards. Although terrifying, flying through the dark night was exhilarating.

The higher we flew, the colder the temperature became, and I found myself shivering to such an extent that my teeth began to chatter.

"Don't worry, we're almost there," Sammy said softly above the sound of his moving wings. I couldn't look down for fear. But soon enough, we were home. He swooped down, staying within the confines of the forest. I recognised the area and knew I was close to home.

As we came to a standstill, he gently released his grip on me. "Are you all right?" Nodding, I hugged him tightly and told him that soon we would all be together again.

"How can I contact you, though?" I asked, wondering how he would know when it was safe to return.

"I'll come back and meet you here again tomorrow night as soon as darkness comes. I'll stay hidden until I see you. Until then, Lilly. Keep safe. Good luck speaking to the rest of the family."

I nodded as I watched him gracefully leap off into the sky again. I could hear his wings gently beating in the wind and wondered if, one day, I would be able to fly like that. I hadn't forgotten that I might possess the gene that could give me wings of my own. Or furry paws. But I was still waiting, nervously, for it to happen.

"Gabriel, Gabriel... wake up," I said, gently shaking his shoulders as he slept peacefully, blissfully unaware of what had just happened to me.

As he came to, he suddenly sat upright and asked, "Lilly, are you all right? What on earth is the matter? Did you have another bad dream?"

I told him that I needed to talk to him urgently, but I also needed to speak to Rose, Wyatt and Meredith... and Jo. "We must call them now and tell them to come over straight away. Something very important has happened."

He turned and looked at his bedside clock. 4.57am.

"Perhaps it might be pertinent to just wait a couple of hours, Lilly. We don't want to worry the rest of the family... unless absolutely necessary. Is it, Lilly? Is it absolutely necessary?"

I thought for a moment and agreed that perhaps it could wait a few more hours. After all, it had waited fourteen years, what was another two hours?

I debated whether I should tell Gabriel about Sammy first but decided against it. I knew how he felt about the man, and there was a possibility that he just might go a little mad at the mere mention of his name. At least with the others there, particularly Jo, they would help calm him down – that was my plan, anyway.

Gabriel wanted to know what was so urgent, but I said I couldn't tell him until the others arrived. He wasn't delighted, of course, but he was understanding. Gabriel was always understanding. It was one of the many things that I loved about him.

We decided to telephone the others at 8am – it was a Sunday morning, and Gabriel had said calling any earlier might have panicked them.

Fortunately, he hadn't noticed my unusual attire by then, so I decided to go to my room and lie down for a while. It gave me the chance to remove Sammy's over large boots and hide them until the truth was revealed later.

Adrenaline pulsed through my body as I lay there, darkness disappearing for another day to be replaced by a gentle light as the sun slowly began its ascent. I thought about Sammy. He had spent fourteen years completely alone. Even though I had felt lonesome during my childhood years, I could have no idea what it must have been like to have had absolutely no interaction with other people during that time.

I wondered how he had managed to hang on to his sanity. Hidden from the world like some kind of freak, when that couldn't be any further from the truth.

This man was a gentle soul who had suffered more than any of us had at the hands of a truly evil witch. It saddened me more than words could describe that he was not part of this family. The family that would have been his had Neleh lived. He would have been my brother-in-law. In my eyes, he was and would always be Neleh's husband.

The others arrived as soon as they could after the phone call. Wyatt had also brought Jo, as I'd requested. The last to arrive was Rose at five to nine.

They all appeared to be consumed with worry, but it wasn't too difficult to get them to calm down. They could see for themselves that I was safe and happy.

I had wondered about Meredith. I knew at times she had been able to read my thoughts, but this time, she seemed totally oblivious as to what was going on in my head. I asked her about it, and she told me that it's not something she can do all the time.

"It only happens occasionally and only when you are very close to me, but I'm not getting anything at the moment," she sighed, clearly wishing she was.

After I'd made them all some hot tea, and requested that Gabriel bring the box of photos they had shown me before, I asked them all to sit in the living room together.

Gabriel handed me the box, and I emptied it until I found the photograph I was looking for. The one of Sammy and Neleh happily together.

"I don't want any of you to worry, especially you Gabriel," I said, "and I don't want you to say anything until I've told you everything."

Gabriel sighed, and I continued, "Please, Grand-father. This is more important than anything. Not a word, okay?"

He nodded and smiled as best he could, unsure about what I was about to reveal.

"A few nights ago, I had a dream, and when I woke up, I discovered that it had caused me to sleepwalk."

The others all looked at each other with worry.

"It's okay. That night I woke up inside the house and nothing happened to me," I smiled before going on, "but last night something very different happened. I had the most vivid dream I have ever had, and I sleepwalked... right into the forest."

"Goodness, Lilly... you could have..." Rose began, but I interrupted her.

"Please Rose, let me finish. I was led there by the ghosts of Serena and Neleh. They took me deep into the forest. I walked for a long time before I woke up, but when I did, I knew that they had been trying to show me something. Well, not something, but someone," I whispered.

I could tell my family were all biting their tongues, except Jo, who was clearly excited and desperate to know the full story.

I held up the photo of Sammy and Neleh and said, "Last night, I met Sammy Morton."

Gabriel stood up so abruptly that he knocked his cup of tea to the floor.

"Lillian Tulugaq. What were you thinking? You could have got yourself killed. And then what? Then what?" he yelled and stormed out of the room.

That was exactly the kind of reaction I had dreaded, which was one of the reasons I had wanted the others to be there with me for support.

As I'd imagined, Wyatt stood and followed him, as did Meredith who returned a moment later with a sponge and began mopping up the tea. She was soon followed by the others. Gabriel was obviously forced to bite his tongue again.

I said nothing until everyone was sitting quietly.

"Sammy is not what you think he is. Sammy is not a killer."

I could hear Gabriel huffing and trying so hard not to speak, so I continued quickly.

"Sammy was a witness to my sister's death. Vivian is the true murderer."

Although there were gasps, I could tell the information was being mulled over by them all.

"And he told you this, did he? And you naïvely believed him? Oh Lilly," said Gabriel softly.

"There's more to it, Gabriel," I said, "Sammy has been in hiding all these years. Not because he was involved in the death, but because she cursed him. She prevented him from being able to return home. She cursed him with wings. Two beautiful big black wings."

Everybody suddenly began to speak at once, and I waited a moment before hushing them so I could continue, "Sammy was the one who saved my life. He rescued me, and you still have that feather to prove it... don't you, Gabriel?"

He stood then, his face white as a sheet, and he walked into another room, returning with the feather that proved what I had been telling them was the truth.

"Goodness. All these years" began Rose, "all these years he has been persecuted in so many ways. He was never even given the benefit of the doubt."

"That's not all," I said, "Sammy and Neleh saw Vivian putting some kind of spell on Serena. He believes that he was putting a spell on her to get rid of her. That's how Neleh was killed. She confronted Vivian, and she was murdered, but not before..." I took a breath.

"Not before what Lilly?" asked Jo eagerly.

"Not before Neleh changed into a cat."

Rose smiled then, "So she did carry the gene. And I thought I would never know the truth."

"The scar that Vivian had on her face in this photograph was put there by Neleh. She managed to swipe at her with her claws seconds before she died."

We all sat in silence for a few moments, letting the news sink in.

"So where is Sammy now?" asked Gabriel at last.

I explained that he'd created some kind of a home within a cave in the forest, far from the town. He couldn't risk being seen by anybody. "He knew that if anyone saw him, he would be taken away like some kind of freak. He is such a gentle man. Even now, after all that has happened to him. Even after being so alone for all these years, he is still a truly wonderful, gentle man. He should be a part of this family. The way he was meant to be," I said sadly.

Gabriel finally conceded and nodded, "I feel absolutely terrible. How could I not have known this?"

"He hid from the world. He didn't want anybody to know," I replied.

"But the Elders. This is something the Elders should have known. We must go and see him," he said.

Again, I explained that it would be very difficult to find his hiding place but told them that he had said he would return not far from the house that evening.

"He wants to meet with you all too," I whispered, as a tear rolled down my cheek, knowing that he would finally be welcomed into our home with open arms. Fourteen years later than he should have been.

That day had turned out to be one of the most surreal days I had spent in Canada so far. For me, it hadn't been so hard to understand what had really happened all those years ago, because I had only learned the truth about myself a few short months before. I knew it was tougher for the rest of the family, though, as they had old beliefs that had to be undone.

Of course, they believed me when I'd told them what had happened – there was no reason for them not to. But it would be when they met Sammy again that the truth would really sink in. When they saw how much suffering he had been through, not just physically, but emotionally too, they would take him in with open arms. I had no doubt about that.

And it was this reason that I couldn't wait for the reunion to take place. I willed the hours to pass by, for darkness to fall.

There was another problem I had to deal with, though. As much as I craved to be with Oliver that day, I knew I couldn't. He would have known there was something going on. Something big. And I couldn't tell him what it was. Oliver was as innocent and naïve about the truth of this world as I had been on my arrival to this magical place. If I told him that there were such things as witches who could cast evil spells, he would think I had gone completely mad. Wouldn't he?

When he had phoned me that morning to organise a time to

come and pick me up, I had to make excuses not to go out with him, and that hurt me. I hated lying to him. But what choice did I have?

It was then that I began to wonder whether our relationship would survive. As much as I was falling for him, I knew that if he were kept in the dark, our relationship would predominantly be based on lies. And what relationship can survive that? But more importantly, it wasn't fair on him. There was love, but a really successful relationship had to be based on many things. Yes, love was at the top of the list, but it was followed closely by trust and honesty. No relationship could survive without all three.

I was forbidden to talk about our family's raven gene and the fact that I had been raised by a witch. I couldn't tell anyone that I knew this world was not just inhabited by normal animals and human beings, but also by werecats, werewolves, vampires, halflings, changelings, shape-shifters and so on. I had to keep the secret, even if it meant ruining my own chances of love.

Sadness overwhelmed me, but I wasn't ready to give up just yet. I had to try and be a normal teenager. Surely over the centuries, other half-human half creatures had successful relationships with other humans... hadn't they?

I needed to find out, and so later that day, I broached the subject with the person I knew would offer me the wisest words, Rose.

"I knew this subject would come up at some stage, dear, and it's a difficult one to answer. Sure, there have been relationships between changelings and humans. But not all of them have survived, I'm afraid. Yet others have," she said with a sad smile, as I caught the remnants of a memory flashing across her eyes.

"What about you, Rose? Did you have someone once?" I asked, eager to find out what she had been thinking about.

We were standing in her conservatory where she kept a number of beautiful flowers. As she spoke, she sprayed them gently with water, carefully breathing more life into the different stunning specimens of roses.

Her face lit up immediately as she said his name. Walter.

"He was the love of my life," she said as she placed the water bottle down and turned to face me. She then opened a cupboard and pulled out an old photo album, the pages had become slightly withered with age.

She handed it to me, and as I opened it, I could see it contained photos from many years ago. Most were black and white. The majority of them were of a very handsome young man with fair hair. There were a few which showed him standing very close to a stunning young woman with dark hair and very familiar cat-like eyes. It was Rose. Although she had aged, she was instantly recognisable. About halfway through the album, the pages became empty. I felt a pang of pain for her; I guessed that he had not lived past his thirties, perhaps not even his mid-twenties, judging by the images.

"What happened?" I asked, intrigued.

It was clearly, even after all these years, still painful to recollect but she spoke gently, "He just disappeared," she said, taking my hand in hers.

So that was why it was painful for her to talk about it – because she knew it might be painful for me too. She knew that her words would reverberate with me. He simply vanished. Just as my own father had.

As she spoke, she flipped to the back of the album where a single photograph had been glued down. This one contained the image of not just the couple in love but of a tiny baby too.

"One day he took her out in her pram for a walk, and they never returned. Nobody saw them. It was a complete mystery," she stuttered, trying to hold back the tears.

"Rose, I'm so sorry," I said, wishing I could do something but knowing full well that I couldn't. When my father had disappeared, it must have been absolute hell for poor Rose. It was as if she was re-living history.

I felt her pain. Not only had she lost the man she adored, but she had lost their only bond, a tiny little daughter.

"How old was she?" I asked.

"Six months exactly," she said as she blotted her eyes with a white cotton handkerchief, "her name was Lori."

"When did they disappear?"

"A long, long time ago, my dear. He was 30-years-old. I had just turned 21," she answered before closing the album and putting it back in its resting place, before continuing, "we had known each other for many years and had begun dating when I was 16. Some people weren't so keen on us being together because of the age gap, but we didn't care what they thought. We were so in love. We were soul mates, and little Lori was the icing on our cake. That's what we used to say," she said.

"Did he know about your... your 'abilities'?"

She chuckled then and nodded, "Things were a little different back then. I didn't know I could change until I was eighteen and it wasn't because I was told. It was because it just happened one day. I was terrified. I didn't know what was happening to me. Luckily it happened while I was at home and my mother was visiting. Walter was out at the time, and my mother had heard a commotion in my room. She walked in, and I was no longer Rose the teenager. I was Rose, the Canadian Lynx. You can imagine my shock when she began speaking to me softly as if it was the most normal thing in the world. She calmed me down though, and I soon changed back to my human form. It was while I was changing back that Walter came home."

"I bet that gave him the shock of his life," I said, and she nodded.

"It was the only time I have ever seen a man faint," she laughed. "When he eventually came to, he thought he'd had a strange dream, but then he saw my ripped clothes and knew it hadn't been a dream at all. He took it surprisingly well. It was a shock to both of us on the same day, and so we had to come to terms with it together."

"So he accepted that it was a part of who you are?" I asked eagerly, thinking that perhaps Oliver would do the same.

"I was very lucky," she nodded before slowly adding, "but his parents weren't killed by wildcats."

The excitement that had been building within me was ripped out of me, and I slumped back in the chair, closing my eyes and fighting back the tears that threatened to break loose.

"Lilly, Oliver and Ben have been through a lot over the years. They have had to come to terms with the fact that both their mother and father were killed by two wild mountain lions. If you told them now that you may well be an animal of the feline variety, they could see you as a huge threat. It's very risky," she said gently. "You're still very young, Lilly. Oliver is your first boyfriend. Are you absolutely certain that he is the one? Because if he's not... and he finds out about this family, all hell could break loose. There are so many things you need to think about, to take into consideration. Ultimately though, it's up to you. We can't tell you what you should be doing with your life. That's for you to decide."

Of course, I knew what she said was true and, although it hurt in the pit of my stomach, I had gone to Rose for a reason. I trusted her, and so I knew I had to think long and hard about my decision.

There was so much going on in my life and perhaps stringing Oliver along was the worst thing I could do. The problem was that my feelings for him were getting stronger. They were strengthened every time I saw him.

But on the other hand, I had to think of him, and I did know that he would undoubtedly be safer not knowing the truth. But how could he continue to be such a big part of my life and not know? I felt so confused.

As I watched Rose continue to prune her beloved flowers, I couldn't help but think what a remarkable woman she was. She had been through so much, losing her true love and their daughter – and had never known what had happened to them – and yet she had remained clear-headed and, well, normal. She had continued to be a strong and loving woman in spite of it all.

It was then that I thought about how Vivian had taken my father and me away from our family, and I wondered whether someone like Vivian could have been responsible for Walter's disappearance too. I didn't mention it though; I had already drudged up enough heartbreaking memories. I didn't want to cause any more grief. As I left Rose's house a little while later, I thought that perhaps it was something I could talk about with Gabriel.

Walking back down the pathway through the trees, I decided to take the scenic route home, stopping along the shoreline to watch a single fisherman catch a small fish off in the distance. I began to think about Oliver and decided that I ought to ask Gabriel for his advice too.

He was pleased that I wanted his opinion on the matter

because he had practically raised the two boys himself and knew how difficult it was to keep the truth from them.

"But I am a strong believer in fate, Lilly, and if Oliver is meant to be in your life, then he will be."

"But how can he be and not know the truth. Surely he needs to know who I really am. Who we really are. Doesn't he, and Ben, deserve to know the truth about the family that raised them?" I asked, almost wishing for him to just say 'yes, let's tell them the truth'.

But he shook his head and reiterated that what will be, will be.

As the afternoon turned into evening, the sky slowly became darker, and my family members began to arrive. My worries about Oliver moved towards the back of my mind as I began to feel excited about seeing Sammy again. I was eager for him to be welcomed into the family after all these years. At least that's what I hoped would happen.

The six of us assembled just beyond the opening to the forest, where I'd followed my mother's ghost the night before, and stood huddled together for warmth as we awaited Sammy's arrival.

Soon we could hear the soft flapping of wings from above. It wasn't a frightening sound, just like a rather large bird flying down from the sky. Only this bird was a man.

As he swooped down quite a few metres from us, he came to a gentle halt, before walking very slowly towards us.

I rushed forward with open arms, and as I approached him, I could almost feel the tension from behind me, but I ignored it completely, hugging Sammy like the long lost brother that he was.

"Sammy," I whispered, "don't worry. I've explained the truth. They know what happened now and they have nothing against you... but it's been such a long time, and it might take a little while for them to accept you and to come to terms with everything. Please bear with them."

His face belied his body language, which was cool and confident. I could see in his eyes that he was nervous. Scared, even.

I took his hand in mine, and together we turned to face my family. We walked towards them and waited.

"Sammy... oh dear Sammy," cried Rose, "we're so sorry", and she rushed forward and took him into a big hug, sobbing. I could see that she wasn't the only one crying. As I looked closely at all their faces, all were wet with tears, and I smiled as they rolled down my own cheeks too.

This is what my mother and Neleh had wanted. They had wanted the truth to be known. They had wanted me to find Sammy and bring him home.

Gabriel took his hand in both of his own then and smiled. He didn't say a word, he just stood looking at the man he had once held responsible for the death of two beloved family members. He now knew that he had been so wrong.

Jo later told me that she had been a little afraid at first. Although she knew of the amazing things our family could do, she had never actually seen anything like him before and had hovered in the background waiting to be introduced, nervously.

Of course, as soon as I'd done so, her nerves had melted, and she was won over by Sammy's gentle soul.

As we huddled together for warmth, we walked back towards the house, checking that there was nobody out and about before we quickly rushed indoors, cautiously hiding that magnificent set of wings. It was the first time that Sammy had set foot indoors in so many years and the simple act led him to break down in tears as he looked around and saw that everything was pretty much as it had been all those years before.

Meredith patted him on his back before quickly jerking her arm away for fear of hurting him. It broke the ice instantly, and he laughed at her reaction, "It's okay", he said, "they won't break. They're pretty strong," as he wiped away the tears from his cheeks.

"Come, Sammy, come and sit down with us. Let's make some hot coffee or tea?" Gabriel asked. We all wondered what he must have survived on all these years, and Sammy smiled, "It's been a long time since I had coffee," he smiled.

"Coffee it is then," said Gabriel standing quickly.

"No, Gabriel, I'll do it. You've all got a lot of catching up to do. Let me do it," said Jo as I walked with her into the kitchen, leaving them to reminisce about the happy times and get to know each other all over again.

Later that evening, it was decided that Sammy would move in with us. Gabriel's house was close enough to the forest and had easy access should Sammy need more space. And of course, should he need to hide from anybody.

Sammy shed plenty of tears that night, as all of us did. As I had hoped, he was welcomed back into the family with open arms. All was as it should have been. But there were still so many questions that needed to be answered. Things we needed to figure out together. A future to plan. A father, a son and a brother to find and bring home.

❦   23   ❦

The next few weeks were fairly uneventful and seemed to go by quickly. Sammy was a joy to be around, and he and Gabriel were developing a close bond. He had even been introduced to the rest of the family after they had suspected something pretty major was going on. Gabriel knew that it was wrong to keep it from them.

Meredith's husband John and their son Cormac as well as Wyatt's wife, Sonya, were told of his existence prior to them coming over to our house. They were told that a discovery had been made that proved, contrary to popular belief, that Sammy Morton was innocent. That he had nothing to do with Neleh's murder or Serena's 'suicide'. They weren't told, however, about the shocking curse that had been placed upon him until the small group arrived at the house.

Because they were aware of the strange creatures that already inhabited our world, they weren't as shocked as I thought they would be. Cormac, however, nearly fell off his chair when Sammy walked in with his huge wings in full view. After a few minutes, though, he declared it to be 'cool' and wanted to know if he could see him fly. Again, the ice was broken, and Sammy no longer needed to be hidden from the rest of the family. Who he did need to be hidden from, however, were two men who had been a big part of the family for many years... Ben and Oliver.

Although it was discussed at length, we all felt the same. With their parents killed by wild animals, they needed to be shielded from the truth. So during those few weeks, I had to prevent Oliver from coming to the house. I knew eventually he would become suspicious, but until then, I would go on as normal.

Unfortunately, things didn't go quite as planned.

It was an evening in early March. Gabriel had gone out to celebrate an old friend's birthday, and Sammy and I were enjoying an evening in, alone. We had eaten pizza and were watching an old film on television. Ever since Sammy had moved in, we had just clicked. After all, we did have a lot in common. We had both spent many lonely years forced to live without so many things. Although I'd had a few creature comforts, there had been none for Sammy.

We had gone without things like TV and pizza, so whenever we had the chance, we would savour every moment.

That night we were being silly and giggling away when there was a knock on the door. Sammy became nervous.

"Hide," I whispered, giving him a few moments to slip away somewhere in the house.

"Who is it?" I yelled through the door, and as I slowly opened it, there was a beaming Oliver.

"Happy Valentine's Day," he said with a beaming smile.

"But it's not Valentine's Day," I answered hoping that Sammy had managed to hide himself well.

He grinned again and produced from behind his back a single rose. Handing it to me, he said, "I know, but as we haven't been able to do much together lately, and we couldn't celebrate Valentine's Day, I thought I'd surprise you tonight. I know Gabriel is at a birthday party so I figured you'd be alone."

He bent down and kissed me softly on the lips. My concern for Sammy, however, meant that I didn't respond the way I should have.

He pulled back and looked at me strangely, "Is everything all right, Lilly?" he asked.

I nodded, but I knew I had never been a very good liar.

"What is it?" he asked.

I smiled, trying to think of something to say when we both heard a noise from indoors.

It dawned on Oliver that I was not alone. He knew I was hiding something, and I had no explanation. I was mortified.

"Oh, God, Lilly. Are you seeing someone else?"

"No, of course not," I whispered in response, though not convincingly enough for him. If only I could just tell him the truth.

Suspicion got the better of him, and he pushed open the front door and walked in, "So who is he, Lilly? Is it someone I know? Someone from school?"

I repeated over and over again that there was nobody else, but he just didn't believe me. He walked into the living room, and when he saw two plates and two glasses, he knew, for sure, that I certainly wasn't on my own.

"Oliver, please don't do this. Of course, I'm not seeing anybody else. You're the only one," I sobbed.

"Then why all the secrecy, Lilly? Why have you been avoiding me for the past month or so?"

Again I was speechless, there was nothing I could say.

When I heard the front door slam, I knew that Sammy had made a run for it.

Oliver followed, and I was terrified that he would see him. I tried to grab him, but I wasn't quick enough.

I followed hot on his heels and knew that he had seen the man leaving the house.

"Who are you?" shouted Oliver.

I watched in horror as Sammy turned slowly and the realisation hit Oliver smack in the face.

"But you're... you're a murderer. You're Sammy Morton. Oh my God, what the...? Wings?" he said. Something clicked within Oliver then, and I could see that he was going to try to catch him.

"No, just let him go, Oliver," I yelled as loud as I could, running faster than I'd ever ran before, chasing after them. The two men that meant the world to me. It was then that something extraordinary happened to me.

As I ran, I could feel a dramatic change within me. A fierce pain shot through my entire body, stopping me dead in my tracks. I screamed out in agony and at the same time noticed that Oliver had stopped abruptly and turned to see why I had yelped so loudly. For a moment, Oliver became the least of my problems as I felt my body trying to shut itself down. It was trying to black out. I fought the feeling to lose consciousness and remained awake throughout the process in which my body began to radically change beyond all recognition.

I had been wondering when this would happen but had not prepared myself for the fact that it might happen during the most inopportune time. Why, oh why did it have to happen while Oliver was there?

The ferocity of the pain continued to attack my every pore, and I felt as though I wanted to die, and although it felt like this change took a long time, I knew deep down that it had almost been instantaneous.

I knew then that I was no longer the innocent young fourteen-year-old girl that had been chasing after Sammy and Oliver in the forest. And as I looked down, I saw the full extent of my new self. I saw that in place of my long pale arms and legs were four limbs of a completely different nature. Long, lean, incredibly strong and covered in soft black fur, I knew that my change into a feline was complete. Judging from my size, I realised that I wasn't your average house cat but a much larger animal. To my horror, it dawned on me that I had become one of the most fierce feline creatures in the region. I had morphed into a black mountain lion, and I will never forget the look of absolute terror on Oliver's face at the sight of me. It would haunt me forever.

I had no idea what to do. For some reason, I had not questioned Rose enough about the physical changes that happen during a transformation, and we had certainly never discussed what I should do when it did occur.

After witnessing Sammy fly off into the distance, Oliver had then seen me become something terrifying, especially in his eyes. I watched as the utter shock of it all caused him to collapse right in front of my eyes.

Terrified that the shock had killed him, I rushed to his side and put my head above his mouth. I could feel his breath, and his heartbeat was strong yet incredibly fast – I could hear and almost feel the rhythmic beating without even touching him. I dared not touch him in case he suddenly awoke. That would be an even greater shock, I was sure of it.

I came to the conclusion that he had most likely fainted. He needed to be taken back to the house but, being on four legs, I knew I couldn't do it myself. I had no choice but to call out to Sammy and hope that he was merely hiding and had not flown too far away.

Forgetting that I couldn't call out his name, I tried to make some kind of noise to get his attention. It was difficult, but I managed a deep howl. He returned almost immediately, landing just a few metres away from us. I could just see his face, and I knew that he was not afraid of what I had become. He had witnessed his own girlfriend change into a cat, albeit briefly, and so the sight of me changing wasn't something that caused too much concern.

As if reading my mind, he approached quickly, bending down to pick up the still unconscious Oliver. He walked as fast as he could back to the house, while at the same time I rushed off into the distance, heading towards the one person I knew would be able to help me in these strange circumstances. I ran as fast as my hind legs would propel me, trying to keep myself hidden, until I reached Rose's house.

I let out another howl as soon as I arrived, causing all of the other cats in the vicinity to howl back. Rose appeared quickly in the doorway, a look of concern across her face.

I approached her, not knowing how to tell her what had happened, but she knew something wasn't right. As she peered down at me fearlessly, I bowed my head and looked to the ground, trying hard to think of a way to let her know that it was me. But I needn't have worried, for she knew immediately who I was.

"So it has happened, Lilly," she said softly, and I nodded, "I knew you would become a special beast. A black mountain lion, eh? Excellent," she chuckled.

Rose then stepped right up to me and bent down, so our faces were parallel to each other. She looked deep into my eyes and sensed the urgency.

I watched as she made the immediate decision to change too, "for speed," she had whispered while still in human form. I nodded and then watched as the old lady morphed into a creature of grace, beauty and speed – all in a matter of seconds, completely silently except for the ripping of her clothes. It appeared that her change had happened painlessly.

It was only when she had become a smaller cat than me that we could communicate effectively. Although we were unable to physically speak to each other, we were able to read each other's minds. I explained to her exactly what had happened, and I listened intently as she responded, telling me that we needed to get to Oliver immediately.

She sprang into action, leaping quickly and effortlessly down through the tall trees in the direction of my home. I followed as quickly as I could, noticing that we were using a different route to that which I had become accustomed. An easier route for beasts that could move the way we could, fitting through gaps within the trees that I would have struggled with in my human form.

I had little time to dwell on the change that had happened to me, but I did notice a few things. My senses were like nothing I'd ever experienced before. Not only could I smell things I would never have even noticed, but my eyesight and hearing were also second to none too. But I couldn't think about that. I needed to think about Oliver. What had I done? We would never be the same again. He would hate me and wouldn't even want to lay his eyes on me, probably for the rest of his life.

I knew there was nothing I could do to change his feelings for me. I just hoped that he would be able to keep our secret. That was even more important than anything else now.

As I followed behind Rose, my mind strayed again, and I couldn't help but notice how gracefully she moved. Graceful in human form, graceful in feline form – she was a true beauty.

Minutes later, as we arrived at home, I wondered how I would change back. I had no idea how I had changed in the first place, so I didn't know what to do. I watched as Rose didn't even give it a second thought. Well practised in the art, I watched as the cat grew larger, the fur giving way to pale skin and the whiskers disappearing from her face, her claws becoming long slender fingers. I was about to discover an unfortunate side effect of the change, though, as she stood up proudly, I saw that she was completely naked.

She looked down at me and smiled, "It's something you'll have to get used to, I'm afraid," she said.

"I've had many years to come to terms with it," and then she opened the front door and tiptoed in quietly. I skulked in behind her, watching her as she opened a cupboard that I hadn't even noticed before and pulled out a pair of black trousers, a grey sweater and a pair of black pumps, which she hastily dressed with.

"I'll explain later," she whispered.

Sammy appeared then, recognising Rose's dulcet tones.

"He's still out cold," he whispered, "I didn't want to try and wake him in case he freaked out again. I think he's okay, though."

Rose nodded and told us to stay out of the room. She didn't want him to wake up and see us before he saw anyone else. She asked Sammy to call Gabriel immediately.

After he had done so, he came over to me and gently put his hand on the back of my neck, "Don't worry, Lilly. I'm sure everything will be all right."

I let out a sigh and sat down on the cold stone floor, wishing I could morph back into human form. I wanted to speak to Sammy so badly but I couldn't. There was no way he could understand me, so I just curled up on the floor, waiting. Waiting for something to happen.

We heard Rose's voice from Gabriel's bedroom, where Sammy had lay Oliver down until he came to. Although we couldn't hear what she was saying, we could tell that she was reasoning with him. Occasionally, his voice could be heard too – but he never shouted. There was no anger there, which was at least something to soothe my worrying head.

It wasn't much later when I heard the sounds of an engine roaring up the driveway. Gabriel was home. I leapt up, not sure what to do with myself, but before I could do anything, Gabriel was at the door, opening it.

As he rushed in, he gasped at the sight of me with Sammy.

Speechless for a second, he suddenly gushed, "Lilly?"

I nodded and rushed to his side, brushing my head against his legs gently. I was afraid he might be angry, but he looked so proud, and he smiled at me warmly for a moment until Sammy filled him in on the evening's events.

"Oliver?" he said, "Where is he?"

"Rose is with him now. They're in your room."

He patted me on the head and told us both to just stay in the living room out of the way until he had spoken to him.

I was desperate to see Oliver for myself. I was desperate to speak to him and plead forgiveness for keeping this from him. But the sight of me wouldn't help my case.

I watched as the door shut slowly behind Gabriel and waited patiently, not able to do anything but pace up and down the living room floor.

"Come and sit down, Lilly. There's nothing you can do," said Sammy kindly.

I shook my head and sighed heavily, wishing that there was something I could do.

Then the phone rang. Knowing that he shouldn't answer it in case it was someone other than a family member, he picked it up without saying a word and listened carefully. It was Jo, however. Relieved to hear a friendly voice, he recounted what had happened, and she told him she would be right over.

Luckily she only lived a stone's throw away, so she arrived within a few minutes.

With a gentle knock on the door, Sammy gingerly peered through the window to make sure it was her. When he saw that it was, he opened the door, and she stepped in, becoming speechless at the sight of me in all my feline glory.

"Wow, Lilly. This is amazing. You're a... you're a mountain lion. A black one!" she exclaimed, stating the obvious. "Do you mind if I stroke your head?" she asked tentatively.

I shook my head, and she moved closer to me, and I felt her hand softly touch the top of my head and move slowly down my back. It was a soothing motion, helping me to feel a bit calmer after everything that had happened.

Suddenly the bedroom door opened and Rose appeared, shutting it behind her.

"It's good of you to come, Jo. I think Lilly needs as much support as she can get right now. I'm afraid Oliver's not taking this very well."

I sighed loudly once again, wishing I could rewind time and

save Oliver and myself all this heartache. Although he was probably feeling something far more than heartache – shock, outright disgust, perhaps?

As the three spoke amongst themselves for a few moments, I tried to will myself to change back, closing my eyes hard and thinking, 'change, change, change'. But nothing happened, and so I had no choice but to wait until it occurred naturally.

"Well, I have said everything that I can say and done everything that I can do. Gabriel is the best person to reason with Oliver at this stage, so I think you and I should go back to my house, Lilly. Jo, can you stay for a while? Gabriel might need you."

Jo agreed and asked whether she should call anyone else.

"I'll leave that up to Gabriel. He will let you know. Just wait for him, okay?"

Again she nodded, "I'll make us some tea, Sammy. You two go. Don't worry. I'm sure everything will be all right."

Rose beckoned me to follow her as she opened the front door, and so we walked in silence for a few minutes before she turned to look at me and smiled.

"A mountain lion, eh?" she said with pride. "Your mother would have been so proud of you, Lilly. Of course, we knew that you wouldn't just be any old cat... or raven," she added.

It was then that I thought about ravens. I had become a cat, not a bird. Gabriel must have been a little disappointed that I had inherited my mother's genes and not my father's. Especially considering there was no other family member, at that stage, that was able to become the bird of our ancestors.

I thought how great it would have been to be able to fly, but as I looked around at my surroundings and smelled the wonderful things I could smell and heard the extraordinary things I could hear, I didn't feel any disappointment. Although I still wondered how I was going to return to my old self, and I dreaded the pain that I had felt earlier that evening, I was still amazed at my whole transformation.

It hadn't happened how I had hoped it would. I had imagined myself something like Professor McGonagall in Harry Potter who could change in the blink of an eye, without an ounce of pain. That is how I'd wanted it to happen and in the company of a select few.

Certainly not in the company of Oliver. But that is exactly what had happened, and I couldn't take it back. My relationship with him was ruined. And there was nothing I could do about it.

Rose had become quiet once again, deep in thought, I imagined as we trampled through the undergrowth beneath the tall trees and headed in the direction of her home. Although I wasn't looking where I was going, I knew we were close because I could hear all of her cats. I could smell them too but more than anything I could almost feel the sound of their hearts, beating gently, keeping them alive.

Of course, I could 'feel' Rose's heartbeat even louder than anything, and it was beating a little quicker than when we had left my house. I looked at her, and it amazed me that this seventy-plus (she still hadn't told me her actual age) year-old woman was capable of such a massive transformation. She was still incredibly fit and agile. She was a force to be reckoned with, and I was intensely proud that I could call her family.

We arrived at the front door, and as she pushed it open, Scully was the first to rush out. The hair on her back raised high as she saw me, and she arched her back. I noticed that her eyes had become as black as coal again as she stared deep into my eyes. I just stood still, waiting for some kind of recognition. It didn't take long. Within seconds, she relaxed completely and approached me, purring happily.

Rose smiled too and patted her on the back, "I knew she would recognise you. She just needed a moment," she said.

As I entered the house, I had similar experiences with the rest of the animals, and soon it was as normal, the cats curling up in various nooks and crannies wherever they could.

Rose walked into the kitchen and sat down, taking off her black pumps and replacing them with a pair of warm slippers.

"Right," she said, "we need to get you back to Lilly, the girl. As much as I love this new look."

I sat beside her and waited for her to tell me what to do.

"And don't worry, I've got clothes for you to wear here," she laughed. "You'll find that it becomes very useful to keep clothes at the homes of all our family members," she laughed.

"Now, the key is to relax. It's really quite simple, but it will take some getting used to."

I tried to do as she said, but nothing happened and so I sat and focused on relaxing and being calm. Nothing. I was still a mountain lion.

"Okay, let's try something different. Lie down completely," I did as she said and curled up on the soft rug beside the kitchen countertop.

"Now close your eyes. Slow your breathing down and relax. Feel as though your muscles are falling away from your bones. That's it. Breathe in slowly. Breathe out slowly. In. Out. In. Out."

Sure enough, as I completely relaxed my body, I felt something happen within me. There was no pain like before. It was incredibly uncomfortable but strangely pain-free. And finally, moments later, I felt my whole body become human again. I opened my eyes to find Rose had gone. I stood up and turned around, conscious of my nakedness. At first, I had felt very warm but soon grew cold.

Rose appeared from another room carrying a pair of pink pyjamas and some thick purple woolly socks. "I told Gabriel you would stay here tonight. I think it's for the best," she said as she handed me the warm clothes. I slipped them on, quickly warming up before I thanked her.

Once dressed, she hugged me long and hard, "It's a tough life sometimes, Lilly. We can never know what's going to happen. But you mustn't worry yourself over Oliver. What's done is done. He will survive."

For the first time since early that evening, I broke down in tears. They flowed for a long time afterwards. No matter how hard I tried to choke them back, my cheeks would become soaked once again. Rose was perfect company. She knew exactly what to say and when not to say anything, and I was particularly grateful for her wisdom that night.

When my eyes and cheeks finally became drier, Rose heated up some milk on the stove while I heaped a few teaspoons of cocoa into a couple of mugs. Hours later, we were still talking about love, life, Serena, Neleh, Walter, Lori, Sammy, Oliver, December and everything else that mattered to us both. We bonded more that night than we had ever done before. Rose had become something of a surrogate mother to me.

$\mathscr{H}$ 24 $\mathscr{H}$

I didn't speak to Oliver again after that. I tried phoning him, but he ignored all my calls. My emails bounced back, and my letters were returned unopened.

Gabriel had reasoned with him and thankfully he had agreed to keep our family's secret, but at a price. The price being that he no longer wanted to be a part of our lives.

I was heartbroken. Not just for me but for Gabriel who cherished him and had done so ever since he was born.

I was also sad for his brother Ben who was completely unaware of what had happened. Oliver had agreed Ben was better off not knowing the truth that surrounded him. He then left Powell River, out of our lives. I knew that the fault lay entirely with me.

Ben had attempted to find out the truth behind his sudden departure, but we refused to give him any more details than absolutely necessary. All he had been told was that Oliver and I had a huge disagreement, so big that he no longer wanted to live here. Apparently, he'd told Ben he had always yearned for more than being stuck in Powell River, so it seemed the perfect time to get away and explore what he really wanted out of life.

Ben simply accepted what he had been told. The excuses made sense to him, and so he carried on life as normal. Well, as normal as could be expected considering his beloved younger brother had effectively run away.

I could tell that it pained him that Oliver had left, but he told me that, regardless of his reasons for leaving, he was also proud that Oliver had decided to stand on his own two feet and was going to have his own adventure.

After several weeks when I asked after Oliver, Ben told me that he regularly talked to him on the phone but when I asked for more details – how he was, where he was, etc., Ben just said that he was doing okay but that he had promised Oliver not to tell me where he was or what he was doing. His only message to me: 'please stay away and don't try to contact me'. When Ben told me those words, I hid away for a while, shed a few tears and did my best to move on, but it wasn't easy.

Although I blamed myself, I refused to let it affect my life negatively. I still had a life, and I intended to live it as best as I could. That didn't mean I didn't miss Oliver, though. I missed him terribly. He had been such an important part of my early life in Canada, and I wished that things had happened differently with him. He deserved it... and so did I.

My life continued, not quite as normal as before, but continued nonetheless. With Oliver no longer in the picture, Sammy didn't have as much to worry about because we rarely had any other visitors to our home. The two of us became very close, he was like a brother to me, and I loved him dearly, and I knew he loved me too. I was the little sister he had never had. There were days we would spend hours in the forest, Sammy showing me how he had lived there for so many years.

Throughout that lonely time, he'd had no choice but to become totally self-sufficient – hunting for food and furs to keep himself warm during the winters, creating shelter, building fires... he taught me all of this and more, at the same time helping me to develop my own fitness and strength too.

Whilst there, deep in the forest with him, usually during the hours of darkness, I spent much of my time as a mountain lion, running stealthily through the trees below with Sammy flying just above the treetops. We would spend hours racing against each other and having fun.

It hadn't really occurred to me until then, but it was like

Sammy was regaining those years of his youth, the ones he had lost. The ones that had been so cruelly taken from him.

As spring turned to summer, my thoughts of Oliver and our times together gradually dwindled, and I began to concentrate on other things and to look to the future.

I hadn't forgotten Gabriel's promise to me, the one he had made earlier in the winter shortly after I broke my leg. I recalled him saying that he would take me on a trip to visit the Elders and he'd said that we would go when the weather had improved... in spring. Yet spring was now nearly over.

He hadn't forgotten. In fact, he was well prepared for my questions and had already begun preparations for our journey together.

With a smile, Gabriel nodded. "There's no need to worry, my dear Lilly. I have been planning our trip for a while, I've just been waiting for the right time, and I believe that time has come."

The thought excited me. Not just the fact that we were leaving Powell River for an unusual journey, but that I was to spend some quality time with my grand-father, something I hadn't really done.

When Gabriel had first mentioned that we should go to the Elders together, it was primarily to help unravel the mystery of who had rescued me after my accident, however, with the truth now fully known, we decided the journey was still an important one.

It was a rite of passage for me. At the same time, he told me, it was important for me to meet the Elders. "You never know when you might need their assistance or advice, Lilly," he had said, almost in a warning.

Of course, there was also the matter of my missing father and the Elders might be able to offer some insight as to what had happened to him and where he might be.

Gabriel explained that it would likely be a difficult trip to take and that it involved a lot of hiking through the mountains and forest trails. But, like him, it had to be taken in human form. I couldn't change into a mountain lion for ease of passage, he had warned me.

"In order for you to grow, truly grow as a young woman, you need to complete the journey as one," he had added.

I knew I was ready, physically and mentally. I was also ready to learn more about the Elders, and he told me he would enlighten me during our journey.

Gabriel had gained approval from the school to take me away for a while, with the simple agreement that I would take some extra classes during the summer holidays.

When I asked Ben if it was okay for me to take some time off work to go away with Gabriel, he had agreed that I could use a break.

We had packed as if for a camping trip. Our backpacks filled with all the gear that we would need on our journey. The first part of our trip would take place by boat. It was a very small boat too – with just sufficient space for the two of us and all of our gear. Having no idea where we were going, this little boat surprised me. It frightened me too. The only other boat I had ever been on was the ferry with Ben when he had collected me from the airport. This was seriously tiny in comparison, and I certainly didn't feel safe. But Gabriel's soft voice and his kind words helped me feel at ease after a few hours on the water. At least it had a small motor, so we didn't have to row.

It wasn't until we were gliding quietly through the water that Gabriel began telling me about the Elders. And from what he explained, they were not quite what I was expecting.

"The Elders live high in the Coastal Mountains, hidden from all eyes other than those they want to see. They are not all human, Lilly. Many of them are changelings, like you. Some are vampires, some are white witches. There are some creatures there that might even frighten you. But you must not be fearful. All of them are good and honest. They are very wise, and they help people like you and me who know the truth about their world. You could say that they are authority figures for our kind. Somewhere we can go for help should we really need it," he said, and I nodded a little nervously.

I took a little time to let the information sink in. We were on a long and arduous journey to meet with vampires and witches? It sounded crazy, but I knew that Gabriel knew what he was doing.

"Are they all really old then, Gabriel?" I asked, wondering why they were known as the Elders.

"Many are very old, yes, although they will not appear to be old to us. The vampires, for instance, are immortal. They appear to be young and beautiful, when in fact they have been in existence for many hundreds of years. Some of the witches are the same. But those of them that are like you, half-human, half-animal, they look old because they are old. But they all have something in common. They are the Elders, and they are called the Elders because they are full of wisdom and knowledge about almost everything," he answered.

"How did they become the Elders?"

He smiled then and told me that he had been invited to join them, but only when he feels ready. This surprised me. I was not quite sure why it should shock me so much because Gabriel was a wise and honest man, full of advice for anyone that needs it. A pillar of the community. But I was shocked nonetheless. And worried. It's a long way from his family. A long way from me. And when would he decide to join them? I hoped that it would not be for a long time to come.

But Gabriel continued to answer my question, not concerning himself with the worried look on my face, "All of the Elders are beings that have been strong and reliable members of their own communities who want to help on a larger scale. They are a kind of authority for people like us. They make rules we must follow, just like our own governments do. There is a large number of groups of Elders found throughout the world. All living in well-hidden communes, like the one we're going to visit in the mountains."

I listened intently and wondered what kind of 'people' they would be, and how many of them would be there. But the thing that really caught my attention was the fact that they make rules that must be followed by the likes of me – anyone that is not entirely human. The only rule I knew of at that point was the fact that we needed to keep our true selves a secret from the rest of the world. Cringing at the memory, I recalled how I'd already broken that secret when I'd accidentally revealed my true form to Oliver. I was lucky that he'd agreed to turn a blind eye to the truth.

We continued to motor along the calm waters in silence for a while, myself deep in thought about the rules and the Elders while Gabriel contentedly hummed to himself. Looking down into the depths of the river below, I was surprised how clear the water was.

Although inviting because of its clarity, it looked icy cold, and I wasn't in the least bit tempted to jump in. Our boat made large ripples behind us as we chugged along, and I watched for a while as it mesmerised me, taking my mind off what was to come.

Looking up from the water, I noticed a number of small green islands around us. I assumed they were uninhabited, but I was probably wrong. Knowing what I knew then, I changed my mind and decided they were probably full of vampires and werewolves, all waiting for fresh blood and meat to feast on. The thought made me shiver, and I decided I needed to cut down on the horror I'd been watching and reading lately. Gabriel watched me and asked what I was thinking about.

Grinning, I told him that I wondered who, or what, lived on the islands surrounding us. I didn't expect him to know the answer, but he did. I should have known. He usually had answers to everything.

"Only a few of them are inhabited full time," he said, "most are used on the odd occasion by passers-by like us. But there are a few islands that have small communities of special creatures," he added, "who would prefer that we avoided them entirely."

"Why would they want us to avoid them?"

"These creatures do not want to be tempted by what they shouldn't have, which is why they live far from civilisation."

I noticed that he neglected to say what kind of creatures they were and I decided I didn't want to know... at least until we had passed through and were well clear of them.

Changing the subject, I asked Gabriel why we were making this journey by boat and on foot. "Isn't it possible to reach the mountains by car?"

He laughed then and reiterated what he had said before. The journey itself was a learning experience. Something that was an important part of my becoming a woman of strength. Not just physically, but psychologically too. I thought about those words for a moment while Gabriel watched me intently. "And besides," he added, "you'd never get a car up there," he chuckled.

I didn't have an answer to that, so we sat in silence for the rest of the boat ride. The corners of his mouth twitched slightly as if he was trying hard not to smile.

We reached the shore a short while later, and Gabriel took off his shoes and socks and hopped out to pull the boat safely out of the water. I jumped onto the sandy beach and helped pull it further inland, where he carefully tied it to a large tree trunk before drying his wet feet and putting his shoes and socks back on before he caught a chill. He seemed to know exactly where things were, and so I asked how many times he had made this journey before.

"Many, many times," he said, "whenever I need to get away, I come through here on my way to the Elders. I came a lot after your mother and Neleh died and when you and your father were taken away. The Elders knew it was the one place I found some peace. But, like I said, it's not just the destination where I found peace. It was the journey too."

It was certainly peaceful, and I could imagine how it would calm the soul after those awful things had happened.

After we'd had something to eat, the two of us set off on foot, leaving the boat and the river behind us. I was a little nervous about the hike – it was my first, after all. But I was grateful for all the exercise I had been getting with Sammy. It had made me fitter and stronger and ready for whatever the world had in store for me.

I thought of Sammy and what the world had in store for him too. He could never be a part of the world he had lived in all those years ago. As long as he had those massive wings, he would have to remain in hiding. It was a sad fact that made me heavy-hearted. As far as I knew, the only way he could have his life back again was if we found Vivian and somehow reverted the curse she had placed on him. I had high hopes for these Elders.

Later that night after much walking, we had set up camp, built a small fire and ate supper, when Gabriel surprised me with another talent I knew nothing about. He carefully took out a small musical instrument from his rucksack and began to play the most beautiful tune I'd heard since my first arrival in Powell River when I'd heard that Portuguese song that had led me to Rose.

The instrument looked like a kind of flute, and I was so shocked when he carefully put it to his lips and played it so beautifully, especially considering he'd never played it in my presence before.

Lying down by the fire and snuggling into my sleeping bag, I stared up at the night sky and listened intently to the music. Even though it was quite chilly, I felt completely peaceful and comfortable. It was a magical feeling, lying there, listening to him playing and watching the sky filled with the brightest of stars. I enjoyed the moment, keeping very quiet until he had finished.

"That was beautiful Gabriel. How come you never play at home?" I asked, sitting up and leaning on my elbows as I looked across the softly burning fire towards him.

"It's something I only do when I come out here," he said before he continued to play some more. The music, combined with the gentle sound of the running water from a little stream nearby, gently lulled me to sleep.

Surprisingly I slept remarkably well that night. I had thought that the cold would prevent me from getting a good night's sleep, but the fresh air must have counteracted it. I awoke feeling fresher and more alive than ever.

Climbing out of my warm cosy sleeping bag, I noticed Gabriel had already packed up his sleeping bag but was nowhere to be seen. All his things were still there, though.

"Gabriel," I called out and waited for a reply, but none came.

Again, I yelled his name even louder and hoped that he just hadn't heard me the first time. But nothing. I decided to sit and wait for a while, hoping that he had just gone for a brief walk while I slept.

It didn't take long for my mind to begin running riot with terrifying possibilities. Vampires, werewolves, witches, bears. Had any of these creatures taken my grand-father? I could feel my body twitching, wanting to change. I knew that my senses would be a hundred times more in tune with the nature surrounding me as a lion. If I changed, I might be able to find the creatures that had taken him. But he had told me this journey was one that must be taken in human form, regardless of what happened.

So I stood still and breathed deeply, just as Rose had shown me. I had to keep calm and relax.

"Ah... you're awake," yelled a cheery voice and my entire body slumped forward in relief.

"Gabriel... I thought something had happened to you."

"You seem to forget that I am becoming an old man. My ears

aren't quite as good as they were when I was your age," he laughed, "I was just washing my face in the stream," he added.

Since discovering the truth about myself, I had become more of a worrier. I decided it was something I needed to work on as we both sat down and enjoyed a nice cup of tea.

"We have a long and arduous hike ahead of us today, Lilly. It's important that we stay focused," he said, adding "but if something should happen, remember what I told you. This is a journey to be made in human form. You are not to transform yourself, except only in the direst of circumstances."

I agreed, wondering why it was so important, but I didn't ask. I was too busy thinking what 'the direst of circumstances' could be. A niggling little doubt crept into my mind that something awful was going to happen.

On the other hand, it could be a test. Could Gabriel be testing me? Was this some kind of ritual that all changelings had to go through? I hoped it was, at least then I didn't have to worry about a nasty experience awaiting us. Did I?

After we had eaten a good, hearty breakfast and set off on foot, we spent the majority of that day hiking through forests until eventually the terrain began to change and the trees became a little scarcer. It was the beginning of the ascent up the mountains. Although I loved being among the forested areas, I enjoyed the change of scenery, and the mountainous region was absolutely breathtaking.

Gabriel and I spoke about all kinds of things as we walked together, him always in front, leading the way. He wanted to know more about my life in London, not that there was an awful lot to tell. He already knew what living there had been like for me, mostly lonely and uneventful.

But still, he wanted to know what my school had been like, whether or not I had ever had any friends if the teachers had been fond of me – everything.

"December Moon was my one and only friend," I had told him. "My life was incredibly dull until she arrived." I smiled as I thought about the quirky girl with the red hair that had brought some sunshine into my otherwise dark life.

I told Gabriel all about her and her own strange, unhappy life.

"Perhaps we could arrange for her to come and visit sometime," he had suggested.

"Oh, that would be wonderful. I'd love for you to meet her. I just know that everyone would love her. She would just fit in with us here if you know what I mean?" I laughed.

Gabriel nodded and smiled at me, and I was suddenly reminded of my father. I don't know what it was, perhaps an expression that Gabriel shared with him. I felt a sudden pang in the pit of my stomach, and I had to stop walking for a moment.

"Are you all right, my dear," he asked as he pulled out a bottle of water and handed it to me.

Taking a deep drink, I nodded. "Yes, I'm fine. You just reminded me of father." He nodded too and smiled sadly, "We will find him, Lilly. If the search takes me to the grave, we will find him," he said sombrely.

I gulped another swig of water and attempted a smile. That was not a thought I would cherish. The search sending Gabriel to his grave, or the search taking that long.

My heart began to feel like it was breaking just a little bit more and Gabriel obviously sensed it, so he changed the subject again.

He began to tell me about his long and eventful life in Powell River, and I learned even more about my family. The heaviness in my heart was lifted, and I became intrigued, as we continued our long walk.

Perhaps this was another reason for our journey. We could finally talk honestly together, just the two of us.

He talked more about his wife, Elsebeth, who had died of breast cancer when she was just 31. It had been a very aggressive form of cancer, and she'd had little time between her diagnosis and her death, "but she was happy that she had the chance to say goodbye to everyone that she loved," he said.

"I'm sorry, Gabriel. It must have been heartbreaking to see her like that. How long ago did she die?" I asked.

"She's been gone about thirty years, but never forgotten," he added, smiling. "She was a remarkable woman. Not unlike Rose, actually. They were good friends."

"You and Rose are very close," I replied, and he laughed, nodding,

"Elsebeth made us promise that we would be there for each other. She wanted Rose to take her place. She felt that I needed a wife and

Rose was the person she nominated," he chuckled, "but Rose and I are, and have always been, just very good friends. I have managed on my own, but Rose is always there when I need her, and vice versa."

I agreed that he and Rose would make a great couple, but understood perfectly that some people are better off living alone – well, kind of alone.

"Gabriel?" I said.

"Mm?"

"I'm sorry about Oliver. I'm sorry that I made him go away. I know that he is like a son to you."

Gabriel stopped walking and turned to me, "Don't apologise for being who you are Lilly. It is not your fault that it happened the way it did. Oliver is a fine young man, he can look after himself, and I know he'll be okay. Like I said to you before, I am a strong believer in fate. What is meant to be, will be, so don't blame yourself" he said, "he'll be fine. And so will we."

We continued walking uphill in silence until the terrain started to become a little more rugged. Gabriel pointed to an area where there were a few more trees and told me that was where we would stop for the night. As we approached, myself a little breathless, I noticed a small cave, the entrance of which was well hidden by foliage.

"This is where I usually stop and sleep," he said as we exhaustedly let our backpacks drop to the ground. I slumped down on a nearby rock until my breathing became slower and steadier, watching as Gabriel began collecting sticks and twigs and larger pieces of wood to create a fire.

He had barely even caught his breath. Feeling guilty for just sitting and watching, I stood up and began to help, but I soon stopped when I had the feeling we were being watched.

I moved closer to Gabriel's side and whispered, "Gabriel, I think there's someone here. I think someone's watching us."

"Stay close Lilly, and act naturally," he replied without looking up as he continued to collect kindling for the fire.

I saw from the corner of my eye that he was discreetly looking around to see who it could be. Suddenly he stood upright and chuckled. I turned to see the source of his amusement and noticed a rather large white wild mountain goat perched slightly above us, watching us with beady eyes.

"Hello, old chap," shouted Gabriel, "I thought I might bump into you again."

The goat carefully and cleverly climbed down from the narrow shelf above us, and as he did so, the top half of his body changed dramatically. Like Sammy, he was half animal, half human in every sense of the words.

His head and arms were that of a human and the rest of him were most certainly that of a goat. His hair was completely white, as was his long goatee. Age-wise, I would have said he was in his sixties.

"Gabriel. Good to see you, old man. Frightfully sorry if I gave the young girl cause for concern," he said in a posh British accent, which completely puzzled me.

"Hello my dear," he said as he walked over to me, with his hand outstretched. I shook it, my mouth open in surprise.

"Close your mouth, Lilly," laughed Gabriel, "this is an acquaintance of mine, Charlie."

"Acquaintance? I would say, friend... would you not?" he chuckled, before adding, "absolutely charmed to meet you, my dear Lilly. You must be the old man's grand-daughter from London, I presume," he said, still holding my hand in his.

I nodded, not quite sure what to say. I'd never seen a half-man, half goat before. Especially not one with such a strong English accent.

"Nice to meet you, Charlie," I eventually managed to spit out.

He finally let go of my hand and turned his attention to Gabriel, just as Gabriel was explaining that he had met Charlie when he'd visited the Elders the previous winter, at about the same time I'd arrived – the reason Gabriel had been unable to collect me from the airport.

"I presume you are on your way to visit the Elders?" Charlie asked while he began to assist making the fire.

"Yes, I'm taking Lilly up to meet them. What have you been up to lately, Charlie?" asked Gabriel.

Charlie stuttered momentarily before explaining that he had

actually been recovering from an injury and so he'd had little choice but to stay on the mountain for the last few months.

"What kind of injury?" asked Gabriel as he lit the fire.

"Oh, nothing to worry about really," answered Charlie in a way that suggested he didn't want to talk about it. Gabriel promptly changed the subject, asking if he'd met anyone of interest there lately.

Charlie moved over to the now roaring fire and sat down, making himself comfortable as he told us about a small group of travellers he'd seen just a few weeks before. Having not recognised any of the group, Charlie had kept his distance, watching from above. They were a group of young hikers. "Kids," said Charlie, "the human variety... not fellow goats!" he added, chuckling.

"I just stood grazing while I watched them attempt to make a fire. They drank lots of beer and acted like idiots," he added, "other than them, there hasn't been much going on around here for quite a while... unless you count the time when a strange young woman stayed the night. It was around Christmastime, I believe."

"A strange young woman?" questioned Gabriel, "I wonder who that was."

"Her name was Tabitha, I think. That's it. Do you know her Gabriel?"

He shook his head.

I was intrigued. Who was this Tabitha? Where had she come from? Where was she going? What was she doing up here alone? And why was she strange?

Going by Gabriel's friendliness to the goat man, I finally accepted that Charlie must be somebody (or something) that could be trusted, so I pulled out my sleeping bag and laid it down next to Gabriel's where I curled up and listened to their conversation to find out more about the folk that often gathered around the mountain.

Charlie had obviously spent some time watching Tabitha, and he revealed that she appeared to be a witch.

"So what was she up to at Christmas, Charlie?" asked Gabriel as he warmed his cold hands over the flames.

"I don't know where she was coming from, but she stopped at this very cave for a night. I was near enough to watch her without being seen," said Charlie as I began to get the feeling that he was something of a voyeur.

"She was alone, to begin with, but was later joined by a young man who wasn't exactly the kind of boy you'd like your daughter to bring home if you know what I mean. He was covered in those awful tattoos, all up his arms and legs. Dreadful things. I thought they were perhaps lovers, but before I knew it, they had a huge argument. I couldn't quite hear what they were fighting about, but it was clearly serious. And then just when I thought they were over it, he turned into a wolf, of all things. I knew then that I needed to make a quick exit, so I went and hid away in my cave until they left. They were gone by the next morning. I was intrigued, to say the least. I'd have loved to know what that was all about," he said.

"Interesting," said Gabriel, "but I don't know either of them. Did you hear what the boy was called?"

Charlie sat motionless for a moment, deep in thought. "Aah yes. It was Zoltan."

Zoltan and Tabitha. A werewolf and a witch. I asked how Charlie had come to the conclusion that she was a witch.

"I just knew... it was written all over her," he chuckled, before adding, "that and the fact that she appeared to be attempting to cast spells before wolfie arrived."

I was so fascinated that I decided I wanted to meet them. I wasn't sure why there was just something about the way they had been described that intrigued me.

Gabriel and Charlie began chatting about things that were of little interest to me, so I decided to have a wander around on my own for a while.

"Be careful, Lilly and don't go too far," said Gabriel as I walked away from them as they continued chatting.

Dusk was approaching, and I knew it wouldn't be too long until it was dark, so I kept fairly close to our camp. Since becoming a mountain lion, my eyesight had improved dramatically, even in human form, but because I wasn't familiar with the area, I certainly didn't want to tempt fate. And I never forgot that I had promised Gabriel that I would remain in human form.

As I walked out of sight of them both, I heard the gentle cooing of an owl. Following the sound, I saw the majestic creature sitting on the branch of a lone tree. As he cooed, he just sat staring off into the distance. I didn't want to disturb him, so I just stood for a few moments, watching. Looking around for somewhere to sit, I noticed a large smooth rock a few metres away but to get there, I'd probably make some noise. I tiptoed as silently as possible and, sure enough, he turned his head to look at me. He probably knew I was there all along.

Sitting down so he wouldn't feel threatened, I watched as he did nothing. He just sat and stared at me while I admired his unusual dark eyes. After a few minutes, he must have got bored of my face, and so he turned to look in the opposite direction before he took to flight and disappeared.

I stayed where I was and, looking around me, I saw what a spectacular place it was. It was amazing how far we had actually climbed, the tops of the dense woods below were quite a distance away. Other than me, Gabriel, Charlie and the lone owl, we appeared to be very much alone. It was an excellent spot to get away from it all, and I could certainly understand Gabriel's penchant for doing that occasionally. Whenever life had a strange twist to it, I supposed. Over the course of Gabriel's life, there had certainly been rather a lot of twists and turns, and the majority of them weren't particularly pleasant.

I wondered about Charlie. Who was he? And how did he have such a posh British accent? It was bizarre. As far as I knew, wild mountain goats didn't exist in the UK, and for creatures that were capable of changing from animal to human, they must have been born into it. Like I was, it was in my genes. There was something about Charlie that was a little strange. Why had he changed the subject about his injury? And why had he been watching us for a while before coming down to greet us? After giving it a bit more thought, I wasn't so sure that I trusted him, so I walked back round to make sure everything was okay. Darkness had fallen, and I didn't want Gabriel to worry unnecessarily about my whereabouts. I also knew that he would be preparing some food before we called it a night.

Sure enough, as I wandered carefully over the rough terrain back to the camp, I could smell the food. I just hoped that the bears couldn't smell it too. But Gabriel knew what he was doing.

Although I watched Charlie carefully while we ate, I concluded that there didn't appear to be anything to worry about and so, exhaustion taking me by surprise, I curled up in my sleeping bag and drifted off to sleep. The sound of Charlie's and Gabriel's words did nothing to keep me awake.

oOo

"Lilly, Lilly."

I awoke with a start, someone was nudging me, "Wake up, Lilly. It's Gabriel. He's gone," said Charlie as he finally managed to drag me out of comfortable sleep with a bang.

His words twisted my stomach into a knot, "he's gone? What do you mean, he's gone?" I asked, jumping out of my sleeping bag. I looked around and saw that Gabriel's sleeping bag was still there, exactly where it had been the night before, a few embers smouldered in the fire but Gabriel was nowhere to be seen.

"Are you sure he didn't just go to get some water or something?" I said, trying hard not to panic, even though I could feel it rising from the pit of my stomach.

Charlie shook his head and stuttered, "I've... I've been awake for over an hour. I thought the same. I assumed that he had gone for water or to the toilet. But he hasn't come back, Lilly. We must leave immediately. We must travel to the Elders together. There we will be able to get some help," he said as he grabbed everything in sight and shoved it into mine and Gabriel's rucksacks.

I didn't even want to think about what might have happened, but I couldn't prevent those negative thoughts from entering my mind. Had a bear attacked him? Surely I would have heard if something so large and ferocious had done, wouldn't I? What about a vampire? Or that man who could change into an alligator, the one Gabriel had first mentioned months ago? My mind was running riot. I thought of Rose, 'Breathe, Lilly, breathe. Slowly, in and out, in and out'. I knew that's what she would be telling me to do.

Charlie stood looking at me, quizzically, "Lilly, my dear. What are you doing? We must get out of here."

"I need to calm down, Charlie. I need to think about this sensibly and not react wrongly. I wouldn't want to rush off only to find that Gabriel isn't far away. I can't just leave now. Anything could have happened," I whispered while I continued to practice the deep breathing techniques.

"That's exactly why we need to leave now. We need to get to the Elders now," he said authoritatively.

"You go, and I'll stay here and wait," I said, standing my ground.

"Lilly, you are coming with me, and you're coming with me now, young lady," he said as his nostrils flared. His face and demeanour changed suddenly, and I began to get the feeling that Charlie wasn't who or what Gabriel thought he was. I began to think that my intuition the previous evening had been spot on. Charlie wasn't one to be trusted.

"Charlie... where is my grandfather?" I asked. "What have you done to him?" I asked.

He turned and laughed a deep laugh, "You're a smart girl Lilly, aren't you? I thought I had fooled you both last night, but clearly not. Now listen to me. If you want your grand-father to remain alive, you had better do as I say."

I knew I had no choice but to do exactly as he said. Until I knew where Gabriel was, I couldn't risk losing him altogether. I nodded, trying hard to keep myself from transforming.

"Pick up your bag and walk ahead of me... that way," he said, pointing in the same direction where I had seen the owl the night before.

I stumbled ahead and tried to think of ways to escape, but I knew I couldn't go anywhere. Because if I did, I might never see Gabriel, alive, again.

❄ 26 ❄

"Why are you doing this?" I asked Charlie after we'd walked in silence for over an hour. "What have you done with Gabriel?"

"Be quiet and keep walking," he said, while I wondered how my grandfather had trusted this beast. He was usually such a good judge of character, how could he have let this happen? But I knew it wasn't his fault. Being so close to the Elders, Gabriel had assumed he could trust him. Clearly, he had been wrong.

Charlie was after something. I didn't know what that was yet, but I would find out soon enough.

The fact that Gabriel was gone and Charlie was kidnapping me suggested I had something he wanted. I dreaded to think what it was. As I thought about this evil creature, I began to notice something familiar on a tree a little further ahead. It was an owl. And it looked an awful lot like the one from the night before. It was watching me. I wondered if it was just an owl or if it had special abilities. I stared at it, hoping that it would somehow swoop down and rescue me. But it didn't. Like before, it swiftly looked away and then took flight.

"Keep moving!" yelled Charlie, and he shoved me, causing me to stumble on the loose stones beneath my feet. As I fell onto my knees, I contemplated whether I should just change and rip the goat to shreds.

But I calmed myself down again, thinking about Gabriel's safety. I pulled myself back onto my feet and rubbed my hands on the front of my combats, to get rid of the grit and dirt. In the distance, I could see what appeared to be another cave. We seemed to be heading in that direction. After another ten minutes or so, as we approached it, I noticed that we were not alone. Somebody was waiting for us.

The person was well hidden by an old black cape that covered them from head to toe.

Charlie spoke first. "Here she is, Master, here she is. Just as you requested. Lilly Tulugaq," and he pushed me so hard that I fell once again to the feet of the stranger.

The fall angered me, and I yelped. It was with great difficulty that I stayed calm.

"Don't you mean Lilly Taylor?"

As she said those words, I felt as if I had been kicked in the stomach. I was winded. I closed my eyes momentarily and then looked up as she removed the cape from her face. I gasped at the sight of Vivian.

This wasn't the woman that I had lived with for thirteen years. This Vivian had thin greying hair and wrinkles. Her shoulders stooped forward, and her back curled over, like a hunchback. This Vivian had become an old hag.

"I might have known that you would be responsible for all of this," I spat. "Where is my father?" I demanded.

"Now that's not a very nice way to greet your dear mother, is it?" she spat as she circled me, looking me up and down with a scowl.

"My mother is dead... and you killed her, along with my sister," I shouted, as I became increasingly angry.

Charlie shoved me down to the floor again and told me to shut up.

I could feel the lion in me trying to take over, but I knew if I transformed then, not only would I lose Gabriel, but I would lose my father too.

"I raised you, and this is the thanks I get," said Vivian.

"You haven't got a clue how to raise a child," I spat back,

adding, "why are you doing this? Where is Gabriel? And where is my father? If you've hurt either of them, I swear to god I'll..."

"You'll what, Lilly? You'll kill me with your bird's claws? I don't think so, my darling. A little raven isn't going to kill me. I'm one of the greatest witches that ever lived," she announced.

"If you're so great, then why do you look like an old hag?" I asked.

"How dare you!" she yelled back, slapping me hard on the side of my face.

"You hit like an old hag," I said with a glare, knowing I was hitting a nerve.

"Get her and bring her in here," she ordered Charlie, who grabbed my arm roughly and pulled me after her. The entrance to the cave was small, but inside it proved to be a lot bigger than it first appeared.

"Throw her in there," she said, pointing to a massive birdcage in the centre of the cavern.

As I was pushed into it, it dawned on me that Vivian had no idea about my true self. She thought I could transform myself into a raven, but she knew nothing about the mountain lion. I began to feel that I could use it to my advantage.

"What are you going to do to me?" I asked her, watching as she read from a large ornate book that looked centuries old.

"I'm going to take your blood and your hair... not that you've got very much of that these days... and use it to make me young and beautiful again." She said it as if it was the most natural thing in the world.

"Is that what you did to my father?" I asked, hoping to find out the truth.

She ignored me, instead standing up and walking over to a large shelf that had been created from an old log, similar to the ones I had seen on the beach at Powell River. On it was a number of vials filled with all kinds of creepy looking things. I recognised a few of them. They were just like the vials in the black room in London.

"Is that my father's blood?" I asked.

Again she said nothing, ignoring me as she continued to search through the little bottles. Her eyesight was clearly failing her, and she had to hold things up close to identify their contents.

"Talk to me, Vivian. Oh, I forgot. You never talked to me before did you? Years of no conversation. And you think you raised me," I said, hoping to irritate her enough so that she'd tell me more.

"What happened to you? Why are you old and ugly, Vivian?" I continued.

"Old... of course, I'm old. I've been alive for hundreds of years, what on earth do you expect. Why do you think I became a witch in the first place? Eternal youth, of course. Don't you know anything, girl?" she shrieked like the old hag she'd become.

"I can't believe I thought you were my mother. You're nothing like my mother. She was absolutely beautiful, and so was my sister. No amount of my blood and hair will ever make you beautiful. You'll never be beautiful, Vivian. Never."

"Damn you, Lillian!" she yelled, throwing a vial at the cage. The glass bottle smashed, and I was spattered with blood. Whose, I didn't know.

"Is this my father's blood?" I asked again.

"No, it is not your father's blood. He's all out of that," she answered with an evil smile.

I gasped. Did that mean he was dead? I felt as if my heart had been ripped out of my chest.

"When I ran out of your father's blood, this is what became of me, if you must know," she said as she looked at herself in a large cracked mirror that had been hung on the wall. She touched her face gently, sadly.

"He gave me beauty, and then he took it away," she whispered.

"Is... is he dead? Vivian, please tell me what happened to him. I need to know," I asked, hoping that she might have just a tiny amount of compassion in her, somewhere.

"Dead... dead? Does it matter whether he's dead or not? It doesn't matter any more."

"It matters to me!" I cried, tasting a salty tear as it fell down my cheek onto my lips.

"I don't believe that Jack is dead. Not entirely anyway," was all she would say.

Although it wasn't what I wanted to hear, it did give me a

glimmer of hope. I just needed to know where he was so I could try to save him.

"Where is he? Is he here? Please, Vivian. Tell me where he is."

She shook her head and looked at me, "I can't tell you."

"Please, Vivian, please," I begged as I shook the bars of the cage.

"Lillian I can't tell you because I don't know where he is," she answered finally. "He disappeared in London. I tried to find him, but he just vanished. I don't know how he got away, but he did. The second time that has happened to me, bloody men," she said, "they always get away in the end," she added more to herself than to me.

So my father managed to escape from Vivian, and he didn't take me with him. My heart had indeed been wrenched from the depths of my soul. He had run away and left me with a witch. What kind of father would do that? I was at a complete and utter loss.

"I have spent months looking for him. Months and months... and nothing. So now I have to find someone else to make me beautiful again. Until I can find myself another man, a special man, you will have to do. You are his daughter. You must carry the same blood as he. You will have to do... for now anyway," she said with a smile.

"But why my father in the first place? There are millions of men in this world, why did you have to choose my father?"

"Oh, Lillian... are you that dim? I need the blood, and sometimes the hair, of only very special people. They have special qualities in their blood. When mixed with other secret ingredients and drunk by me, it returns me to my youthful glow and extraordinarily good looks. You have your father's genes, so you must have that quality, my dear," she said as she approached the cage with a small dagger in her hand.

"Charlie, grab her hands," she said as she opened the door to the cage and pulled me half out. Charlie appeared behind me and managed to hold both my hands while she cut off a tiny tuft of my hair. I breathed a temporary sigh of relief as she walked away and dropped it into a small pot. But then she turned and walked back towards me and pulled my leg so that it hung out of the cage door.

She grabbed my hiking shoe and sock and tugged them from my foot. Pulling up my trousers, she very gently placed the blade against my skin and then pressed hard so that blood oozed out from just above my ankle. I winced, trying hard to stay calm.

She placed a small bucket underneath my foot and waited for the blood to drip into it.

Adrenaline pumped through my veins, but I took long deep breaths to prevent myself from changing. I needed to know where Gabriel was before I could do anything.

"Vivian, what have you done with Gabriel?" I asked. "Please tell me that he's okay. Have you hurt him?"

"I have no need to harm the old man," she said, and I was surprised. The evil things she was capable of made me think that she hurt people on purpose, whether she needed to or not. But perhaps she only did so when she needed something. That was until she continued, "The same can't be said for Charlie though," and she laughed heartily as if she'd cracked a joke.

She released my leg, and I pulled it back quickly. Charlie slammed the door shut and locked it.

"Charlie, where is Gabriel?" I asked, hopefully.

But he just sniggered and said nothing.

"There's just one important ingredient that I'm missing. I'll be gone a while. Charlie, keep an eye on her – she might try to change into a bird, although the cage should prevent her from escaping," said Vivian before she grabbed her cape, threw it on and exited the cavern.

"Charlie... how did you get here? I know she must've cursed you. You're an Englishman that she made into a mountain goat. Isn't there a part of you, hidden somewhere in there, that hates her? A part of you that wants some kind of revenge for what she did to you?" I asked softly.

But again, he ignored me and sat staring off into space.

"Charlie, please help me. If you can't, please just tell me where Gabriel is."

"Shut up, Lilly. Shut up!" he yelled as he bent to pick up a small stone from the floor and then flung it against me. It pinged off the side of the cage and bounced against the wall before landing on the floor by the cave's entrance.

He wasn't going to tell me, so I sat in silence and waited for Vivian to return. My leg began to throb, a dull ache where she had sliced into it. Fortunately, the cut wasn't too deep, and the bleeding had slowed. I feared that if I didn't escape, she would bleed me to death. My father had obviously come close to that, but he had managed to get away before death had come. How I had no idea. He must have been so weak by that time and to get out of that room must have been near on impossible. I wondered if someone had helped him. But why? And how? And more importantly, who?

I would find out what had happened to him, and I would find out where he was. I would also find out why he had deserted me and left me in the hands of an evil witch.

I pulled my legs up to my chest and rested my head on my knees, and before I could stop myself, I began to cry. I cried for Gabriel, I cried for my father, and I cried for me. I knew I could escape, but I was so scared that Gabriel would end up dead if I did.

That's when I heard the sound from outside. A soft, cooing noise that reminded me of something. The owl. It was the sound of an owl hooting, the same sound I had heard the night before. I recalled how the bird had watched me but had then looked away and flown off into the distance. And then again, while Charlie had been dragging me to the cave, I had seen it, but it hadn't taken much notice of me. It was a soothing sound, but that's all it was.

The sound, however, began to get a little louder and then there was silence. As I looked towards the entrance to the cave, I could just about see it perched on the branch of a tree close by. It was looking towards me.

There were a couple of birds circling above the owl, and I gasped when I recognised what they were. Ravens. Charlie looked over at me, suspiciously, and I coughed to try and hide my surprise. He stood and walked around the cage before he returned to sit down and just as he let down his guard to relax a little, one of the ravens flew into the cave as quietly as possible. He didn't notice. I watched it surreptitiously as it stood on the floor behind him, waiting. Whoever it was, it had found me. But had it found Gabriel?

As I waited, wondering what it would do, I heard footsteps and the sighing of an old woman. The simple act of walking left her breathless.

Vivian had returned.

The raven was startled, clearly not expecting her to return so soon, so it hopped backwards and hid away in a dark corner while Vivian walked into the cave carrying the final ingredient that would help make her young and beautiful once again.

"So you're still human are you, Lilly? I'm surprised at you. I figured you might have tried to escape. Not that you would be able to. I raised you not to run away, didn't I? You never could get away from me," she laughed as she began concentrating on her strange recipe for beauty.

I listened and watched closely as she read to herself as if from a bizarre recipe book.

"Let's see, two sprigs of rosemary, Lillian's blood, hair from a horse's mane and the sinew from a horse's leg, the hair from Lillian's head and a few tablespoons of pure spring water from the Pantheon Mountains... yes, I think that's about it."

She placed all of the ingredients into a small bowl and mixed it up with a wooden spoon before placing it over the fire that Charlie had been busy preparing.

It was a surreal experience, watching this old Vivian becoming more and more excited as the recipe developed. She became almost childlike, skipping around the fire, clapping her hands in anticipation. This was a Vivian I had never seen. The only Vivian I had ever known was sombre, strict, mean... and beautiful.

It didn't take long until I could hear the ingredients bubbling away. Vivian removed it from the fire and sieved it into a wooden chalice before picking it up and turning to me.

"Cheers, Lillian darling," she laughed, before placing the cup to her lips and drinking it hungrily without taking a breath. She then threw it to the floor and wiped her lips with the back of her long black sleeve.

"Time to change," she added before she took off the long black cloak and revealed her naked body.

The old hag was covered from head to toe in deep-set wrinkles, and her skin hung in folds all over her body. This was the body of an ancient woman, not the Vivian I remembered.

She didn't stand naked for long. She stepped carefully into a crisp white gown that Charlie held open for her. All the time, she maintained a wicked smile on her lips. The smile of a madwoman.

Even though she was barely recognisable, seeing her in white reminded me of the times we had lived together. She had never worn any other colour. She always presented herself, from head to foot, in white. White trousers, white blouse, white pumps, sometimes even a white headband. Every day, something else white. She had long white dresses, skirts, jeans even.

She had presented herself so beautifully, while at the same time, had presented me in such an ugly way. Dowdy, old, used clothes that didn't fit properly. In yellow, the one colour that did nothing for me. The one colour that made me look ugly. That's what she'd tried to do. She'd wanted to make me look uglier so that she could feel even more beautiful. Me, Mellow Yellow. It had all been done on purpose.

As she stood there, looking at herself in the mirror waiting for something to happen, I noticed the raven had managed to sneak closer to me. It stared at me, and I could see something startlingly familiar in its eyes. Then suddenly, it winked at me, and I knew exactly who it was. Jo. She often winked at me. She had finally made the transformation. But how had she known where to find me? Then I thought of the owl. If the owl knew where I was, it would undoubtedly know where Gabriel was. I smiled at her and winked back. Relief flooded through me, and I felt as if I could finally make my escape, but before I did, I waited to see what would happen to Vivian.

She stood smiling at herself in the old mirror on the wall, waiting for her transformation to begin.

After a few minutes, I could see that it was working. Her saggy skin began to tighten up, and the colour of her hair slowly began to change from grey to bright red. Her sallow eyes began to gleam and her lips, and not to mention her breasts, plumped up. All age spots disappeared, and I began to see the Vivian that I remembered.

She breathed in a long, happy breath and sighed out in happiness before she began to laugh uncontrollably.

"I'm back, and I'm even more beautiful than before," she

giggled, as she touched her face and her neck and then her breasts and bottom.

"Why didn't I think of doing this before? I should have used your blood from day one. Instead, I wasted years on that father of yours, and before that, I wasted years on Walter, when I could have used the blood from his damned daughter. And I let her go. How stupid of me," she said to herself as she continued to admire herself in the mirror.

As she said the words, I thought of Rose. How her husband and daughter had disappeared all those years ago, when in fact they had been kidnapped, just like my father and I had been. And they had been used for the one single reason: to achieve her own flawless beauty. It disgusted me.

But Vivian had just let it slip that she had let the daughter go. Just when I thought I could make my escape, I discovered something new. Something else I needed to find out more about. And I needed to find out the truth for Rose.

Just as I began to think of ways to investigate what had happened to Walter and his daughter, Lori, Vivian shrieked.

"What is this?" she cried, turning to me, "What is happening to me? Lillian, what have you done?"

I watched, stunned in silence as whiskers began to sprout from her cheeks and out of her ears. Her hands and feet began to mutate, and suddenly I knew. She didn't know the truth about my own transformation. She didn't know that I was capable of changing into a mountain lion. The combination of my feline and raven genes must have been affecting her in ways she could never have foreseen.

I couldn't help but smile at her affliction.

"How... is this possible?" she sobbed as she stared at her reflection in the mirror. Part witch, part cat. Not at all attractive.

"How could I have been so damn stupid? The girl, your sister. I thought I'd just miscast a spell on her the day I killed her. But I hadn't, had I? She'd really changed into a cat herself. No!" she cried while I nodded, smiling.

"But that means..." and before she could finish, I transformed myself into a mountain lion, breaking the cage into a hundred pieces right in front of her eyes. I pounced on her and pushed her to the ground, ready to get the revenge I had craved ever since I'd learned the truth.

"Lilly!" yelled another voice as I saw a very naked Jo had changed back into human form and had managed to throw Charlie to the ground too. He had hit his head on a rock, knocking him unconscious in the process.

"Lilly... no. Let the Elders deal with her," she shouted as I held a razor-sharp claw close to her jugular vein. "Lilly, you're not like her. You're not a killer," she said, but I couldn't move. All I could think of was Serena and Neleh, the years I'd spent practically a prisoner in my own home, my poor father and Sammy, Walter, Rose and Lori and what she had put us all through. And Gabriel. Poor Gabriel, wherever he was. She had done all of this damage just so that she could be beautiful and young. I wanted her to die more than anything but, as I looked up at Jo's face, I knew it couldn't be by my hands. She was right, I wasn't a killer. I wasn't anything like her. I wasn't a monster.

I leaned back away from her and instead pulled her up and pushed her hard against the cave wall, winding her. Jo took over. Finding some rope, she tied Vivian up so there was no way she could release herself. Not even a witch could escape. But Vivian didn't even struggle, she was too busy sobbing about her appearance.

I made the transition back to my human self, using the breathing techniques Rose had taught me. After a moment, I was human again. Jo and I clothed ourselves with tops and trousers from my rucksack.

She gave me a long hard hug, while the other raven just sat outside, perched quietly on the same branch the owl had been on earlier.

"I'm so glad you're okay, Lilly. We were all worried sick," she said.

"But how did you know?"

"Both Sammy and Meredith felt something was wrong, so we contacted a close friend, one of the Elders, who sent someone to search for you," she said.

"Let me guess that someone was an owl?" I asked, and she nodded, "so you saw him then?"

I nodded and then remembered Gabriel. I asked her if he was okay, and she reassured me that the owl had witnessed everything and had gone to fetch help straight away.

"Gabriel was in quite a bad way, but he's recuperating with the Elders. They sent one of their raven friends to tell us what was going on. But at that stage, we didn't know that Vivian was involved. So I'm so relieved you're okay Lilly."

"Thank you for coming so quickly. But how? When did you learn to transform?" I asked.

Jo explained that the family's only chance of getting someone here quick enough was for her to change into a raven. "I couldn't wait for it to happen naturally so Rose helped me make it happen for myself, that was this morning," she said proudly.

I was amazed at her transformation, and even more surprised that she had taken it upon herself to come and help us.

"Sammy wanted more than anything to come and help, but it's daylight. It was too much of a risk. We practically had to tie him up to stop him from following me," she said.

"A few of the Elders are on their way now. They should be here soon. Come, let's wait for them outside."

We tied Charlie up and dragged them both out into the sunlight where we sat on a large boulder as we awaited the arrival of the Elders.

As we sat, I saw that the other raven and the owl were waiting patiently with us and so I stood up and walked over to them. Bowing my head, I thanked them for all their help, "I don't know if you can understand me or not, but I just want you to know how grateful I am."

Both birds nodded their heads at me, and I knew then that, through some kind of magic, they could understand my every word.

"I know Meredith can occasionally read minds, but I thought that was just when we're close," I said to Jo as I returned to her side, "how was she able to do it this time?"

"This is the first time that she's been able to pick up on something so far away. I think the fact that Sammy was picking up on the same feeling helped," she answered.

"So were your mum and dad okay with you coming all this way to help?"

"They were obviously really concerned about you and Gabriel. They were worried sick when I told them I wanted to come, but they understood that it was something I had to do. They were really proud that I finally changed though," she said.

As we sat chatting to each other awaiting the Elders, I was developing a horrible feeling in the pit of my stomach. I had been trying to ignore it, but it just wouldn't go away. Some of the things that Vivian had said had crushed me, and no matter how hard I tried to push them to the back of my mind, I struggled to keep them there.

As I watched Vivian still sobbing to herself, I thought of the evil things she had done, not just in my lifetime but way before that too. She had taken the two loves of Rose's life and ruined any chance of her finding love again.

Rose had no idea what had happened to Walter and Lori, but now it seemed that her husband was probably dead and her daughter could be anywhere in the world, probably never to be found again. She was just a baby when she was cruelly ripped from Rose's life – just as I had been when I had been taken, so she would probably have no idea as to the true identity of her real mother.

Rose would need answers and Vivian was the only person who would be able to give them. Once she was handed over to the Elders, perhaps the answers to these questions could finally be resolved. I hoped so. Not just for Rose's sake, but for Lori's too. Wherever she may be.

I worked out that Lori would be in her late forties now. Perhaps she had children of her own. I hoped Rose would find her one day. She deserved to know the truth. Just as I had deserved to find out the truth about my life. But my father had escaped Vivian's clutches and left me behind. He'd abandoned me, and now I didn't know if he was dead or alive.

If he was dead, was he finally resting in peace with his beloved Serena and Neleh? If that was the case, wouldn't he have come to me in a dream, just as they had? Perhaps the Elders would be able to help solve the mystery.

As I sat there with Jo, my mind quietly wrestling with itself, I noticed a small group of people approaching in the distance. The owl and the raven immediately withdrew from their branch and flew towards them. We knew it must be the Elders and so we stood up and waited for them to come closer.

$$\text{27}$$

They were a group of five; three men and two women. An odd-looking bunch, but I wouldn't have expected anything less.

The eldest was an old white-haired man who ambled along slowly with a walking stick. What I noticed most about him were his massive grey eyes. He resembled a caricature rather than a real person. But they were friendly eyes that twinkled and smiled at us, even though his mouth, initially, did not.

Walking slightly behind him was a younger man, of about forty years, with red hair and green eyes and covered in freckles. His pale, almost translucent skin suggested he didn't venture out into the sunlight very often. But again, he had a friendly and, despite the colour, a warm face.

The third man was barely twenty years old, and I knew he was a changeling – I guessed a werewolf. His strong, attractive features and golden eyes gave him away. He was quite tall but very stocky and, although wolf-like, I wasn't afraid of him. I could tell he was trying to appear fierce, but I could see right through him. He was a softy at heart.

The eldest woman was probably in her sixties, and she commanded a certain presence. She was more striking than beautiful and had shoulder-length grey and black hair. I could imagine her as a school teacher, strict and bossy. A little bit intimidating.

And the last woman was a bit of an enigma. Her face and body suggested she was around the same age as me, yet she had grey hair, short and spiky. For some reason, I was drawn to her, there was a certain familiarity to her. I could tell she was feisty, rebellious... fun.

"Lilly, my dear child. We are so relieved to find you safe and well," said the old man with the large eyes as he held out his arms and pulled me into a gentle hug, "your grandfather is also safe and recovering well, so you need not worry too much about him now. Hello Jo. It's good to see you again. You won't remember me though as you were just a toddler when we last met," he chuckled, hugging her softly too. "I am one of the Elders. I am Finley. We came to help, but by the looks of it, you are not really in need of any assistance. You appear to have everything tied up rather well," he said, with a wink, as he approached the two sorry creatures and gave them a prod with his walking stick.

When Vivian lifted her face from her knees, Finley did a double-take before turning his attention back to us. "Oh, let me introduce you to the others," he said as they all stepped closer as if they had been awaiting his instructions.

"Rupert here is our newest addition to the Elders," he said as the red-headed man stepped forward and shook my hand. "Good to meet you, Lilly... Jo," he smiled, shaking Jo's hand, too before stepping back.

"And this lovely lady is Ursula. She has been with us for many years," and the older, slightly frightening-looking woman stepped forward, nodding her head at us both before stepping back.

"And our other friends here are not members of the Elders but were with us when we heard about what was happening, and they wanted to come along and offer any assistance. I think they're perhaps a little disappointed at missing out on all the action," he laughed.

The two stepped forward and smiled at us, clearly pleased to see some younger people.

"Hi. I'm Tabitha, and this is my boyfriend, Zoltan," said the young woman with a grin, "we had hoped to get in on a bit of action. There hasn't been much going on lately," she laughed, and I felt immediately at ease. So these were the people Charlie had seen arguing at Christmas. Zoltan stepped forward and shook Jo's hand, and then he turned to me to shake my hand, but as our hands touched, he let out a deep snarl and snatched it back.

I immediately felt defensive and took a step backwards, pulling Jo with me.

"Don't worry about Zoltan. I got the same reaction from him when we first met too. You've probably realised that he is, in fact, a werewolf?" asked Tabitha and I nodded, "Well sometimes the wolf overpowers the man, and that kind of thing happens," she laughed, "but you'll find that he's pretty harmless... to us, anyway."

He turned to look at me and smiled apologetically. I forgave him easily.

While we had been talking, the others had been into the cave to investigate what was there. I heard them whispering to each other about how they had not known of the cave's existence. How a witch had been under their very noses and they'd not seen what was going on. It perturbed them, which, in turn, worried me a little.

When they came back out into the sunlight, Rupert pulled both Vivian and Charlie up from the ground, ensuring the ropes were tied tightly enough, and then we prepared to set off towards the Elders' home. I grabbed our bags, and we began our hike back up the mountain. Jo walked ahead with Finley and Ursula; Vivian and Charlie were pulled in the middle of the group by Rupert, and I walked behind with Tabitha and Zoltan.

Tabitha was eager to know what had happened and so as we walked, I relayed our adventure to her. When she commented on my British accent, I also told her about my life before and how I had managed to find myself in Canada in the first place.

She was intrigued by my tale and impressed that we had managed to capture the witch. "I would have probably killed her," she said.

"Well, I was pretty close but, as Jo told me at the time, I'm not a killer. Vivian needs to take full responsibility for the evil things she has done. The Elders will make sure of that," I answered.

"Yeah, I guess you're right. You've got more self-control than me though," she added.

"I doubt that. I'm sure had it been you, you would have been able to stop yourself."

We continued to tell each other about our lives, and I discovered that Tabitha had been raised in New York but had moved to Canada as soon as she was old enough to fend for herself.

"I always felt like I had some connection to this part of the world you know," she said.

"Well, it's not difficult to connect, is it? Just look how breathtaking it is," I said as we stopped momentarily to take in the utter magnitude of the view surrounding us. Tabitha laughed then and agreed with me, but I knew she had meant it differently. There was some kind of pull that brought her here. She didn't know what or why but she wanted to find out.

"But how did you find the Elders? How did you know about... you know... all this supernatural stuff?" I laughed, not knowing of a better way to describe it.

"My mother told me, actually. She had a lonely childhood, brought up by a strict mother and a father she rarely saw. When her father took off one day, her mother went crazy and started casting crazy spells. My mother freaked out and managed to run away. But after a few days, she decided to go back, and when she did, she found nothing. Her mother had gone too. She'd just upped and left. Never to be seen again," she explained.

"So that's how your mother learned?" I questioned, thinking it wasn't really enough to make you believe. But Tabitha shook her head, "Oh no... God no. It was when her father returned one day that she finally understood about it all. He was different. Mum told me that he actually scared the hell out of her. He was so incredibly pale, and his eyes would change colour from yellow to red. He told her that he had been made a vampire."

"Oh," I exclaimed, "well, that would do it."

Tabitha smiled, "My grandfather was a vampire. He told my mum he loved her more than anything else in the world but that he had to go away. He said it was too much of a risk for him to stay near her. He couldn't bear her being in danger."

"Wow, that must have been hard," I whispered.

"She knew he was telling the truth and so she accepted it. She started doing loads of research into the supernatural, paranormal...

whatever you want to call it. Eventually, she started discovering all kinds of freaky stuff. So I learned all about it from a very young age, I guess."

Her mother had never married and still lived in New York. Tabitha was the result of an intense affair she'd had with a very wealthy man who had adored her. "But my mum didn't want to settle down, she likes her own company, and she likes to travel a lot... for research purposes. My dad never married either, so occasionally they get together. He's been very good to her, and to me. He's a good man," she said.

I thought of my own father and felt a tug of sadness at the pit of my stomach. I wish I knew the truth. Where was he? Was he alive? Did he desert me on purpose? So many questions and so few answers.

As we had been chatting, we had fallen behind. The rest of the group were quite far ahead, and so we walked on in silence, increasing our pace until we caught up with them.

A few hours later, in darkness, we arrived. It wasn't what I expected.

The main entrance to the mass of caves beneath the mountains was well hidden. If I'd have been there alone, there was no way I'd have known anything was there.

But a large group of people and creatures were waiting for us. I later found out that the raven and the owl had flown on ahead and notified them of our impending arrival.

I wasn't prepared for such a large group, but everybody was very pleased to see me safe and well. Many of them patted me on the back and welcomed me into their home. However, my number one priority was to see Gabriel, and so I asked to be taken to him.

"Ursula will take you both to him. Now I must sit down. It has been a long day and a long walk for my old legs," chuckled Finley as he was led in the opposite direction.

"Come, girls. Zis vay," ordered Ursula in a thick German accent. It was the first time we had heard her speak.

"You're German, Ursula?" asked Jo tentatively.

"I am, yes," she answered and continued walking at a fast pace.

"How did you get here?" I asked, hoping to get her to loosen up a little.

She stopped and turned to us. "Now is not ze time for conversation," she said, turning brusquely as she carried on walking, taking large strides. We struggled to keep up, especially after such a long hike up the mountain.

Jo shrugged her shoulders, and we walked quickly in silence, having little time to take in our surroundings. What I did notice though was that the sequence of caves rolled easily and smoothly into each other, and it was warm. I had expected something cold and damp, but it was quite the opposite. It felt homely.

"Come!" yelled Ursula, "Gabriel is in here," and she pulled back a heavy thick green curtain to reveal a large oval-shaped room covered in wall hangings and thick warm rugs on the floor. Two old red leather sofas were facing each other, with a mahogany coffee table carefully positioned between the two. Behind was a large king-size bed and in it, lay Gabriel. He was surrounded by pillows. He grinned the moment he saw us. I noticed then that he was on a drip.

"Girls, girls... I was so worried. Lilly, I am so sorry," he said with open arms, but he winced as he moved.

"Gabriel, I was terrified something awful had happened to you," and I suddenly broke down in tears, "for a while, I thought you might be... might be... dead."

"Dear Lilly. I'm okay. Everything is all right now. Come now, no more tears."

But they continued to fall, preventing me from speaking. Jo, instead, spoke for me, telling him all that had happened.

"Jo, you have been so courageous, my dear," he said to her.

"But I didn't do anything... Lilly was the one who captured Vivian."

Finally able to speak I said, "But I couldn't have done that had you not captured Charlie, Jo. And when you winked at me, I knew you were telling me Gabriel was safe. I couldn't have done any of it without you."

This time, it was Jo's turn to shed a few tears. After a few minutes, we laughed and hugged each other.

"You are both the most courageous girls I know, and I am so proud that you are my grand-daughters. Now that you are safe, we need to send a message to the rest of the family to let them know.

They're probably worried sick," he said, adding, "if only this place had a cell phone mast. There's no signal around here."

We giggled with him then and pondered the quickest and safest way to get a message back. Ursula, who had been waiting outside, stepped in and suggested we send a changeling. Jo offered to fly back home, but she was too tired. She needed rest.

"I vill talk to Finley. Ve vill decide who to send, okay?" she had said before walking back out again.

"She's a strange one," I said to Gabriel quietly, and he laughed loudly.

"Perhaps a little. But she is an incredible woman. She is responsible for saving the lives of hundreds of people during the First World War," he said clearly in awe.

"But surely she's too young to have been involved," I asked confused.

"Ursula has recently celebrated her two hundredth birthday," he said, impressed, "when she was 61, she was bitten by a vampire."

I gasped, not expecting it at all.

"She wasn't directly involved in the war itself, but there was a very nasty vampire around at that time, Olivier Duran was his name. He was ruthless, killing anybody and everybody. Ursula made it a point to stop him. She prevented hundreds of murders. That's how the Elders discovered her. They're always on the lookout for those that help other people like that. So they sent a couple of people over to France, and they worked together to stop Duran."

"Wow," said Jo, "that's impressive. Did they kill him?" she asked.

He shook his head, "Unfortunately he managed to escape. He hasn't been found since though, so we're hoping that he now keeps his killing to a minimum."

"But how does Ursula survive? She needs blood, doesn't she?" I asked, and Gabriel nodded, assuring us we weren't in any danger from her.

"She has extraordinary self-control. She usually feeds off the blood of other animals, occasionally from the stock they keep in the medical supply here."

Tabitha appeared with Zoltan, "Can we come in?" she asked.

"Of course, come in, come in," said Gabriel.

"Zoltan is probably the fastest here at the moment, and so he'd like to deliver your message to your family if that's okay with you," said Tabitha.

"That would be wonderful. It's very kind of you to offer, Zoltan. Thank you. Perhaps we should write a letter. That would be best. Jo dear, please hand me the inkpot and some paper... thank you."

After he had written a lengthy note to our family and Zoltan had taken it away, Jo stepped out with Tabitha for a while as I stayed with Gabriel.

"Gabriel?" I asked.

"Yes, dear?"

"What did Charlie do to you?" I whispered.

"It's not important now. You can see I'm okay," but he decided to tell me after seeing the stubborn expression on my face.

"I believe that he drugged me before I went to sleep. I think he must have put something in my tea. It paralysed me, but I was conscious of what was happening. He removed me from my sleeping bag... and told me that he was going to... deliver you on a plate to Vivian." A tear fell from his eye as he spoke. "And then he pushed me down the mountain. I couldn't even lift my hands to protect my face from everything that I fell on, stones, twigs, branches, rocks. I seemed to fall forever. It was cruel. Very cruel. But I am safe, and I am recovering. And more importantly, you are safe and well," he said as he lifted a bruised hand to my face and softly brushed my cheek with his fingers.

"I fear I will never forgive myself for putting you in that position," he added.

"No Gabriel, no... please don't think like that. There is nothing to forgive. She would have got me somewhere else if it wasn't here on the mountain. She was desperate for my blood, Gabriel. But she got what she deserved in the end," and I told him how my blood had affected her, how her face had changed beyond recognition. All the beauty she craved, gone for good.

He smiled, and I could see in his eyes that he was exhausted.

"I should let you sleep now, Gabriel," and I kissed him gently on the cheek and went to stand up, but he took my hand before I could go.

"Lilly... did she tell you anything about your... father?"

I sat back down, took his hand in mine and held it tightly.

I had hoped to wait until he was better before I told him the truth, but he needed to know. Just as I had needed to know. And so I told him. That she had almost killed my father, 'almost bled him dry' and then he had escaped, without taking me with him. I told him that we didn't know if he was alive or if he was... dead.

Gabriel and I sat sobbing together, thinking of the man he had been and wondering what kind of man he had become – dead or alive.

"Lilly, please sit here with me for a while. At least until I fall asleep," and I nodded as he closed his eyes while I sat quietly by his side.

Gabriel had been asleep for an hour when Jo tiptoed back into the room. When she saw that he was finally asleep, she ushered me out.

"Come on, Lilly, it's time for supper. You must be starving? I know I am. But first, we've been given these clothes to change into," she said as she handed me a small bundle consisting of a long red dress and black pumps. I noticed she'd been given a similar dress in green with a slightly different pair of black shoes. We quickly changed, before I followed her back through the maze until we found ourselves in what must have been the main dining 'room' within the caves. The ceiling was particularly high, but as there were no windows, it would have been very dark were it not for the hundreds of candles placed at regular intervals along the walls and along the centre of an unusually long dining table.

I wondered how the Elders had managed to get all of this beautifully fine furniture all the way up the mountain, but before I got the chance to ask, we were greeted by an abundance of friendly faces – all of the people that had been waiting for our arrival outside the cave.

It was the first time I had managed to get a good look at them, and I was surprised at how many ordinary-looking people there seemed to be. Of course, there were a fair few rather strange looking ones too. Some looked very old indeed, needing assistance just to move across the floor to their seats where they struggled to sit down, with their old joints creaking.

I noticed a woman with bright red hair and skin so pale that I could almost see through it. I wondered if she was related to Rupert. She was chatting quietly to an older woman who appeared to have dark scales all over her face, and when she reached for her chair, I saw that her fingers were webbed. As the candlelight caught her face, the dark scales appeared to sparkle. She noticed me staring and smiled kindly. I blushed and looked away, embarrassed.

The last creature to walk in came as a bit of a shock. He was huge, about seven feet tall and covered from head to toe in fur. He looked like a giant ape, except that he walked precisely like a human and his facial features were soft. He was laughing at something someone had said in front of him. He laughed like a human too.

They all sat at the table and Rupert called Jo and me over to sit at either side of the head. We had figured that Finley would be sitting there, assuming him to be the head of the Elders, but we were wrong. He was sitting a few chairs down from us, chatting quietly to Tabitha who grinned when she saw us.

We waited a few minutes, and then everybody stood up – apart from the really old ones. We followed suit and stood up too, waiting for something to happen. We didn't have to wait long. A very attractive young man appeared. Jo gasped at the sight of him and blushed, making me smile.

"Good evening, my equals," he said in a deep smooth voice, "I trust you are all well? Please sit." We all sat down and waited. "This evening we are honoured to be joined by two of Powell River's greatest changelings. Two courageous young women, Lilly and Jo. Welcome," and then everybody lifted their glasses to us, and we blushed crimson.

"We also have with us another very special guest, but he is recovering from a brutal attack. Fear not for him, though. The girls' grand-father Gabriel is recovering well, and I believe he is currently sleeping. But we shall lift our glasses to him none-theless." And we all raised our glasses and said 'to Gabriel' before everybody began talking amongst themselves while Jo and I sat nervously to the side of what appeared to be the Elders' number one man.

"I'm sorry I wasn't able to come down to help today. I have literally only just arrived back home. I have been away for a few days. But I have been told of the news, and I know of your bravery... and yours Jo, too. Remarkable. Absolutely remarkable. So young and so brave. Excellent." We smiled shyly and wondered who this man was.

"Forgive my manners. I haven't introduced myself, have I? I am Carmelo. I founded the Elders many hundreds of years ago. It is a pleasure to meet you both," he said.

"It's an honour to meet you, Carmelo, but it's a little difficult to understand how you can be hundreds of years old," I said.

"I am surprised you do not know about me, but yes, I am 435 years old. I am what people call, a vampire," he smiled.

It made sense. From the research I had done, I understood that vampires were usually beautiful people, and Carmelo certainly was that. As I looked at my surroundings, I wondered how many other vampires lived in the caves, and I shivered involuntarily.

"Please do not be afraid of us here, Lilly. We are not the kind of vampires you should be frightened of. In fact, you should not be afraid of anyone that lives in these caves. You can trust everybody here. Although they are not all Elders, some live here because they have nowhere else to go. You can probably imagine how difficult it is to blend into the crowds when you look like Theodore over there," and he pointed to the ape-man, "or Carla," and he pointed to the lady with the webbed fingers.

I nodded and asked why he had created the Elders in the first place.

"After two hundred years of having nobody to go to for advice, or nowhere truly safe to go to when I needed to hide, I decided to create somewhere myself. I searched for a few years to find the right place and the right kind of people and creatures, and we slowly built this place here in these caves. Our kind know this is a safe haven of peace."

"Wow... that's impressive," I uttered as I took in more of the surroundings, amazed that this was created because of one man's, or should I say one vampire's, dream.

"That's absolutely amazing," said Jo dreamily.

"Thank you, Jo," he said, smiling as she sat staring at him.

"Perhaps I can show you around when we have finished dining," and he looked deep into her eyes as if he was looking right into her subconscious mind. Jo nodded gently, and that was the moment I realised that Jo had fallen head over heels in love with a 435-year-old vampire.

A vampire and a raven? Anything could happen in this world.

After the majority of us had eaten (the vampires just kept us company), Carmelo and Jo headed off for a walk together, and I went to check on Gabriel. As he was still fast asleep, I quietly tiptoed out and went to explore a little bit.

"Oops, sorry, Tabitha. I was just having a wander around," I said as we had rounded a corner and, both deep in thought had bumped straight into each other.

"Sorry, I was in another world there for a minute. I was actually looking for you. I wanted to talk to you about something," she said as we found a comfy old leather sofa to sink into.

"What is it?" I asked, seeing that she was preoccupied.

"I was thinking about what you mentioned on our way up here. When you spoke about your transformation, you said that it had all started happening with the strange dreams."

I nodded, wondering what was bothering her.

"Well, it's just that a few weeks ago I started having really bizarre dreams, a bit like yours."

"Everyone can have strange dreams and nightmares. Mine were only significant because of my blood relatives. Well, my genes, I guess. Why are you worried?"

"I've been dreaming that I am an animal too, a lynx, actually. Oh, it's probably silly. It's probably nothing."

"No, go on, what else?" I asked.

"Do you remember Zoltan's reaction to you when he touched your hand?"

I nodded.

"When he first touched me, he had the same reaction. Apparently, that only ever happens whenever he is very close to cats. He didn't tell me before because he didn't think it was relevant, but after having met you, I just wondered whether, somehow, I have the same ability."

I was intrigued so we decided that we would speak to Gabriel the following day. It sounded like something important was going on deep within her.

I told her about what Charlie had seen at Christmas – that he had thought she was a witch.

"Charlie was there?" she whispered, and I nodded. "And he saw our fight?" She laughed. "Zoltan and I are always at each other's throats. We fight like cat and dog... oh..." as she said it, she realised what she was saying, and we both began laughing. "Maybe you really are then," I giggled.

"But a witch? He got that wrong," she insisted.

"He said you appeared to be casting spells," I said, and this time she nodded.

"Yes, that's right. I always try to do the right thing and then find out that it wasn't the right thing. That's why I've come back to the Elders now. I want them to teach me where I'm going wrong."

I didn't have a clue what she meant, and so she tried again, "I want to help fight evil, basically. But there have been times when it might have looked like I was evil when I was just trying to go 'undercover' if you know what I mean. But it never worked, and the Elders ended up having to rescue me."

When I understood, I felt like I had met a kindred spirit in Tabitha.

Later that night as I lay down in a warm and comfortable bed, with Jo gently breathing as she slept peacefully in the bed next to mine, I came to the conclusion that Tabitha was truly a good person, she just needed some guidance. I fell asleep with the most minimal of fuss after such a hard and gruelling few days. Content that we had finally caught the woman responsible for so much pain, but sad that my father was still lost.

Jo woke me up the following morning. She was still in bed, but she was desperate to talk to me.

"Lilly, are you awake? Lilly? Lilly?"

"No, I'm still asleep," I grumbled and turned away from her.

"Lilly. Wake up."

I was awake, and I knew I wouldn't be able to go back to sleep again, and so I turned to face her. Her face was bright as if she'd been awake for hours, and she looked excited. I knew why, of course.

I shook my head and chuckled to myself.

"What? What's so funny?" she said frowning.

"Jo... you're glowing."

"I am?"

"One word, Jo."

"What's that?"

"Carmelo." The second I said it, she glowed even more, and her eyes lit up. "I can't believe you're falling for a man who is hundreds of years older than you," I said as I lifted myself up in bed.

"He's twenty-five... he just happens to have been twenty-five for a very long time. And... I'm not falling for him. Don't be ridiculous," she said, trying not to giggle.

"It's written all over your face, Jo. I could tell the second it happened last night at the dinner table."

"It is? And you could? Oh, Lilly... I've never had this feeling about anyone before."

"How long did you stay up with him last night?"

"For hours and hours. We talked for ages, and then he walked me here. He was such a gentleman, Lilly. I can't stop thinking about him," she said almost to herself as she peered up at the cave's ceiling.

The dreamy look on her face reminded me of how I had felt when I was with Oliver. I missed him, and I still had that horrible feeling of emptiness in the pit of my stomach whenever I thought of him. I wished things had happened differently and that he had accepted who I was. Perhaps we would still be together if he had. But I couldn't think about him. He hadn't accepted me, and I wouldn't dwell on it. I had moved on. At least I'd thought I'd moved on.

"But doesn't it bother you that he's a vampire, Jo? He survives by drinking people's blood," I asked.

"Technically, he survives by drinking the blood of animals. He hasn't drunk human blood for a long, long time," she answered, and I knew that she had already made up her mind about him. Deep down, I doubt that it would have bothered her even if he drank human blood. She was in love, and when love hit you like that, nothing else seemed to matter.

Later that day, when Gabriel was feeling a little stronger, I took Tabitha to see him. For a split second, he'd looked at her as if he knew her. When I asked him about it, he just said that she looked familiar, that's all.

And then we told him about her dreams and her concerns. He was quiet for some time and Tabitha, and I exchanged glances.

"Tabitha, tell me about yourself. Tell me about your family, where you have come from, how you ended up here." And so we made ourselves more comfortable, and she began to tell him all about her upbringing, everything that she had told me the day before.

After about an hour, Gabriel turned to me and asked if I would mind making some tea for us all, "I'm quite thirsty, and you must be too, Tabitha, after all that talking," he laughed. I did as I was asked and went in search of some tea.

On my way, I noticed Carmelo and Jo laughing and talking together as they walked through the maze of the caves. They were holding hands like lovestruck teenagers, and I could easily see that he had fallen for her in just the same way she had fallen for him. She glimpsed at me and winked when he wasn't looking. I laughed and carried on looking for the cave's main kitchen.

I followed the sounds of voices and the clanking of pans and sure enough, found a large room containing everything necessary for the preparation of food and drink.

Two elderly women were gossiping while they prepared what looked like soup over a large open flame. Before I could introduce myself, I heard them talking about Carmelo. "I've never seen him act this way before. This young girl seems to have bewitched him," said one.

"But don't they make a lovely couple. It's about time he found true love. It's been a long, long time since Dharma died," said the other.

I cleared my throat to make myself known, and they both turned and smiled widely at me.

"Hello, dear. You probably heard that" chuckled one.

I nodded, and she continued "But it's true. That cousin of

yours, Jo, seems to be brightening Carmelo's day. He's quite smitten. It's been an awfully long time since he knew love. What can we do for you, dear?"

We spoke for a little while longer before I thanked them and left the room, carrying a tray with tea for the three of us.

When I eventually found my way back to Gabriel's room, he was alone. Tabitha was nowhere to be seen.

"Where's Tabitha?" I asked, noticing that he was smiling more than he had been before.

"I sent her to find Carmelo."

"What for?" I asked, and he told me that there was something important he needed to speak to him, and us, about.

As I set the tray down, I asked Gabriel what he thought about Carmelo.

"He is perhaps the most remarkable man I have met, the most remarkable vampire anyway," he chuckled, "why do you ask?"

Not sure whether to say anything or not, I decided that rumours were already doing the rounds so he should know.

"Because it seems that Cupid has shot him with his arrows," I grinned.

"Cupid is here? When did he arrive?" he asked seriously.

I shook my head in disbelief, "Cupid is actually real?"

Gabriel began to laugh, and I grinned.

"Very funny," I said, gently punching him on his good shoulder. "What I meant to say was, it appears that Jo and Carmelo have bonded."

Gabriel smiled and relief flooded through me. "You're okay with it?" I asked.

He nodded, "Since you arrived Lilly, my outlook on life has changed quite a lot. You have helped me become more open-minded," he whispered gently, stroking my face as he spoke. "Especially since you brought Sammy back into our lives."

Before I could answer, Tabitha returned with Carmelo and Jo in tow.

"Gabriel. How good to see you. My apologies for not coming to see you sooner. I was away for a few days and only returned yesterday evening, and I certainly did not want to disturb your sleep last night," said Carmelo as they gently shook hands.

"And you have had far more important matters to attend to, Carmelo," Gabriel replied, looking at Jo, who blushed and smiled at the same time.

"Ahh, so the cat is out of the bag," laughed Carmelo.

Gabriel nodded and said, "Well, it's funny that you should use those words exactly Carmelo because I believe that the cat is quite literally out of the bag... that's what I wanted to talk to you about. I believe that Tabitha here is, in fact, of the feline variety."

Jo moved forward to sit at the foot of the bed, clearly curious. Carmelo followed, standing behind her with his hands lovingly on her shoulders.

Tabitha sat on one side of the bed, and I sat on the other.

Gabriel took a sip of his tea and then handed it to me to put down.

"I believe Tabitha is part of our family."

We all gasped.

"But how?" I asked.

"Tabitha has kindly filled me in on her life, but it wasn't until she mentioned, right at the very end, the name of her mother... Lori," he said, and he turned to look at her, "that's why you looked so familiar to me when you first arrived. You are Rose's grandchild, Tabitha. You are Lilly's second cousin."

And we both shrieked and laughed and leaned over Gabriel to hug each other.

"That means that Lori is still alive!" I gasped, "We must return home to tell Rose."

"This is wonderful news, Gabriel. Would you like me to send news to Rose?" asked Carmelo.

But Gabriel declined, "I think this is something that needs to be done in person by Tabitha and Lilly. But thank you, Carmelo. In the meantime, I need to decide what I am going to do. And you, Carmelo, and you, Jo, need to decide what you are going to do too. If you understand my meaning."

Jo turned to look at Carmelo, and he smiled down at her.

"Perhaps you would like to discuss this in private?" asked Gabriel.

"Well, actually. We've already decided," Jo answered quietly, "I'm going home to finish high school, and then I'm going to return to live with Carmelo and help with the Elders," she said, and Gabriel smiled.

"That is a wise decision, my dear. It also gives your parents a few months to come to terms with this situation and to accept Carmelo into the family... but don't look so worried Jo, I believe that your parents will understand. After all, this family has a long history of love at first sight," he chuckled.

His earlier words hadn't gone amiss with me, and I asked nervously, "But what about you, Gabriel? What do you mean you need to decide what to do?" as I remembered that the Elders had invited Gabriel to live with them in the mountains.

"We will leave you two alone, for now, Gabriel. So you can talk," said Carmelo as he, Jo and Tabitha, walked out of the room.

"So what did you mean, Gabriel?"

"Lilly, I already knew that I would one day come and be with the Elders. I just thought that it wouldn't be for a few more years, but since this has happened to me, I feel like an old man. I don't think I will ever fully recover from the fall. I think you know that too," he said sadly. "This is my destiny, and I have, therefore decided not to return home with you."

I sobbed, not just because he wasn't coming home, but because Vivian had hurt us once more. She had injured my grand-father, and although he would recover, his body would never be as it once was.

"What am I going to do without you?"

"You'll be fine. You'll be absolutely fine. And with your amazing ability, you can come and visit me whenever you want to, okay?"

I nodded sadly. "But what will I tell the people in town?"

"I will give you letters to give to my close friends. I will tell them that I had to move away to take care of an elderly relative in the north. They will understand."

"But what about Ben? He'll be devastated," I whispered.

"I will tell him the same thing. He will get over it. He is young."

I knew he would, but he would be hurt not to see Gabriel for one last time. Not to be able to say goodbye. I knew how he would feel, and I didn't want him to have to go through that.

"Through you, we can exchange letters. Then it won't be so bad for him, okay?" and I agreed.

❧ 29 ☙

Three days later, we were ready to set off home, but there was one thing I needed to do before I left. I asked Carmelo if I could see Vivian. Although he wasn't keen, he did understand that I needed some kind of closure. And since coming to Canada, I had changed. Not only was I becoming a young woman, but I had also become much stronger, and I felt the need to stand up to her once more.

"It is very cold where she is being held beneath the mountains. You will need a cape or a coat to keep you warm," said Carmelo.

"Here, have mine, Lilly. I'll wait for you up here," said Jo as she removed the coat she had put on in readiness for our departure.

I took it and wrapped it around my shoulders before I followed Carmelo and a few others deep down into the mountain where she and Charlie were being held until their trial.

"What will happen to Charlie?" I asked him.

"Some of our witches are working on a spell to try and undo the curse she has placed on him. If we can do so, we will return him to his original self, and he will be set free, although he will have no memory of what happened to him."

I wasn't sure I liked the idea. He was responsible for seriously injuring my grand-father after all.

"Lilly, please remember that this poor man was not really responsible. He has been changed at the hands of one of the evilest witches we have ever seen. If we change him back, he will be a different man. However, if we cannot reverse the curse, we will have no choice but to hold him accountable with his mistress, Vivian."

Charlie was being held in a cell beneath the mountain. It was clean and comfortable, and he was being fed and looked after. As I peered through the tight bars, I tried to see him as the man he used to be. An Englishman who had been kidnapped and cursed and forced to do the evilest things. I suddenly had a vision of London all those months before when my father and Vivian had vanished, I had a flash of a newspaper headline, 'Entrepreneur Charles Austen Missing'. I wondered if this could be the same man.

"Charles? Charles Austen?" I said gingerly, hoping for a response.

Charlie looked up, and for a second, there was recognition in his eyes.

I explained this to Carmelo, who assured me that it might help the witches return him to his former self, and I felt some relief. I knew I couldn't lay the blame with the poor man. Full responsibility was with the witch who was being held even deeper into the mountain. Even with Jo's coat enveloping me, I felt chilly and shivered as we approached another cell which was smaller and not quite as comfortable as Charlie's. There were several people outside on guard, but from what I could see, there was little need. Vivian was still pining for her beauty. The looks that would never return, thanks to me.

She sat curled up on the floor in the corner, even though there was a perfectly comfortable bed. As she looked up, I saw that the scar had returned to her face. The scar given to her years ago by my brave sister just seconds before her death.

She sat rocking backwards and forwards like a child, repeating the same words over and over again.

"I am beautiful, I am beautiful, I am beautiful..."

"No, Vivian, you're not beautiful. Not at all," I said, wanting to inflict more pain. "You will never be beautiful again. I've seen to that. You will spend the rest of your life ugly. You have whiskers on your face, hair on your hands and a scar that will never disappear.

You deserve even more suffering for what you have done. You deserve to rot in hell."

In what seemed like less than a split second, Vivian was standing inches from me. Her fingers had poked through the bars of the cell, and she had seemingly picked something from the coat I was wearing. I looked at her face and saw that her eyes had turned red. She was whispering something, something incomprehensible. A spell.

"No!" I screamed.

Carmelo moved like the speed of light towards us, he opened the cell quickly and grabbed her, holding her by her neck up against the wall. She could barely speak, and I feared that it was too late. What spell was she trying to cast?

He loosened his grip for just a second, and she began to laugh, an evil sound that echoed throughout the mountain.

"Too late," were her final words before he tightened his grip. I heard a crack, and her head flopped to one side. She was dead.

But it was not over. A scream was heard from the top of the steps, and a desperate voice shouted, "Carmelo, Lilly, hurry!"

Running as fast as I could, I dreaded to think what we would see when we reached the top. But I knew that it must be Jo. She had been standing there waiting for us. She had given me her own coat and Vivian had removed something. A hair.

Tabitha was crouching down, holding Jo's body in her arms, "She just collapsed. She said she couldn't breathe and she collapsed. Do something. Quick. She's dying!" she cried.

I couldn't see straight. The image before me made me feel physically sick. Jo was going to die. It was Vivian's ultimate revenge. The death of a loved one. Perhaps she had thought that I would die. She probably thought it was my hair she had taken. She was wrong. It was Jo. My lovely cousin Jo was on her deathbed.

I cried, sobbing loudly while Carmelo held her in his arms as the life slowly drifted from her body.

"Carmelo!" shouted a familiar voice. Gabriel. "Carmelo, you must save her. You know what to do. It's the only way. Carmelo... you must. It is meant to be."

I was confused, how could she be saved? She was on the brink of death. Seconds until Jo no longer existed in this world.

Carmelo turned to look at me, "I'm sorry," he whispered before he leaned forward and lifted his own arm, slicing into the skin with his talon-like nail. Blood appeared to the surface, and he carefully placed it to Jo's lips.

"Swallow, Jo. You must swallow the blood to survive."

I couldn't take in what was happening, and before I knew what was going on, my vision blurred, and I fell to the ground.

�֎ 30 ֎

"Lilly, Lilly," said a soft voice as I felt a damp cloth being dabbed across my forehead. I looked up to see Tabitha smiling down at me. Zoltan stood at her side.

I had been carefully laid on the bed in which I had slept the last few nights. "How did I get here?" I asked, and then I turned my head to see the empty bed to my side.

"Jo!" I shouted and jumped up. I suddenly had a vision of her death, and I felt like I'd been kicked in the stomach. It almost winded me, and I had to sit back down again.

"I'm so sorry, Lilly. Carmelo had no choice. It was the only way she could live."

"I'm okay," I said, "can I see her?" I asked.

Zoltan shook his head, "They won't let anyone see her for a while. She needs some time to adjust to the change. They're not quite sure how it's going to work, her being a changeling and all."

I told them I needed to see Gabriel and so we walked to where he was waiting, sitting in a large armchair outside the door of the room where Jo was being cared for.

"Oh Gabriel," I said when I saw him. I rushed to his side and knelt down, putting my head on his knee.

"There there. Don't worry, she'll be fine. I'm just sorry you had to see that," he said reassuringly.

"It's all my fault, Gabriel. I wanted to see Vivian for the last time. It wouldn't have happened if I hadn't gone down there to speak to her." He gently stroked my back and assured me that it wasn't my fault at all.

"It would have happened one way or another, Lilly. At least Jo is alive, in a manner of speaking. And this, this is something that she would have eventually wanted. She would have asked Carmelo to do it. Don't blame yourself, Lilly. Don't do that."

I heard noises from the other side of the door, and then it opened, and Carmelo walked out, closing it behind him. He looked sad. My stomach twisted, fearing the worst.

"Jo is going to be fine," he said. "Lilly, I'm so sorry. I hope that one day you will find it in your heart to forgive me."

I stood up and stepped towards him. I put my arms around him and hugged him tightly, "Carmelo, there is nothing to forgive. You saved Jo. That is what matters. I just wish I hadn't wanted to speak to Vivian. This may never have happened otherwise," I whispered.

"Lilly!" shouted a voice from the other side of the door. Although it sounded like Jo, the voice was slightly different, smoother somehow but in pain. "Lilly!" she yelled again.

Gabriel looked concerned, "Is it safe, Carmelo? Surely not so soon?" he asked.

Carmelo explained that when somebody becomes a vampire, they usually need weeks, sometimes months or more, to adjust to the transformation. They have a thirst for blood that cannot be quenched until they have mastered the art of control.

"So at this stage, Gabriel, no, it is not safe," he added.

"But she wants to see me, and I want to see her," I said, stepping forward and putting my hand on the key to unlock it.

"No!" Gabriel yelled, "No, Lilly. I will not lose you," and he tried to stand up. He was very weak, though, and he struggled.

"Gabriel, please. If Carmelo comes in with me, and perhaps Ursula, I'll be safe. I need to see her. I'll be safe," and he nodded his head and gave in. Tabitha knelt by his side and took his hand in hers tightly, and they sat and waited patiently while I turned, took a deep breath and opened the door.

Jo was lying on a bed, handcuffed. I was sure though that if she really became desperate, she could easily break them off her wrists. I'd heard how strong vampires could be.

I stepped further in and whispered her name.

She turned to look at me, "Lilly," she cried. She looked as if she was in a lot of pain, and it hurt me to see her like that.

Even in pain, she looked absolutely stunning. The combination of vampire, woman and raven had an extraordinary effect on her. She was beautiful before, but now everything about her beauty was increased a hundredfold. Her black hair had grown longer and even darker if that was at all possible. Her blue eyes had turned so deep in colour that even though they continued to be blue, they were almost black. Her pale skin sparkled, and her nails had become like talons.

"Jo... I'm so sorry," I whispered.

Jo shook her head, "Lilly, eventually, this is what I would have wanted. I wanted to be with Carmelo, and this would have been the only way. It was just sooner than I thought it would be, that's all," and she squirmed and winced again. "Vivian is dead now. That's what really matters. When I can, I will come home, okay?" and I nodded as the tears rolled again. "Lilly... thank you. Tell my family I love them and that I will be home when I can. Please tell them the truth. Tell them they can't come here until I have control, okay? I love you Lilly, and I will see you soon," and she tried to wink at me. "Now go... please go," she said as she pulled uncontrollably on the handcuffs, while Carmelo and Ursula held her down.

"I love you too, Jo. I will see you soon," and I tried to smile as Ursula moved towards the door and opened it, ushering me out as I attempted to hold back the tears.

❧ 31 ❧

I had been home for just over three weeks. It was strange living in the house without Gabriel, but I had accepted the fact that he was meant to be with the Elders, and I would see him again soon. Sammy and I had decided that once Jo was strong enough to come back to see us all, we would return with her to visit the Elders, Gabriel in particular.

I had hoped that when Vivian had died, her curse on Sammy would be lifted. Even the witches with the Elders had said that the curse should disappear, but when I finally returned home, Sammy was still the same. A man with two big black beautiful wings. Wings to be proud of, I told him. We were all confused about why the curse had not disappeared, but nobody had the answer.

The curse on Charlie, however, had vanished and he was now a free man. Carmelo saw to it that he had found his way back to London safely. I had seen his return home on the news on TV. He maintained that he had absolutely no idea what had happened to him or where he had been.

His family were shocked and amazed when he came home safe and well, and I was happy for him. Truly. Vivian was responsible, not him.

I was adjusting to life without Gabriel at home. It was a strange time in my life, especially considering that Sammy and I were now living with two others. Tabitha and Zoltan had moved in, making it an unusual household – a changeling, a werewolf, part raven part human and a potential changeling in the making! Although we were an odd combination of people, we got on tremendously well together.

Rose had been ecstatic to see me when I came back. I'd decided not to mention my momentous discovery until Tabitha was there with me. I knew she would arrive a day later so Rose and I enjoyed some time together, just the two of us. We spoke about Gabriel, Jo and Carmelo and of Vivian's death. When I left her that night, I was so excited about what would happen the next day.

I had knocked on Rose's front door later the following day and greeted her with a hug before she noticed I wasn't alone.

"I've brought someone to meet you, Rose," and Tabitha stepped forward with the biggest grin on her face. Rose's face changed immediately, and she had to sit down.

"Oh my goodness," she said, knowing immediately that she had a strong connection with this young girl.

"This is Tabitha... your grand-daughter."

Rose let out a gasp, both her hands moving to her cheeks.

"My... grand-daughter? You are Lori's child?" she whispered, and Tabitha nodded. Crying, Rose stood up, steadied herself and took her in her arms. "Lori is alive?" she asked, and again, Tabitha nodded and smiled. "I have a picture of her," and she put her hands in her coat pocket and pulled out a small wallet. Opening it, she revealed the face of a woman smiling happily and Rose began to cry tears of joy as she hugged her long lost grand-daughter for what seemed like ages.

We spent hours and hours talking about our lives, Tabitha explaining to Rose what had happened to Walter and to Lori and how she had come to be in Canada again. When we finally called it a night, we had left Rose looking more peaceful and happy than she had ever looked before, eager to get to know the grand-daughter she never even knew existed. And ecstatic that she would finally get her daughter back after all these years. The daughter that she had never given up hope on, and the daughter she had never stopped loving.

A few days later, I visited the graves of my mother and sister. It was my first visit there and, although Tabitha had driven me there,

I had wanted to be alone by their graveside. As I bent to place a single red rose on each of their tombstones, I thought about my father.

Although I had still not discovered what had happened to him, I was one step closer. I knew that he had not died at the hands of Vivian. There was still a chance that he was alive, and I knew that one day, I would find out the truth.

Read on for an excerpt of Book II in THE RAVEN WITCH SAGA: DECEMBER MOON

❦ 32 ❦

DECEMBER MOON EXCERPT

December Moon had no idea that she was a witch.

She had never given it a single thought. Why would she?

Well, she hadn't given it a single thought until the day before her fifteenth birthday when she had silently wished that the gymnasium would flood. She was sick of humiliating herself with her rather serious lack of elegance on the floor... pointed out, rather loudly, by her fellow gymnasts. The other girls looked impressive, as they fluttered about the room like brightly coloured butterflies, full of elegance and composure. December, on the other hand, thought herself more akin to Alice in Wonderland's caterpillar.

Imagine December's surprise when she began to hear the gentle whooshing sound that usually accompanies an overflowing bathtub. A noise that slowly became louder and louder, until water literally began pouring into the gymnasium from all directions. And it wasn't even raining.

"What the...?" Miss Finnegan screeched.

"Everybody form an orderly line and exit the gymnasium as soon as you can!" she yelled in her posh English accent to her students, after turning puce from blowing so hard on the red whistle that always hung around her taut, blotchy neck.

December knew something wasn't quite right with the whole scenario, considering the gymnasium had never posed a flood threat before and the fact that there was no plumbing anywhere near the building. The changing rooms were situated at the far end of the school... a design she had never quite understood.

As all the girls and boys panicked and flocked to the exit in one mad rush, December slowly took her time. It was only water, after all, and a little bit of water never hurt anyone. *Well, it had never hurt me*, she thought. Exactly at that moment, the water that had begun seeping into her black plimsolls and wetting her feet, receded, leaving her feet and ankles entirely, and strangely, dry.

Eyes wide in amazement, December surveyed the scene around her as one last student ran across the large mat in the centre of the room, it squelching beneath her feet. She was the last to leave. Even Miss Finnegan hadn't waited to make sure all her students had escaped unharmed and dry.

The water continued to pour in from each corner of the room, large droplets plopping around her from the ceiling and walls. Bits of green painted plaster broke away from the wall and fell down, bobbing up and down in the ankle high water below. December looked down at the floor and noticed that water was everywhere except within a small circular area surrounding her feet. As she moved, the dry circular area moved with her, like a bouncing bubble.

Before she could work out what was happening, gymnasium equipment began to fall and crash to the floor with the force of the running water.

How can this be? She thought. Then she remembered her silent wish, *surely not? No, there had to be a rational explanation to all of this. I couldn't possibly be responsible.* But the dry bubble around her told her a very different story.

As much as December wanted to hang around and enjoy watching the gym fill up with water, abruptly putting an end to her least favourite subject, she knew Miss Finnegan would eventually notice she was missing. So she skipped from the flooded room and out into the unusually bright sunlight of the October English afternoon.

oOo

It had been nearly a year since her best friend, Lilly, had left her behind in England and moved to Canada. It had proved to be a long and lonely year for December.

After Lilly's parents had completely vanished, she had moved to the other side of the world to a town called Powell River in the province of British Columbia. December had been so sad that her friend had to go, but she was also really pleased for her. They had stayed in touch and Lilly had sent numerous emails telling her all about the beauty that surrounded her and the wonderful loving family that had welcomed her with open arms over there.

December suspected that there was more to Lilly's new found happiness. She suspected there was something her friend wasn't telling her. After a few years of being the very best of friends, December knew Lilly too well to not know when something was going on, but she hadn't asked her about it. She knew that Lilly would tell her, whatever 'it' was, when the time was right.

For now, December had her own boring life to worry about. Since Lilly's departure, her life had returned to the same awful day-to-day experiences of having to stay out of her Aunt Penelope's way and dodge the cruel comments by some of her more horrible class-mates. She secretly daydreamed about the day that her own mother would return to take her home, to rescue her from her only other family member; the rich aunt, who had only agreed to look after her because her late brother, December's father, had requested it.

That and the fact that there was probably money involved, she thought later that day, when her chauffeur arrived to collect her from the school that was just across the road from Lilly's apart-ment. The apartment from where her parents had disappeared.

Looking up, December half expected to see that strange woman in white who had stood in exactly the same spot day after day to make sure Lilly had gone to, and returned from, school.

She shivered as a dark black cloud moved overhead. The hairs on the back of December's neck prickled and stood on end. *Strange*, she thought. It was almost as if she herself was being watched. December turned and looked all around her. The usual stream of students flowed from the school gates. Some of the boys kicked about a football and laughed as the ball hit one unexpectedly on the back of the head. "Oy!" he shouted, with a laugh as he picked it up and kicked it as hard as he could back at his friend.

A couple of girls giggled at the group in an attempt to get their attention.

On the other side of the street, there was the usual bustling of stallholders trying to sell their many wares, everything from freshly cut flowers to second hand books. People were going about their business. December could see no-one looking at her.

She shrugged her shoulders and hopped into the back seat of the black Range Rover.

"Have a good day, Miss Moon?" asked the driver, a man of about sixty with shoulder length hair as white as his crisp shirt. While on duty, he wore it in a neat pony tail at the nape of his neck.

She rolled her eyes at him and grinned.

"After all these years, I wish you'd call me December, Monty. You should know by now that I'm nothing at all like that aunt of mine," she tutted, smiling, although the smile didn't quite reach her eyes.

"And my day was, well, let's just say that it was interesting."

He nodded and returned her smile, showing a toothy grin. "Sorry Miss, it's habit, I suppose. Your Aunt Penelope would hate to hear me call you anything other than Miss Moon. Oh, I did it again, didn't I?" he laughed while shaking his head.

"I've been driving you to and from this school for years...Mi... December, and I don't recall you ever describing your day as interesting, not since Miss Taylor left, anyhow. Want to talk about it?" he asked as a gap in the traffic finally allowed him to pull away from the kerb by the school.

Monty was the only other person December felt she could talk to. He had been in the Moon's employment since she was a toddler and he had probably been more like family than any of her actual family members. Although it was clear that her Aunt Penelope wasn't keen on him, she had kept him on, purely at her dying brother's request.

As they drove through the London traffic and headed in the direction of Battersea where they had lived her entire life,

December regaled Monty with the strange story of the flooded gymnasium. What she did neglect to tell him, however, was the fact that even when the water completely surrounded her, she was kept dry by an unexplained bubble at her feet. A bubble that she was keen to get to the bottom of...

ABOUT THE AUTHOR

Suzy Turner wrote her first chick lit novel in her early twenties, but it wasn't until much later that she decided to focus on writing full time. It was during a visit to Canada in 2009 when the ravens within the dark eerie forests of British Columbia called to her. The story of Lilly Taylor was born soon after and the first novel in The Raven Witch Saga was created. Suzy has since published several more urban fantasy books (under her pen name SG Turner) and contemporary women's novels.

Having lived in Portugal since childhood, Suzy, who is originally from Yorkshire in England, loves to travel. She finds inspiration wherever she goes. Old decrepit buildings, graveyards, cathedrals and castles are just a few of the things that can be found within the worlds of her urban fantasy books, and her contemporary women's fiction novels are filled with fun friendships, ordinary people in extraordinary circumstances and quirky characters you'd want as friends.

Suzy lives in the Algarve with her husband, three cats and a dog, where she does yoga every morning and bookish stuff for pretty much the rest of the day!

For more books and updates, visit www.suzyturner.com or www.chilloutpress.com

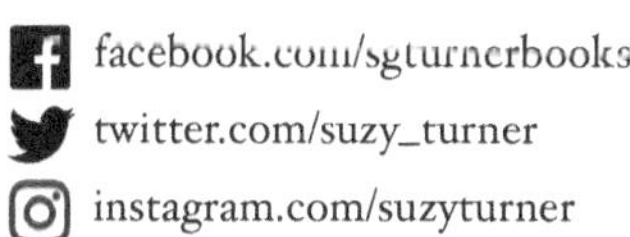

ACKNOWLEDGMENTS

A huge thank you to Cristina Alcock, Jill Ibrahim, Elizabeth Martens, Emma Naylor & Eloise Walton. I don't know where I would be without your excellent suggestions, editing and proofreading skills. You're all absolute angels!

Michael, thank you for believing in me, even when I doubted myself (which was more often than I care to admit). You're my rock.

And lastly, thank you to all my lovely followers, fellow bloggers, writers, twitterers and facebook friends for just being there when I needed advice or a little pick me up. It's wonderful to have friends like you behind me.

Mum... you may have been gone from our lives for many years,
but you will never be forgotten.
This book is for you.